Pr~~aise for the~~
Washington Whodunit Series

"The mystery is perplexing—for Kit and company, and for me—and well done. I was impressed by the complexity of the murder plot. I enjoyed the political theme, and all the details about lobbyists."

—*Jane Reads*

"To someone who has mastered that uniquely Washington skill of bobbling two cell phones and a glass of wine without spilling a drop, solving a murder is practically child's play."

—*HillRag*

"A solid choice for political junkies and readers of Maggie Sefton, Fred Hunter, and Mike Lawson."

—*Library Journal*

"The fourth volume in author Colleen J. Shogan's simply outstanding 'Washington Whodunit' series, *K Street Killing* is a consistently entertaining read with many an unexpected twist and turn by a true master of the genre."

—*Midwest Book Review*

"Shogan does a good job depicting the creaky, squeaky wheels of government, and Marshall plays politics and sleuth with equal dexterity in this capital Capitol Hill mystery."

—*Publishers Weekly*

"Loads of inside scoop about the workings of Senate offices—complete with all the gossiping, back-stabbing, and procedural maneuvering—plus an appealing young sleuth, sprightly pacing, and an edge-of-your-seat showdown on the Hart-Dirksen underground train."

—*Literary Hill*

Other Books in the Washington Whodunit Series

Stabbing in the Senate

Homicide in the House

Calamity at the Continental Club

K Street Killing

Gore in the Garden

Larceny at the Library

Dead as a Duck

Lethal Legacies

Lethal Legacies

A Washington Whodunit

COLLEEN J. SHOGAN

CAMEL
PRESS
Seattle, WA

A Camel Press book published by Epicenter Press

Epicenter Press
6524 NE 181st St.
Suite 2
Kenmore, WA 98028

For more information go to:
www.Camelpress.com
www.Coffeetownpress.com
www.Epicenterpress.com
www.colleenshogan.com

This is a work of fiction. Names, characters, places, brands, media, and incidents are either the product of the author's imagination or are used fictitiously.

Cover design by Scott Book
Design by Melissa Vail Coffman

Lethal Legacies
Copyright © 2022 by Colleen J. Shogan

ISBN: 978-1-68492-030-3 (Trade Paper)
ISBN: 978-1-68492-031-0 (eBook)

Library of Congress Control Number: 2022932141

Printed in the United States of America

To my devoted readers

Acknowledgments

WHEN I WROTE the first book in the Washington Whodunit series, *Stabbing in the Senate*, I conceived of it as a standalone mystery. After all, as a political scientist, I was a nonfiction writer and considered my foray into fiction nothing more than an enjoyable detour. Never in my wildest dreams did I imagine that I would write eight books about Kit Marshall, exploring the nooks and crannies of Capitol Hill and many of the treasures of our nation's capital. The Washington Whodunit series has been one of the most delightful surprises in my life.

My mother frequently said that when Hillary Clinton wrote the book *It Takes A Village*, many people snickered at the title. Nonetheless, she argued, Hillary was right. Whether it's raising a child or publishing a book, anything worth doing doesn't happen in a vacuum. Without a doubt, it took a village to write and publish the Washington Whodunit mysteries and I want to thank everyone who helped along the way.

My husband Rob Raffety encouraged me to write the first book and keep writing. Without his insistence, I wouldn't have even tried to write one sentence of fiction. My entire family, including my parents, aunts, uncles, brother, sisters-in-law, nieces, cousins, and in-laws, were supportive throughout the whole venture. I want to thank my literary agent Dawn Dowdle, who liked the idea of a Capitol Hill amateur sleuth from the start. She has provided me with excellent professional writing advice for almost a decade. Jennifer McCord has offered valuable editorial guidance throughout the whole series. The stories and characters have been improved considerably due to her observations. Annie Dwyer was a devoted publicist for many of the books. Also, thank you to the acquiring editors who bought sub-rights to my books, whether it was mass market paperback, audio, or large print. It helped the stories reach even more readers, which is the primary goal of any writer.

The writing community in Washington, D.C. and the surrounding area is tremendous. The writers I met at the Old Europe dinners in Georgetown were incredibly helpful and provided sage commentary when I was searching for an agent and publisher. The Washington Independent Review of Books helped me understand the business of writing, which was instrumental. The friends I have met through Sisters in Crime are great people as well as talented authors. I've never been part of a more collaborative group of professionals than the mystery writers I have met along the way. Lastly, my friends and former colleagues at the Library of Congress deserve special mention. It was the perfect place to work when launching a new creative endeavor. Special kudos to those people who offered zany ideas about future fictitious murders and where they could take place!

It is bittersweet to bid adieu to Kit Marshall and the gang, at least for now. I hope I have provided hours of reading enjoyment to my dedicated fans. I wrote these books because I love mysteries and I strongly believed an authentic, nonpartisan, and historically inspired Washington-based series would be a welcome addition to the genre. I also wrote the books to offer a more positive view of our nation's capital. As I write this, our country is more politically divided than ever, yet I can't help but cling tightly to the belief that there are many real-life Kit Marshalls out there, dedicated to doing what's right and seeking justice for those who have been wronged. Thank you for coming on this journey with me.

Chapter One

—❧—

"**M**OVE IT MORE TO THE RIGHT!" I said, motioning with my hands in the preferred direction.

"Now it's too far. Shift it in the other direction," ordered my longtime pal and colleague, Trevor.

"Put it down, for goodness sake!" commanded my best friend Meg Peters, who was staring straight ahead through designer sunglasses with a hand shielding her forehead from the springtime sun.

It wasn't every day the Lincoln catafalque left the United States Capitol Visitors Center for an outdoor display. But these weren't ordinary times. We were prepping for the beginning of our weeklong history extravaganza, *Spring Into History*, and the wooden structure that held Abraham Lincoln's coffin in 1865 was the number one attraction.

As the seven-foot-long base of pine boards hastily assembled after Lincoln's assassination came to rest at the foot of a large outdoor tent situated on the north lawn of the Library of Congress, we exhaled a collective sigh of relief. The workmen from the Architect of the Capitol, who had been in charge of transporting the historic structure wrapped in a black funeral cloth, stepped back from their handiwork.

"Are you the person running this operation?" asked a middle-aged man wearing the standard-issued AOC baseball hat. He directed his question towards me, likely because I looked the part.

I was dressed in my standard Capitol Hill uniform, which most female chiefs of staff in the House of Representatives adopted, a black pantsuit, a brightly colored yet conservatively professional blouse, and modestly styled heels. Sensible and functional. Perfect for negotiating deals during the day and enjoying happy hour in the evening hours. Kit Marshall was always ready for whatever the world tossed at her. At least that's the image I desperately tried to project.

I was about to respond a polite "Yes, sir" to the Architect of the Capitol employee, but as the words were about to come out of my mouth, a crisp, commanding feminine voice beat me to the punch.

"I am in charge of this operation."

Heads swiveled in the direction of the pronouncement. I didn't have to change my point of view to know who was speaking. It was Bev Taylor, the young and ambitious director of the United States Capitol Visitor Center.

The man in the AOC baseball hat looked her up and down. Bev was dressed similarly to me, with a black suit and heels to match. Like me, she had placed her medium length brown hair in a stylish ponytail because the temperature had just hit seventy degrees in our nation's capital.

"Are we good here?" he asked. "We're getting close to overtime."

Bev moved closer to the Lincoln catafalque and scrutinized it. Then she stepped backwards several feet. The guy from the Architect of the Capitol rolled his eyes.

"Are we sure it's in the right position?" asked Bev. She turned to face myself, Trevor, and Meg. "Or should we put it on the opposite side of the tent and rearrange the seating?"

I fought the impulse to roll my eyes. Instead, I took a deep breath.

"Bev, we discussed this detail during our planning meetings. Everything is set up for the configuration we chose," I said. "Including the security cameras."

Bev sighed. "I suppose you're right." She turned toward the AOC worker. "You can go now." She motioned with her hand to dismiss him and his colleagues.

I heard the poor guy mutter under his breath. "Let's get out of here before she changes her mind. She's a real piece of work!"

Once they had exited the tent, Bev directed her attention to us. "Are we ready for tomorrow?" It was more of a command than a question.

"Meg and I will be here by eight in the morning, well before the public opening of the tent at nine," I said. "It's hard to know how many visitors will line up to get a close, unimpeded look at the Lincoln catafalque."

"Most people only get the chance to see it behind glass inside the Capitol Visitor Center," said Trevor. "The only other time you can see it is when someone who has died is lying in state inside the Capitol Building."

The catafalque was a macabre spectacle, yet it was the artifact owned by the Capitol Visitor Center that would certainly generate the most interest from a general viewing audience. The catafalque was constructed to support Abraham Lincoln's casket after his assassination. As Trevor noted, it has been previously used inside the United States Capitol rotunda and Supreme Court for those honored with the tradition of lying in state, a very select group of individuals that included former presidents, Congressman John Lewis, Justice Ruth Bader Ginsberg, and Senator John McCain.

Our plan was to begin our weeklong *Spring Into History* series of events with the outdoor display of the Lincoln catafalque. The rest of the day included a stellar lineup of Civil War era historians and Lincoln experts who would give lectures inside the tent. While we hoped the speakers would generate interest in American history, we knew that making the Lincoln catafalque accessible would drive the crowds to our event. At least, that was our goal.

"Of course, there will be a large crowd," said Bev, smoothing her hair. "No one has ever done anything like this before. It takes *vision to* bring history to the masses like this."

"Let's just hope our *vision* isn't wearing rose-colored glasses," said Trevor. I could always count on Trevor for old-fashioned dry wit.

Meg walked over to Trevor and put her arm around his waist. They had been a couple for a while now, giving new credence to the adage that opposites attract. "We're promoting this as heavily as we can with Library of Congress networks," said Meg. "And I've talked to several members of Congress who plan to view the catafalque tomorrow."

"I'm sure it will work out well," I said quickly. It would be an understatement to say that Bev had been difficult to work with during the planning of *Spring Into History*. Instead, she reminded me more of the hurricane season of late summer. Before you knew it, the whirlwind had arrived, and it was often too late to save yourself.

"I have the run of show for tomorrow," said a female voice behind me. I'd almost forgotten about Jill. She was an intern from a program geared at recent college graduates who otherwise wouldn't have been able to afford the low salary of an entry-level position on Capitol Hill. I hadn't planned on participating in the program, but Jill had asked to work with me due to her interest in American history, congressional operations, legislative branch support agencies, and administration. My boss, Congresswoman Maeve Dixon of North Carolina, was the chair of the committee in charge of such matters. Hence my involvement with *Spring Into History*, alongside the Capitol Visitor Center, the Library of Congress, and a variety of other museums and historical societies. It was the first time we'd attempted such an ambitious collaboration across the nation's capital, and I prayed we could pull it off. Cooperation often proved elusive in Washington, D.C. these days, but we aimed to buck the trend. After the final retreat of COVID-19 and the return of public gatherings, we certainly had reason to try our best.

I turned around to acknowledge Jill, who had proven an asset rather than a liability during such a busy time. These days were crazier than normal because Maeve Dixon was splitting her time between Washington, D.C. and her home state of North Carolina, where she was running for an open seat in the United States Senate. As her chief of staff, when Maeve was focused on her Senate run, it was my job to keep an eye on her current responsibilities in the House of Representatives.

Jill handed me the piece of paper, which had broken down tomorrow's schedule in fifteen-minute increments. It outlined each component of the festivities, beginning with the public viewing of the Lincoln catafalque at nine o'clock. Neatly typed and bulleted, it was exactly what I needed to guide me through a complicated day ahead.

I allowed myself to smile, probably for the first time today. "Thank you, Jill. This is well done."

Meg looked over my shoulder. "You should hire Jill on the campaign. Chester McNuggets won't know what hit him."

"Jill's organizational skills would be an asset for any employer," I said. "And Meg, you know our opponent's name is Chester *Nuggets*, not McNuggets," I said, not bothering to suppress a smirk.

Meg waved her hand dismissively with her red manicured nails. "Nuggets, McNuggets, Big Mac, whatever. Maeve Dixon should be eating his lunch."

Trevor squeezed Meg's arm. "That was a funny pun, darling."

I ignored their romantic banter, focusing instead on Meg's remark about Chester Nuggets. She was right. Nuggets was a popular talk radio host in North Carolina, so he had a following. Yet he had no record of public service. Since Maeve Dixon had served honorably in the military and catapulted to a chairmanship during her short tenure as a member of the House of Representatives, most people would expect that she'd have a definite advantage in the race. However, as my boss was discovering, politics is about more than amassing an impressive resume. Nuggets had gotten to his station in life because he had a way with words, including a penchant for ridicule masked by entertainment and biting humor.

I sighed. "She *should* be beating him handily, I agree. Every time she tries to talk about the important policy issues, he diverts attention away from a serious discussion."

"How so?" asked Trevor. "He can't play that game forever."

"He doesn't have to play it forever," said Meg. "Only until November."

"This week, when Maeve tried to speak about health care, he challenged her to a monster truck duel," I said.

Trevor blinked rapidly and adjusted his glasses. "He what?"

"Monster trucks," I repeated. "You must have seen them on television. They have the big wheels."

"I know what they are, Kit, but why is that part of a Senate campaign?" asked Trevor.

"Now you understand what we're dealing with," I said. "It's pretty hard to debate someone for the Senate who isn't interested in talking about what senators actually do."

Bev cleared her throat and pointed to her watch. "I hate to interrupt this fascinating conversation," she said, her voice dripping with sarcasm. "We are due at the Belmont-Paul House in less than thirty minutes."

Intern Jill nodded and moved her long auburn hair out of her eyes as she glanced at her iPhone to check the time. "Bev is right. We need to leave here soon, or we'll miss the start of the reception."

"Anything else we need to do before departing?" I asked, glancing around the tent.

"The Capitol Hill police will take it from here," said Bev, pointing toward an officer who was now standing near the entrance. "Someone will be here all night to guard everything."

The chairs were arranged for tomorrow's lecture, the lectern was in place, and the Lincoln catafalque was positioned appropriately with the black funeral cloth resting on top of it. Everything appeared in order, although I had a nagging sense I'd forgotten something.

"Have we crossed everything off our list?" I asked Jill. Quite frankly, I don't know how I'd survived this long without an assistant. Maybe I could convince Jill to stay onboard after her internship program ended. I made a mental note to ask Maeve Dixon if I could consider the possibility if we had enough money in our office budget.

Jill consulted her phone. "It looks like we're all set with the tasks for today."

"Thank you, Jill. Let's see if we can find time to debrief tomorrow." I wasn't sure when we would be able to find the time, but it was the right thing to say to an intern. I made a mental note to ask Jill about what she was learning. I remembered the two-hour training I took a few months ago, called "Intern Mentorship 101." Things had been so crazy with the Senate campaign and the history extravaganza, I wasn't quite sure I'd lived up to all the expectations.

The training had clearly indicated that a mentor should give an intern "room to run" but should also provide "consistent feedback" and "acknowledge achievements." I'd certainly done the former by giving Jill a number of responsibilities with *Spring Into History*, but I might have to catch up on the latter.

"Let's head over to the reception," said Meg. "I don't want to be late. I need a drink, some nibbles, and then I want to tour the house."

Jill nodded. "I'll meet you there." She disappeared in a flash before I had a chance to offer her a ride. Jill had a lot on the ball and reminded me of a younger version of myself. When I was starting out in politics, I'd do anything for anyone in charge, as long as it wasn't illegal.

The Belmont-Paul House was a National Park Service site located adjacent to the Hart Senate Office Building on the corner of Second Street and Constitution Avenue. It was a lasting memorial to women's equality and the home of suffragist Alice Paul's National Woman's Party (NWP) since 1929. Purchased by NWP supporter Alva Belmont, the house was now known simply as "Belmont-Paul" in the Capitol Hill neighborhood. Over two hundred years old, it served as a museum for the women's suffrage movement and related activism in the United States. Bev and I hadn't agreed on much during the planning of *Spring Into History*, but we both wanted the Belmont-Paul House to host our opening night reception.

"I'm going to move my car nearby," I said. "Doug is joining us for the reception and if I park on a side street near the house, we can go home directly from there."

Doug was my husband, a professor extraordinaire who specialized in American history. Until quite recently, he had led the scholarly center at the Library of Congress. Only a few months earlier, he reversed course and accepted an offer to return to Georgetown University, where he'd become Dean of Faculty Affairs. His boss, the Dean of Georgetown College, was slated for retirement soon and Doug was the heir apparent if everything went smoothly during his current appointment.

"Good idea about moving the car," said Trevor. "I'll do the same."

Normally, I advocated for exercise, which meant walking between meetings, appointments, and events on Capitol Hill. However, it was the end of the day, and my legs were already tired. I might have the strength to walk the half-mile to Belmont-Paul, but I definitely wouldn't have the energy for the return.

"I'll get a ride with Trevor," said Meg. "See you there." She wagged her fingers at me and looped her arm underneath Trevor's. All was quiet on the western front—that is, Meg and Trevor's previously rocky romance. I hoped it remained that way for the next week. I couldn't handle the grueling schedule of *Spring Into History* and another dramatic flareup from my best friend along with her mercurial beau. As an organizer for activities taking place at venues across our nation's capital, next week would be an important one for my career. Little did we know what history had in store for us.

Chapter Two

As soon as I climbed into my car and drove out of the House of Representatives parking garage, my phone rang. Due to the wonders of technology, I was able to answer the call without taking my hands off the steering wheel. My dashboard console showed it was my boss Maeve Dixon, which meant I needed to take the call pronto.

"Hello, Madame Chair," I said in my cheeriest voice. The congresswoman liked it when staff acknowledged she was the chair of a congressional committee.

"Kit, I'm glad I caught you."

I could hear sing-song music in the background. Was that a merry-go-round? "Where are you? There's a lot of noise."

Even across a Bluetooth connected phone, I could hear Maeve Dixon's audible sigh. "I'm at a spring fair outside Charlotte."

"Oh, that makes sense," I said. "Make sure to eat some cotton candy."

She ignored my remark. "Chester Nuggets is putting pressure on me about this monster truck thing."

I shook my head, glad that we weren't on a video call where Maeve could see me. "We talked about this yesterday. There's no reason to engage him on this. What does a monster truck contest have to do with being a United States Senator?"

"It's about relatability, Kit. That's what my campaign consultants are telling me."

I clenched my jaw. Campaign consultants were always dispensing advice, whether you needed it or not. Maeve Dixon wanted to become a senator, but did she want to change who she was in the process?

Two could play at that game. I'd been around the world of politics for a while, and I could speak in the language of professional campaign gurus as good as the rest of them.

"If you do this, Chester Nuggets will be defining you. I don't need to tell you that letting your opponent define you is the biggest mistake you can make when you're running for office."

The line was silent for several seconds. I'd said my piece. Maeve Dixon knew she could count on my unvarnished opinion, and I wasn't going to let her down in an hour of need.

Her voice was clear, yet softer, when she finally spoke. "You're right, Kit. I needed to hear that. I'm going to stick to my guns and insist that Nuggets engage me on the issues at hand."

I'd just found a parking spot on Third Street, only a block away from the Belmont-Paul House. As I carefully parallel parked, Maeve must have heard the beep of my rearview backup camera.

"Are you driving somewhere?" she asked.

"I'm about to attend the kick-off reception for *Spring Into History*," I said. "Remember, you wanted me to assume a leading role in planning it because you couldn't be involved."

"Good luck with that. It sounds like a lot of fun," said Maeve wistfully.

"You need to stay focused on the campaign now. In six months, we'll be planning your swearing-in ceremony for the Senate."

What I didn't add was that if she lost, Maeve Dixon would be out of a job. She wasn't running for reelection for her seat in the House of Representatives. It was the Senate or bust. As Dixon's chief of staff, her fate and mine were intertwined. If she won, I hoped Dixon would ask me to stay on as her top staffer in the Senate. If she lost, my backup idea was to make a play for the committee staff director job in the House of Representatives. She wouldn't be the chair of the committee, but I would have the experience to advise her successor. It was another reason why this upcoming history extravaganza had to go well. I was planning to tout it as a signature achievement in case I needed to implement Plan B. Yes, I know what you're thinking. I probably strategize, analyze, and calculate way too much. However, no one really looks out for your career besides you.

Maeve's voice brought me back to reality. "Kit, are you still there?"

"Yes, sorry about that," I said. "My mind must have drifted for a moment."

"I don't have anything else to tell you. I hope the history events turn out well. Give me a full report each day."

"Will do, Madame Chair." I clicked my iPhone off and checked my makeup in the mirror. My mid-length brown hair had seen both better and worse days. My eyeliner, lipstick, and foundation could use a freshening. After finding my worn makeup bag inside my mammoth purse, I made the appropriate fixes to my appearance and decided I was ready.

The Belmont-Paul House was only a short walk away. I couldn't help but smile as I approached the National Park monument. It was a red-brick federal-style house tucked right behind the Capitol and adjacent to the Senate office buildings. I guessed that many people walked by it every day and didn't realize its significance.

A park ranger greeted me at the entrance steps. "Welcome to the Women's Equality National Monument," she said cheerily. "Are you here for the reception?"

"Yes, absolutely." I extended my hand. "Kit Marshall. I'm the chief of staff for Maeve Dixon, who chairs the House Administration Committee."

The park ranger smiled. "We love our congressional supporters," she said, in an even cheerier voice. Maeve wasn't on the committee that oversaw the National Park Service, but there was no reason to burst the friendly park ranger's bubble.

I walked into the entrance area of the house, where there was a registration table for the event. I did a double take. There was Jill, already seated and checking in attendees.

"Weren't you just on the Library of Congress lawn with me?" I asked.

"I hurried over here because I volunteered to staff the table for the first thirty minutes." Jill's face was a little flush. She must have jogged.

"I could have given you a ride," I said. "But I suppose your way was faster."

She nodded. "Your husband checked in five minutes ago. He's already inside the tent."

I took the badge with my name and affiliation from her. "Thank you very much. I hope you get a chance to enjoy the reception, Jill."

When I was an intern or low-level staffer, the grunt work always was crappy, but I almost always got to watch or enjoy the event I was working. That was when I deployed my magic and networked to find my next gig.

"Oh, I will," she said. "That's why I signed up for the early shift at the table."

I smiled. "Smart girl. Keep up the good work." Then I remembered my duties. "Let's not forget to chat tomorrow after the morning event."

Jill's expression brightened. "Don't worry, Kit. I won't forget."

I walked down the hallway and through the open door to enter the tented courtyard. It wasn't a very large outdoor space, but it was the only historic home on Capitol Hill that could accommodate a large event like our reception. I spotted my husband's slightly puffy brown hair easily in the sparse crowd. Doug's hair had been downright bushy for so long, particularly during the pandemic shutdown, but when he returned to Georgetown as a dean, he determined he had to "act the part." He was dressed today in a royal sharkskin patterned suit with two buttons, paired with a fitted white dress shirt and silk floral tie to match. He gave new meaning to the phrase "dress for success."

He spotted me from across the space and wiggled his fingers to make sure I saw him. I noticed he was juggling two glasses of white wine. My husband knew me too well.

I rushed over to him and took one of the glasses from him and gave him a kiss on the cheek. "Thank you for getting me a beverage. I needed it."

"I figured," said Doug. "Given everything that's gone on with the planning of this shindig."

I took a deep breath. "I think we have it all under control." Doug couldn't see that with the hand not holding the wine glass, I had my fingers crossed behind my back. I certainly hoped that was the case.

"Professor Hollingsworth." A deep male voice sounded behind us.

We turned around, although I already knew who it was. Edgar Beaufort was a former colleague of Doug's in the History Department at Georgetown. He was a specialist in African American history, with a particular focus on slavery and labor. Doug and Edgar had started at Georgetown at the same time, which meant that Edgar was likely near Doug's age of thirty-five. He was likewise dressed to the nines, with his slim cut suit showing off his athletic physique. Edgar might spend time in the library, but he also must have a standing appointment at the gym.

Doug extended his hand. "Good to see you, Edgar. I heard you've been invaluable to Kit as a historical consultant."

Edgar accepted Doug's hand. "Forgive me. I misspoke. It's *Dean* Hollingsworth now." He smiled, his white teeth glistening.

Doug waved his hand. "Don't be silly. I'll always be a historian first."

"Sure, that's what they all say." We shifted our gaze to a woman's voice who had joined our growing circle. It was Mila Cunningham, our other historical consultant.

"How nice to see you, Mila," said Doug. My husband was a pretty good charmer. He knew what was appropriate to say and when. Since I knew him so well, I could detect the edge in his voice. Mila made Doug nervous.

Mila was in the same general age range as us. Her light brown hair was stylishly cut, and her makeup was impeccable. An attractive woman, for sure, and certainly intelligent. However, Mila was always working an angle. Ambition was admirable and I detested it when women were labeled "difficult" if they showed initiative or drive. Unfortunately, Mila overstepped that line. I wasn't sure what her endgame was, but I thought it probably had something to do with fortune and fame. Doris Kearns Goodwin should check her rearview mirror to make sure Mila wasn't stalking her in the background, waiting to pounce.

"I see Edgar already beat me to the punch," said Mila. "I suppose you're claiming credit for the programming." If looks could kill, Mila would be doing twenty-to-life for homicide.

Edgar's upper body stiffened. "I was doing no such thing."

Mila waved her hand dismissively. "That's what they all say." She took a sip from her wine glass and looked around. "At least they spruced this place up for us. It's seen better days."

I narrowed my eyes. "If I'm not mistaken, it was built in 1800, Mila. I think it looks remarkably intact for a house of considerable age."

Mila sniffed. "I suppose you're right. The collections from the National Woman's Party and Alice Paul are impressive to see."

I turned toward Doug. "I'd like to see the exhibits inside the house." I stretched my neck to look around the outdoor tent, which was filling up. "But I don't see Trevor and Meg yet."

Doug gestured carefully with his half-filled wine glass. "Trevor will be here soon, I'm sure. His boss James Bennett has just arrived."

I followed Doug's gaze and spotted Bennett entering the tent. In his early sixties, he was the consummate Beltway insider. He was dressed in a sleek dark suit and walked with a confident swagger only boasted by those who had existed in the capital swamp for years and thrived in it. I watched as he worked his way across the reception, flashing his teeth and shaking hands with as many people as possible.

"I'd better say hello," I murmured to Doug.

He nodded. "I'll follow you in a moment."

I took a deep breath and walked in Bennett's direction. He was the Chief Administrative Officer, known as CAO, of the House of Representatives. That sounded like a boring job, but it was critically important to the operations of Congress. The CAO provided support services, including training, technology, and childcare, to the more than ten thousand people who worked in the United States House of Representatives. He was also, as Doug pointed out,

Trevor's boss. As the CAO, he was one of our partners for *Spring Into History*. Since he only spent time with people who mattered, he didn't engage in the day-to-day planning with us. Instead, he'd designated Trevor as his representative.

In the absence of my boss, I represented the congresswoman. I patted down the inevitable flyaways in my free-flowing brown hair and weaved through the crowd. Finally, I was standing face to face with the CAO.

"Mr. Bennett, a pleasure to welcome you to the inaugural event for *Spring Into History*."

I was about to remind him who I was, but he didn't give me the chance. "Kit Marshall," he said in a booming voice. "Chief of staff and sleuth extraordinaire." He motioned around the tent. "You're responsible for all of this, I suppose. Has Trevor helped you or has he been a royal pain in the butt?" He laughed at his own joke.

I didn't quite know where to start. With men like James Bennett, it was easy to become overwhelmed. He had a personality reminiscent of *House of Cards*. In other words, eat or be eaten. He never was on the receiving end of that equation.

I decided to start with the obvious. "I'm surprised you remember me. I believe we only met once or twice before."

"It's my job to remember people, Ms. Marshall. But it might not matter in a few months. Your boss may be moving to the other side of the Capitol."

"It's a close race with Chester Nuggets," I said. "To answer your question, though, Trevor has been a big asset to the planning. We really appreciated his input."

Bennett snorted. "From what I know, you've known Trevor for a long time, so you probably have grown to tolerate him. But I can tell you he's not the most popular guy in the office."

Like fine scotch, Trevor was an acquired taste. I was about to reiterate this fact with James Bennett, but he gesticulated wildly in the opposite direction. He turned back to close out our conversation.

"Sorry, kid. Gotta run. I spotted one of our vendors. I think they're sponsors of this soirée, and I need to go say hello and thank them."

Before I could even say goodbye, Bennett had dashed off, likely in pursuit of his next quarry. The CAO was not the most popular person in the House of Representatives. Did he get the job done? Yes, and at the end of the day, that's what mattered to members of Congress and thousands of congressional staff who worked there.

As I turned around to head back to Doug and our historian friends, I almost ran into Trevor and Meg. Trevor looked as though he'd just swallowed a lemon.

"Were you talking with my boss?" he asked in a demanding, almost accusatory, voice.

"Don't worry. I only said good things about you, so relax. I wanted to say hello to him because your office is such an important partner for our history week."

"He wouldn't know the difference between a suffragist and a conservationist," said Trevor with a sneer on his face.

Meg tapped his arm. "Now, Trevor. You should settle down about your boss. He has given you a great opportunity to work on all kinds of important projects in your office."

"It's just like him to show up at the big event and act like he was responsible for the whole idea," said Trevor.

I shook my head in disbelief. "Trevor, we work in Washington. Isn't that what *everyone* does?" Usually, Trevor was the one reminding me of the harsh political realities of a situation.

Trevor clenched his jaw, not speaking for a moment. He closed his eyes briefly and inhaled. "I rarely say this, but you are absolutely correct, Ms. Marshall."

Even though I'd known Trevor for years, worked alongside him in the Senate, went on vacation with him last summer, and solved several murders with his help, he still routinely called me "Ms. Marshall" instead of my first name. Some habits die hard. At heart, Trevor was an old soul. If he could get away with it, I think he'd stroll around Washington with a pocket watch, a top hat, and a walking cane.

"Well, even a broken clock is right two times a day," I said matter-of-factly.

"Be careful not to aim too high," said a booming voice from behind me.

I turned around to face Chase Wintergreen, who was the chief of staff to Congressman Amos Duncan. It was hard to guess Chase's age, although I suspected he was somewhere in his forties. His face was without wrinkles, but there was a tightness to it that indicated to me that he'd had work done, perhaps a little too much Botox. His sandy-colored hair was coiffed perfectly and he wore a light tan suit with a striking dark purple dress shirt and matching patterned tie. Chase looked like he had been born to work on Capitol Hill, and he knew it.

Chase had wormed his way into our working group for *Spring Into History* because his boss was first in line to become the next chair of the House Administration Committee. Both Chase and Amos Duncan were delighted that Maeve Dixon was running for Senate. They had practically done everything but measure the curtains, and quite frankly, I wouldn't be surprised if they had snuck into our office space at night with a yardstick and swatches of fabric.

Doug made his way over to our group and offered his hand to Chase. "Doug Hollingsworth. I used to work at the Library of Congress but now I'm back at Georgetown University." He motioned towards me. "And the main reason I'm here is that I'm married to this amazing lady."

"Of course, of course. It's a privilege to finally meet you, Dr. Hollingsworth. Kit has told me so much about you," he replied. "Chase Wintergreen. I'm also a congressional chief of staff."

I winced. Even when Chase was trying to play nice, he sounded smarmy. It wasn't a mystery to know what he wanted. Amos Duncan would become the chair of the committee and he would become the committee's staff director. That meant he wanted me out of the way. The problem was that if I didn't join Maeve Dixon in the Senate or she lost, I would be a serious candidate for the committee staff director position. This made me Chase's rival.

"Your boss is on the same committee that Kit's boss chairs?" Doug asked. For a historian, Doug had grown to understand the insider game of politics in our nation's capital.

"That's correct," said Chase. He took a breath before continuing, but I knew what he was going to say before he said it aloud. "If everything goes according to plan, Representative Amos Duncan will become Chairman Amos Duncan next January. And I hope to work as his lead staffer on the committee."

Doug smiled politely and kept his mouth shut. Meg, however, was not a wallflower.

"There will be a lot of competition for that job," she said, blue eyes blazing.

Chase stuck out his chest. "I'll be well positioned for it." His gaze shifted. "My partner Tom has just arrived. Please excuse me."

Meg tugged at my sleeve. "Does that guy know you might want to stay in the House of Representatives as the committee staff director?"

I rolled my eyes. "He does. I think he's trying to intimidate me."

Meg snorted. "He picked the wrong woman." She waved her hand in a circular motion. "And who would try to intimidate a woman in this place? It's sacred ground for powerful females."

I chuckled. "Good point, Meg. Speaking of sacred ground, should we try to view the exhibits before it gets too crowded?"

Doug, Meg, and Trevor nodded in unison. We exited the tent and returned to the inside of the Belmont-Paul House.

The same National Park Service ranger who had welcomed me earlier greeted us again. "My name is Lily. Can I provide you with a historical overview of the house?"

Doug answered instantaneously. "Yes, please."

I glanced at Meg, bracing for her to show her exasperation with Doug. She consistently chastised him when he showed eagerness for American history. To my surprise, Meg did nothing of the sort. Instead, she nodded in assent. My best friend was ready for a women's history lesson.

We stepped into the hallway of the first floor where Lily began her presentation. "Built originally in 1800, this is one of the oldest houses on Capitol Hill. A man named Robert Sewall was the first owner of the house. It was burned in 1814 by the British and rebuilt in 1820. In the early twentieth century, it was sold to Vermont senator Porter Dale and his wife."

Lily took a breath. "That gives you some background on the house. The history as a women's rights headquarters begins in 1929, when the Dales sold the house to the National Woman's Party, led by Alice Paul."

Trevor glanced around the house, which was quite spacious. "How did Alice Paul afford this house? Wasn't she a Quaker from New Jersey with little personal wealth?"

Lily laughed. "You know suffragist history. She was. Paul didn't purchase the house. The primary donor to the National Woman's Party, a woman by the name of Alva Belmont, gave the money to purchase it."

"So that's why it's called the Belmont-Paul House today," said Meg.

Lily grinned. "You got it. Alice Paul and others had the important ideas about women's equality, but Alva Belmont had the resources."

"But now it's a National Park Service property?" I asked. In my job, it was important to understand the bureaucratic government details that no one else cared about.

"That's right. It became a National Historic Landmark in 1974. There was an important reason why it needed that designation." Lily motioned for us to move closer. She lowered her voice to a whisper. "Senators wanted to tear down the house and build a tennis court."

Doug shook his head in disapproval. "Even though the National Woman's Party had occupied the house since 1929?"

Lily smirked. "I'm not sure that women's history was on their mind. Nevertheless, the house was saved and in 2016, the National Woman's Party donated the house to the National Park Service, and President Obama made it a national monument dedicated to women's equality."

"And that," said Doug, pausing for emphasis before finishing his point, "is why it's important to know history."

"Don't quote me, but for once, I completely agree with you," said Meg, with a gleam in her eye.

Lily proceeded to give us a highlighted tour of the house. The area where we were standing was known as the "Hall of Portraits." We examined busts of famous suffragists, a statue of Joan of Arc, Susan B. Anthony's desk, Elizabeth Cady Stanton's chair, and an original banner from the women's suffrage movement. Lily also told us about the exclusion of Black women as leaders in the most prominent suffrage organizations.

"There's many more artifacts, pictures, and sights to see in the house," Lily said. "We have so many guests here today, I need to attend to the next group."

"Don't worry," said Meg. "Kit and I will be back another time for the extended tour."

Lily grinned. "I'll take you upstairs next time so you can see Alice Paul's bedroom. She lived in this house for over forty years."

"You have our word. We'll make an appointment with you to see the whole place," I said.

Doug pouted. "Are you going to invite me? After all, I'm working on my new book about important women in American history."

I linked my arm in his. "Of course, you're invited. As long as you can tear yourself away from Georgetown to join us."

Never one to be left out, Trevor cleared his throat. "I would appreciate an invitation, as well."

Lily chuckled. "You don't need one. This is a National Park Service site, remember? Anyone can visit."

"Trevor, we won't forget to bring you," I said quickly. "We'd better get back to the reception. It's been a long day and I want to check in with Bev Taylor before we head home."

"Is that absolutely necessary?" asked Trevor.

"Yes, it is," I said firmly. "I know you don't like working with Bev . . ."

Trevor cut me off before I could finish my sentence. "I can work with almost anyone." He grabbed the lapels of his suit jacket and straightened them for emphasis. "But Bev Taylor is too much."

We walked through the house and were near the entrance of the tent. "Is Bev the woman who runs the Capitol Visitor Center?" asked Doug.

"That's her," said Meg, gesturing across the way.

Doug gazed in the indicated direction. "She looks a lot like you, Kit."

"I suppose there's a resemblance," I said, touching my black suit. "We're dressed in similar attire today."

"Bev and Kit might look alike, but that's where the similarity ends," said Trevor.

"Take a deep breath, Trevor," I said. "I'm going to wave her over."

I motioned across the room and caught Bev's eye. She walked over to our group, joined by intern Jill.

I introduced Doug to Bev and Jill. He shook their hands politely. "I've heard both of you have worked very hard on this project. Congratulations are in order."

"There's no reason to congratulate anyone yet. The first public program starts tomorrow. That's when we'll know if we're successful," said Bev, with a huff in her voice.

"You really know how to accept a compliment," said Trevor. "I might need to nominate you for Miss Congeniality."

Bev sneered. "You've been nothing but an impediment during this entire planning process, Trevor. First thing tomorrow, I'm going to talk to your boss James Bennett about removing you from this team."

This repartee was not what I had in mind when I called Bev over. Before I could interject to calm everyone down, Trevor raised his voice. "You will do no such thing."

"And how are you going to stop me?" asked Bev. "He'll listen to me. I'm the CEO of Visitor Services for the Capitol and I report directly to the Architect of the Capitol. Who are you? Some special assistant." She took a step closer to Trevor and pointed two fingers at his chest. "*You're nothing*."

"Enough! We can't have this type of bickering the night before our first big event," I said. "Tomorrow morning, we are going to have thousands of visitors viewing the Lincoln catafalque and then an entire day of historical lectures and discussions. And we cannot have it ruined by a petty fight within our core team."

Bev stepped back. "We'll get through tomorrow. But the next time I see Bennett in the Capitol, I'm going to talk to him about your attitude, Trevor." She put her hand on her right hip. "You're on thin ice."

I put my hand on Trevor's shoulder. "Let it go," I said softly. "This feud ends now before someone else hears it and we end up in H-O-H." I was referring to the popular feature in the Capitol Hill newspaper *Roll Call* called "Heard on the Hill." It reported all the inside gossip. Most the fodder for the column happened at receptions just like this one. *Roll Call* had readers turning in tips daily. No one wanted to embarrass themselves or their bosses with an unflattering appearance in the popular column.

Meg approached Trevor from the other side. "Kit is right. There's no point in causing a scene." She fixed a frosty stare in Bev's direction before adding, "At least right now."

With Trevor under control, I turned to face Bev. "I wanted to check with you one last time. Any last-minute problems or tasks?"

Bev was about to speak, but Jill cut her off. "The boxes of programs. They need to get dropped off at the site so they're ready to hand out as soon as people are lining up."

Our historians Mila Cunningham and Edgar Beaufort had produced a brief history of the Lincoln catafalque. We planned to distribute the programs, which listed all of the *Spring Into History* events, while people were lined up tomorrow.

"I can take them," I said. "I can deliver them on our way home. They should be at the tent tonight so we will be ready tomorrow morning."

"The printer just dropped them off. I'm sorry they didn't arrive earlier," said Jill, her eyes downcast.

"Don't worry about it," I said sympathetically.

"We'll get the box, and I can carry it to Kit's car," said Doug.

"I parked only a block away," I said. "In fact, I think we're probably ready to call it a night."

Bev nodded curtly. "Make sure you take the box inside the tent, Kit. We don't want it disappearing overnight."

"I'll do it personally," I said.

Doug, Meg, Trevor, and I followed Jill to the foyer of the house, near the check-in table. She pointed to a large box. "That's it. Can you manage it?' she asked.

Doug picked it up. "It's heavy, but I can make it a block."

"See you tomorrow, Jill. Thank you for all of your hard work today," I said.

Jill scurried off as we exited the house and proceeded down the walkway. Doug might have underestimated the box's heft. We made it to the sidewalk on Second Street when he had to put it down.

"Give me a second," he said, his forehead wet with perspiration.

Trevor put his hand on Doug's arm. "It's too heavy to move any distance. I'm going to get my car. Meg and I can take the programs over to the tent."

"Actually, I need to get back to the Library of Congress," Meg said. "We're hosting a reception tonight and a few members of Congress are expected to attend. My deputy from congressional relations is there now, but I told him I would drop by after this is over."

"Do you want me to drive you back to the Jefferson Building?" asked Trevor. The Jefferson Building was the oldest Library of Congress building on Capitol Hill and where receptions were typically held.

"I can walk," she said. "Soon enough, the summer heat will be here, and a leisurely stroll won't be any fun."

Trevor gave Meg a peck on the cheek. "See you tomorrow morning, bright and early, Kit," she said.

"I'll be there, with bells on," I said.

Meg smiled and wiggled her fingers at us before heading south on Second Street in the direction of the Library of Congress.

"Trevor, are you sure you want to take these programs?" I asked. "We can manage to my car between the two of us."

"No," he said firmly. "I'd like to take another brief look at the tent without Bev Taylor buzzing in my ear. I want to make sure everything is set up properly for tomorrow, so you and Meg don't have any surprises when you arrive."

Trevor's innocuous comment turned out to be the understatement of the decade.

Chapter Three

WE WAITED FOR TREVOR TO RETRIEVE HIS CAR and helped him load the box of programs into the backseat. Ten minutes later, Doug and I were driving west along Constitution Avenue, returning home to our condo in the nearby northern Virginia suburb of Arlington.

"Do you feel confident about tomorrow's big debut?" he asked.

My hands tightly clenched the steering wheel of our Prius, the vehicle we shared. It wasn't the late rush hour traffic that stressed me out.

"I'm confident in our plan, but it's hard to know if anyone will show up. There's never been a joint effort across various Washington, D.C. institutions to host a weeklong celebration of American history."

"You've done a good job publicizing it. Besides, it's a rare opportunity to see the Lincoln catafalque up close and not behind glass in the Capitol Visitor Center. And people are *still* excited to participate in events after the end of the pandemic."

"My boss is counting on me to make sure it goes off without a hitch," I said. "It's also a good resume builder. Who knows? I might be out of a job after November."

Doug placed his hand gently on my right hand, which was resting on the divider between the seats. "Kit, we've been down this road before. After everything we've been through in the past two years, I'm confident it will turn out as it's supposed to be."

He was right. I'd lost my job after my first boss, Senator Lyndon Langsford, had been murdered. Then I'd been through the ups and downs of Maeve Dixon's congressional career, including a tight reelection race a few years ago. There was COVID-19 and an insurrection at the United States Capitol. Now, it was a Senate campaign fight. I wasn't new to stressful territory, yet the anxiety persisted. It came with the career choice.

We pulled into the parking garage underneath our building and minutes later, Doug unlocked the door to our condo. Usually, this was the time when we braced ourselves for the boisterous greeting of our dog, Clarence. However, Clarence hadn't been himself recently.

The lock clicked open and sure enough, our chubby beagle mutt was not there to meet us. We walked inside and found Clarence lying on the sofa. His tail thumped several times to acknowledge our presence, but it was a mere shadow of the enthusiasm he previously exhibited when we arrived home in the evening.

I sat on the couch next to him and petted his head. "Clarence, how are you doing?"

He licked my hand and looked up at me with his big brown eyes, which conveyed an unmistakable sadness.

I sighed. "I wish we could figure out what was wrong with Clarence."

"There's nothing physically wrong with him, Kit. The veterinarian is certain of it."

We'd taken Clarence to the doggie doctor and had every possible test and examination done. There was no physical ailment, and he was still a relatively young dog. The next step was engaging a pet psychologist. We hadn't done that yet, but I wondered if Clarence's future included a canine shrink. During the pandemic, we'd spent more time with him at home. It had been a while since we had returned to our regular routine.

I got up and went to the refrigerator, removing leftovers from last night's Chinese takeout that we could heat up for a quick dinner. Clarence followed me into the kitchen and sat politely next to his dog dish.

"Whatever is wrong with him, it hasn't affected his appetite," I said. "All hope is not lost."

After we ate our dinner, it was a quiet evening at home. I watched a mystery movie on Netflix while Doug retreated to his office and worked on his next book. After taking Clarence for his nightly walk, I turned in early so I would be ready for tomorrow's hustle and bustle.

The alarm on my iPhone woke me at six o'clock the next day. I usually liked to linger in bed for a few moments, but there was no time to spare this morning. I leapt out of bed, prepared to hit the shower.

"You can take Clarence out this morning after you get up, right?" I asked Doug, who showed no signs of life.

I waited for several seconds. Nada.

"Doug, you'll take Clarence out soon?" I repeated.

He responded by rolling over and waving me away, which I interpreted as "yes." Twenty minutes later, I was dressed and sipping a frothy homemade cappuccino from our monster espresso machine. It was the only kitchen appliance I knew how to operate. However, I did know how to order delicious takeout or delivery, a critical life skill.

I texted Meg to make sure she was on time, and she responded in the affirmative. I had to leave the car for Doug today, so that meant I would be slogging it on the Metro, the city's subway system that extended into the nearby suburbs. It was notorious for breakdowns and even minor explosions, so it was important to plan accordingly. However, the transportation gods were in alignment today. A quick check of the local traffic and news app confirmed that all trains were running on schedule. It was time to rumble.

I checked in on Doug, who was snoring lightly. Clarence was cuddled next to him, breathing in deep rhythmic unison. How I envied the life of the academic! At least *one* of us got to sleep in— or *two* if you counted Clarence.

The closest Metro station was only a few blocks away, another reason that our condo was the perfect location. Doug had wanted to buy a single-family home deeper in suburbia and I had successfully resisted, at least thus far. The longer I could enjoy the conveniences of living close to the city, the better.

An uneventful thirty minutes later, I arrived at the Capitol South station, ascended to street level via the escalator that was thankfully operational, and proceeded to walk the short distance north to the green patch of land where *Spring Into History* would begin.

As I started the short stroll up First Street, I texted Meg.

I've arrived. R U here?

Three dots indicated she was replying.

Headed your way.

Meg took a different subway line to work than me, so she was likely walking south on First Street. We should meet almost exactly midway, which would place us right on the north lawn of the Library of Congress.

Sure enough, just as I passed the Neptune Fountain and the west side of the Library's Thomas Jefferson Building, I spotted Meg. It was hard to miss her. She was decked out in a red sheath dress, a blue blazer, and glistening white pearls I could see a football field away.

We met directly adjacent to the event tent. "Well, someone decided to adopt a patriotic theme for today," I said.

"You should talk," said Meg, pointing to my outfit. I wore a blue and white polka dot dress, which I'd accentuated with a stylish red scarf.

"Birds of a feather flock together, I suppose."

Meg waved her long red nails. "If the most negative remark today is that we dressed alike, the event will be a resounding success."

"Well, should we go inside and make sure everything is in order?" I asked.

"Sure. There doesn't seem to be a line yet for viewing the Lincoln catafalque."

I glanced at my iPhone. "It's still early. Just over an hour before we open to the public."

Meg nodded and we proceeded to walk over the entrance of the tent. A Capitol Hill police officer was standing outside. We both flashed our federal government identification badges.

The cop grabbed a clipboard resting on the ground. "Marshall? Peters? Check. You're both cleared. Please proceed." He pointed with two fingers for us to enter the outdoor tent.

Meg and I surveyed the scene from a distance. Everything looked exactly as we'd left it last night. I spotted the large box of programs, conveniently placed adjacent to the aisle. The folding chairs had been assembled for the lectures later in the day, and the catafalque was situated at the far end of the tent.

"It looks perfect," said Meg.

"I wonder when the crowds will start to arrive," I said.

Meg pursed her lips. "Pretty soon." She checked her watch. "I bet people will start lining up any moment."

"Maybe no one will show up," I murmured.

Meg playfully slapped my arm with her hand. "Don't be silly, Kit. Of course, we'll get a crowd. People love looking at spectacles, especially anything having to do with Abraham Lincoln and his assassination."

That was exactly why we pushed for the catafalque to headline our first day of events. I surveyed the perimeter of the open tent, trying to figure out if any early birds had arrived. My gaze stopped on the Lincoln catafalque at the opposite end of the tent.

Now it was my turn to grip Meg's arm. "Does the catafalque look out of place to you?"

She followed my gaze and squinted. "I'm not sure," she said. "I have a confession to make."

I took a deep breath and held it in. "Which is?"

"I think I need to get glasses. But I've been avoiding it because I don't think I'll look as sexy in them." She sucked in a breath. "And I'm afraid of that laser surgery."

"We'll deal with that later." I made a mental note to force Meg to schedule an appointment with an optometrist after *Spring Into History* was finished.

Meg scrunched up her face as she scrutinized the catafalque across the tent. "It does look a little . . ."

She paused for a moment, and I took the opportunity to finish the sentence for her. "Bulky, right?"

Meg nodded. "Yes. Bulky."

A black broadcloth covered the seven-foot wooden catafalque, similar in style to the fabric used in 1865 for Abraham Lincoln's funeral.

"Let's take a closer look," I said.

We walked down the aisle of the tent and arrived at the viewing area of the catafalque. There was a ten-foot perimeter around the display, marked by brass stanchions and red velvet rope. Even without stepping over the barrier, it was apparent that *something* was underneath the black funeral cloth covering the catafalque.

Meg spoke in a shaky voice. "What's lying on the catafalque?"

I bit the inside of my lip. "I don't know. Should I get the police officer?"

We looked back toward the entrance of the tent. If he was still there, it wasn't obvious.

"Someone could be playing a cruel hoax," said Meg.

Relief instantly washed over me. "You're right. It might be a clever trick."

"Are you going to . . ." Meg pointed at the catafalque. "Check it out?"

Guests would be arriving soon for the display. We needed to remove whatever was underneath the cloth so it would be ready for visitors by nine o'clock.

"This is ridiculous," I said, with more confidence than I felt. "I don't have time for practical jokes."

I unhooked the red velvet rope from the stanchion and walked up to the catafalque. After taking a deep breath, I pulled back the black broadcloth. All I needed to see was the brown cascading hair before pulling my hand back. This was no hoax. There was a dead body resting on the Lincoln funeral stand.

Chapter Four

I DIDN'T HAVE TO say anything. Meg saw my reaction. Her voice was high-pitched. "This is no joke, Kit."

I moved backwards, now behind the unhooked stanchion and next to Meg. My right hand, which had pulled back the black broadcloth, trembled uncontrollably.

Meg put her arm around me. "Did you see who it was?"

I shook my head back and forth. "It's a woman, I think. But her head . . . it was turned away from me."

This wasn't the first dead body I'd discovered, but the closeness of the corpse and the fact it was lying on the Lincoln catafalque had thrown me for a loop.

I needed to take a moment to get a grip on the situation, so I did what my online yoga instructor told me to do. I took five deep breaths, inhaling and exhaling in a steady rhythm.

"Are you hyperventilating?" asked Meg. She tightened her grip around me. "Kit, are you going to faint?"

I ignored Meg's questions and focused on my breathing. Sure enough, I felt better after the oxygen I'd ingested reached my brain. I'm sure my yoga teacher hadn't thought of discovering a dead body when she recommended deep breaths, but I'd have to tell her it worked.

"I'm okay now," I said. The gears turned inside my head. "We need to tell that police officer what's happened."

We hustled to the entrance of the tent and looked in both directions. I spotted the police officer standing by the sidewalk, talking to another cop.

I waved my hands above my head. "We need help!"

The Capitol cop and his friend paid no attention to us. Meg shook her head in exasperation. After putting two fingers in her mouth, she emitted an ear-piercing whistle.

Both police officers turned in our direction. "Finally," Meg muttered.

"You need to come over to the tent," I yelled, cupping my hands around my mouth so they could hear us.

In no apparent rush, the police officer who checked our names earlier walked over to us. "What's the problem, ladies?"

Meg and I looked at each other. No matter how we said it, he was going to think we were loony. Best to blurt it out and get it over with.

"There's a dead body inside the tent," I said.

"On top of the Lincoln catafalque," Meg added.

The cop scratched his chin. "A dead body?" He looked us up and down. "Have you two been hitting the mimosas before coming to work today?"

Meg and I were partial to a good Sunday brunch with bottomless champagne and orange juice, but that certainly wasn't the case this morning.

I pulled my iPhone out of my purse. "Either you walk over with us so you can see for yourself or I'm calling Sergeant O'Halloran."

I hated to pull rank. It was the type of insider Washington, D.C. move that I normally detested. But there was a small matter of a dead person and certainly the cancellation of today's display. To add further complication to the situation, visitors had started to arrive and were lining up outside the tent at the designated spot.

The cop removed a handkerchief from his pocket and wiped his forehead, where perspiration had started to appear. "Okay, okay. No need to call the boss. Let's go inside the tent and you can show me the dead body."

We began to walk back towards the tent entrance. "I'd better call Bev Taylor," I said. "She'll want to know what's happened and why we're going to have to delay the viewing today of the catafalque."

"Good idea," said Meg. "I'm going to stay out of her way. She's *not* going to like this."

We entered the tent as I dialed Bev's cell phone. I couldn't text her with this type of news.

Meg and I reacted at the same time. A familiar ringtone we'd heard before. We both stopped in our tracks.

"Don't you want to show me the dead body?" asked the cop, his chest thrust out and his arms crossed in front of his body.

I ignored his comment and turned toward Meg. "Do you recognize that cell phone ring?"

"Didn't you just dial Bev?" she asked.

I nodded slightly and pointed toward the Lincoln catafalque. "It's coming from over there."

I wasn't sure the cop followed what had happened, but at least we now had his full attention. He walked past the stanchions and pulled back the black broadcloth. I could hear his gasp from ten feet away.

He stepped backwards but didn't replace the broadcloth. The phone kept ringing.

The cop turned around to face us. "Are you calling the dead woman on her phone?"

I gulped and held my phone out. "I think so. If I'm not mistaken, that's Bev Taylor, the head of the Capitol Visitor Center."

He steadied himself and returned to the catafalque. He placed his hand on the victim's neck and waited. After ten seconds, he shook his head and pulled out his radio.

"This is Officer Menendez. We have a ten-one-hundred here. I repeat. Ten-one-hundred. My location is the tent on the Library's north lawn. Copy."

The radio crackled with a response. "Menendez, a ten-one-hundred? Are you sure? Copy."

"Affirmative. Send backup immediately. Copy."

"That's a ten-seventy-six, Menendez. Copy."

The officer placed his radio back in his side holster. "Help is on the way," he said. "Sorry that I didn't believe you earlier."

"It's okay. I would have done the same," I said.

Keeping my distance, I glanced over at the catafalque. Bev's phone had stopped ringing. I couldn't see her face, thankfully. But the long brown tresses were a dead giveaway, no pun intended. Between last night and this morning, our fearless leader of *Spring Into History* had somehow met her untimely death.

Meg was furiously texting on her phone. "Who are you contacting?" I asked.

Even though she now worked at the Library of Congress in congressional relations, Meg was still the social butterfly of Capitol Hill. Normally, her vast network of contacts came in handy for invitations to the best receptions, parties, and exclusive events. But we needed to remain quiet about what happened to Bev for the time being.

"Trevor," she said. "Don't worry. I'm keeping it under wraps. He needs to know about this."

At first, Meg's response confused me. Why did Trevor need to know? Let's face it. He wasn't exactly besties with Bev Taylor. I looked over at Meg. Worry lines appeared on her face. Then, I suddenly understood her concern. Meg was already several steps ahead. It was highly unlikely that Bev had died of natural causes, given the arrangement of the body on the catafalque. That meant Bev had been murdered. If so, the hunt for the killer would begin as soon as the police descended. Who had argued publicly with Bev Taylor the night before? Trevor.

I touched Meg's shoulder and motioned for her to follow me to the edge of the tent, out of Officer Menendez's earshot. "Are you worried that the police would consider Trevor a suspect?" I asked, keeping my voice low.

Meg's brow wrinkled. "Of course," she hissed. "Everyone knew they detested each other. He picked a fight with her last night at the reception. Then he delivered those programs for you to the scene of the crime."

I'd forgotten that Trevor had offered to drop off the box of programs. That meant he had been here last night. Motive, means, and opportunity were the keys to solving a murder. Trevor had motive and opportunity thus far.

"Relax, Meg. We don't even know when Bev died. Or why," I said.

My best friend stopped texting and looked at me. "Let's find out as many details as possible when the police arrive," she said. We heard the sirens growing louder as they approached.

"As always," I said softly. We joined Officer Melendez when the cavalry arrived.

I spotted a familiar figure enter the tent. It was the portly figure of Sergeant O'Halloran. He was the investigating police officer for the previous murders I'd helped solve on Capitol Hill. The good news was that he knew me and Meg. The bad news was, well, that he knew me and Meg.

"I should have guessed," he said as he walked down the aisle. "Kit Marshall, Congress's own Nancy Drew. And for good measure, her best friend, Blondie." O'Halloran knew Meg's name but preferred to call her "Blondie" after her flaxen hair, which irritated Meg more than anything. Sure enough, Meg's fists were predictably clenched at her sides.

"Sorry to see you again under these circumstances." I really meant it. I genuinely liked O'Halloran. Unfortunately, our paths always crossed when a dead body surfaced, making our relationship rooted in the darkest side of humanity.

"Not as sorry as she is," said O'Halloran, motioning towards the catafalque.

"I believe the victim is Bev Taylor, who runs the CVC," I said.

"You can make a positive identification on her?" asked O'Halloran. He reached inside his suit jacket pocket and pulled out a packet of gum and popped a stick inside his mouth. "Want some? I'm chewing sugarless gum these days instead of eating candy and doughnuts. Trying to lose a few pounds."

I shook my head. "You'll have to check the body, but we're pretty sure it's Bev." I explained calling her cell phone and hearing it ring.

"Okay, okay. It's probably her but we'll make sure. You ladies need to back up while we do our work." A litany of law enforcement had descended inside the tent.

Meg and I took a few baby steps backwards, enough to satisfy O'Halloran while remaining in range of any audible observations he made.

A medical examiner joined O'Halloran and they removed the broadcloth. Now I knew our supposition was correct. The victim was wearing a black pantsuit with heels, the same outfit Bev had been wearing yesterday.

The detail hadn't been lost on Meg. "She never made it home," whispered Meg. "She's wearing the same clothes as yesterday."

I nodded. "That means she was killed last night, rather than earlier this morning."

"It's not good for Trevor." Meg was right. If Bev had died this morning, it wouldn't have mattered that Trevor dropped off the box of programs the night before. But it was looking more likely Trevor had found himself at the scene of the crime at the most opportune time.

"She could have been killed late last night, hours after Trevor was here," I said, trying to brighten Meg's spirits.

Meg and I stopped chatting when we overhead Sergeant O'Halloran speaking to the medical examiner.

"Do we know the time of death?" he asked.

The M.E. shrugged. "I'll know more when I perform the examination, but rigor mortis has set in throughout the body." He lightly touched Bev's hands. "For example, her fingers are already stiff."

"And that means?" inquired O'Halloran. "Refresh my memory. I don't have a medical degree, remember?"

The M.E. chuckled. "I'd say about twelve hours since time of death." He pointed a finger at O'Halloran. "That's a guess, not fact."

O'Halloran looked at his watch. He was working backwards to figure out the timing. Meg had already done it. "She likely died between eight and nine o'clock last night," she said in a shaky voice.

That would have put Trevor right at the scene of the crime within the appropriate time frame. So much for forensics eliminating him from suspicion.

The M.E. glanced in our direction. "Let's keep quiet," I whispered. "We still don't know how Bev was killed and I want to find out before they chase us out of here and take our statements."

We tried to look inconspicuous as the M.E. completed his preliminary examination. We couldn't hear the entirety of the conversation between the two men, but we could make out the words "stab wound" from the conversation. We exchanged knowing glances. That was enough information. Someone had murdered Bev Taylor in cold blood and then displayed her body on the Lincoln catafalque.

A uniformed police officer approached us and asked to take our statements. He escorted us away from the body and proceeded to ask us a million questions about how we found poor Bev and every single movement before and after our gruesome discovery. Normally, the person or persons who find a body are automatically considered suspects, but Officer Menendez must have vouched for us. Besides, we knew that Bev had been lying there for a long time before we found her.

We were just wrapping up with the interview when intern Jill appeared.

"I had to talk my way into the tent," she said breathlessly. "The entire block is surrounded by police. Is it true what I heard?"

I nodded and put my arm around Jill's shoulder, giving it a light squeeze. "Yes, I'm afraid so. Bev Taylor was murdered here."

Jill put her hand over her mouth. "How terrible! Do they know who did it?"

"The police are just beginning the investigation," said Meg. "But it seems as though it happened last night."

"After the reception at the Belmont-Paul House?" asked Jill.

"Probably," I said. "Around that time, although nothing is official yet."

"Weren't you here to drop off the box of programs?" Jill frowned. "Did you see anything?"

"I gave the box to Trevor," I said. "He offered to do it for me, so I never returned to the tent."

"Well, I guess the police will want to hear what he has to say," said Jill.

Meg groaned. If intern Jill could figure out Trevor was a suspect, certainly Sergeant O'Halloran wouldn't be far behind.

"Let's not rush to any conclusions about what the police will or won't investigate," I said. "Someone like Bev was bound to have enemies."

"But the murderer had to know that Bev was going to be at the tent," said Meg. "The person had to be familiar with *Spring Into History*."

Meg's comment got me thinking. We had security cameras installed inside the tent because of the Lincoln catafalque display.

"Does Sergeant O'Halloran know about the security cameras?" I asked. "We might have the murderer on digital video."

"Good point, Kit," said Meg. "Maybe this won't be one of these long, drawn out investigations we're used to dealing with."

"Let's hope you're right," I said. "I'm going to ask O'Halloran about it."

Jill stopped me before I could leave. "What should I do? Do you need me to do anything?" Her face displayed worry.

I moved into mentor-mode. "Just keep your head down," I advised. "Let me talk to the Sergeant and see what he knows."

Jill nodded in quiet assent, and I marched over to the sergeant, who had finished up with the medical examiner. He was paging through his spiral notebook. Not a techie, O'Halloran employed old-school methods. He preferred to write his case notes using pen and paper.

"Sergeant O'Halloran," I said. He looked up from his scrawl. "Have your officers retrieved the footage from our security cameras?" I pointed in the vague direction where they were placed, attached at the rafters of the tent.

"Look closer, Ms. Marshall," said O'Halloran. He returned his gaze to the notebook.

I looked in the approximate direction of where we'd placed the two cameras. Sure enough, nothing was there.

"What happened to them?" My pulse quickened as I thought about the ramifications of the discovery.

"Someone knocked them down," said O'Halloran. "We'll check

the digital footage, but I'm sure the person responsible, likely our murderer, did it from behind the line of sight of the two cameras."

"No one was captured committing the crime at hand?" I asked. I already knew the answer.

"I seriously doubt it," said O'Halloran. "But you tell me, Ms. Marshall. What detail does that reveal about our perpetrator?"

A few years ago, O'Halloran wouldn't have asked me that question. Since then, I'd earned his trust. I appreciated his attempt to sharpen my sleuthing skills. At this point, he didn't even bother to urge me *not* to investigate.

"The killer knew where the cameras were located," I said. "It implies an inside job. The murderer didn't have a lot of time to commit the crime." I glanced toward the entrance of the tent. "Maybe when the police officer on duty took a restroom break."

O'Halloran smiled. "Good observations, kid. I'm guessing the killer knew something about the setup of the tent." He pointed his pen directly at me. "Which means you need to tell me more about this Springtime History or whatever it's called."

"*Spring Into History*," I said.

He waved his hand. "Whatever. I don't need to know the name of it. I need to know who knew about the cameras."

"Of course, the Capitol Hill police officers who installed them for security purposes," I said.

"Yeah, I'll check on those guys, but I doubt they're the guilty party. Tell me about the political types who knew about it."

"That would be our planning committee," I said. "Besides Bev, it was me, Meg, James Bennett, Trevor, Chase Wintergreen, Mila Cunningham, and Edgar Beaufort."

O'Halloran was furiously scribbling in his notebook. He stared at what he'd written. "I know you, Blondie, Bennett, Trevor, and Wintergreen. But who are the other two?"

"You wouldn't know them. They're our two consulting historians," I said. "They helped us plan these events, such as which speakers to invite and what topics to focus on."

"Outsiders to Capitol Hill," said O'Halloran. "But they still knew about the setup in the tent?"

"They did. We discussed the security cameras at one of our planning meetings. It wasn't cheap to have them installed inside the tent, but Bev insisted on it. Our two historians agreed with her."

"Very interesting, Ms. Marshall. I don't think I have anything else for you now. If you've given your statement, you're free to go," he said. "Obviously, we need to cancel today's events scheduled for inside the tent."

I knew that was coming. "What about the Lincoln catafalque?"

"We'll take care of it. Right now, it's part of a crime scene. But we'll make sure it gets back to its home inside the Capitol Visitor Center once we're finished with it."

"Thank you," I said, relieved that at least the catafalque was in good hands.

As I turned to walk back to Meg and Jill, Sergeant O'Halloran called after me. "Don't forget, Ms. Marshall. If you have information about this crime, you contact me immediately."

I gave him a mini-salute. "Likewise. And I'll be sure to keep my boss informed. She's going to want to know what happened and who was responsible."

O'Halloran didn't respond. He knew the drill. The Capitol Hill police were beholden to Congress and my boss ran the show when it came to the day-to-day operations, at least when it concerned the House of Representatives. There was no escaping politics in Washington, D.C., even when it came to murder.

"James Bennett is asking everyone to meet inside the Capitol Visitor Center," said Jill. "Can you walk over there now?"

"Sergeant O'Halloran said Meg and I were free to go, as long as we provided our statements, which we have," I said. "Meg, will you join us?" I figured she might need to return to the Library of Congress.

"I've already checked in with Dorian. He knows what's happened," said Meg.

Dorian was Meg's boss and the chief of staff for the Librarian of Congress. We'd worked with him on an earlier case when a national treasure had been stolen from the Library of Congress in conjunction with a murder in the Librarian's ceremonial office.

"And he doesn't want to speak with you personally?" I asked. After all, the Library of Congress was a lead sponsor of *Spring Into History*.

"Dorian can wait," said Meg, pausing for a beat before adding, "Trevor will meet us over at the CVC."

Ahh. The real reason for Meg's desire to join us at the Capitol Visitor Center. She was concerned about Trevor and the fact he might be considered a suspect. I couldn't blame her. When Doug and my brother Sebastian were murder suspects on previous cases, I was particularly keen on figuring out the real killer so I could clear their names. Trevor was Meg's serious, exclusive boyfriend, but he was also my friend. I didn't want anyone to suffer through a murder accusation unnecessarily.

"In that case, we should get moving," I said. "I'll catch up with both of you over there. I need to call Maeve Dixon and then Doug."

I extricated myself from the swarm of police officers and crime scene technicians and tried to find a spot that provided a modicum of privacy. I pulled out my phone and dialed my boss's cell phone number. It rang several times before she picked up.

"Kit, I'm about to head inside a community center in Raleigh for a meeting with voters." Her voice was rushed. "Can this wait?"

"It cannot, Congresswoman. But I will be brief." I recounted this morning's events to Dixon, who remained silent as I provided the details about the victim and the circumstances surrounding it. I made sure to let her know that the details were cloudy, and I would be returning to the scene of the crime for more details.

"My congressional committee is a partner for these series of events," said Dixon. "That means I want you to stay on top of this investigation. I also have oversight of the Capitol Visitor Center, and now the director has been murdered." Dixon paused for a moment. "Do you think I should return to Washington?"

"Perhaps when a memorial service is scheduled for Bev. You should attend."

"Good thought," said Dixon. "In the meantime, I am going to call the chief of the Capitol Hill police to make sure Sergeant O'Halloran knows to keep you in the loop."

"That would be most appreciated," I said. "It always helps to have orders from the top brass."

"I need to go now, Kit. Please keep me informed." The phone call ended abruptly. Maeve Dixon was busy and businesslike. She often terminated conversations without saying goodbye. I'd gotten used to it.

Now I needed to call Doug. News about a murder on Capitol Hill would hit the airwaves soon, and I didn't want him to worry.

He picked up on the first ring. "Kit, aren't you attending the event this morning?"

"Unfortunately, it was cancelled." I explained the grisly discovery of Bev Taylor's body.

After listening to my story, Doug sighed. "Kit, I know you're going to investigate, but please be careful. Someone must have stalked poor Bev, waiting for the right moment to kill her inside that tent."

"I'm afraid Trevor might be considered a suspect," I said. "He was in the tent around the time of the murder. Remember, he dropped off the box of programs for us?"

"And Trevor exchanged angry words with Bev only hours earlier at the Belmont-Paul House," said Doug, putting together the pieces of the puzzle.

"You got it," I said. "It's a recipe for disaster."

"Do you think the event this evening will go on?" he asked.

The *Spring Into History* extravaganza schedule included a Georgetown University lecture tonight on campus.

"I don't know, but I'm headed into a meeting with James Bennett. I'm sure we will decide how to proceed."

"I'll check with Edgar Beaufort about its status later today," said Doug. "I'd better get back to work."

"I hope to see you later tonight," I said.

"Kit, please be careful. If you're right, then the list of people who could have killed Bev is quite short. And you know everyone on that list."

Doug was understandably concerned about my safety, but his final comment reminded me that if everyone involved in our planning committee showed up for our emergency meeting in a few minutes, the killer would likely be present.

After placing my phone inside my purse, I crossed First Street and descended the stairway to the entrance of the Capitol Visitor Center, which was an underground facility built to improve the tourist and learning experience of the United States Capitol and the legislative process. Its construction had been controversial due to inflated cost (a whopping $621 million) but now it had been operational for over a decade, no one could imagine life inside the Capitol without it. Thousands of tourists, school groups, and foreign visitors toured the complex daily, and they learned about the history of Congress inside the CVC.

Approaching the entrance, I noticed there was no one else around, except Meg and Jill, who were waiting for me.

"Is it closed?" I asked.

"I forgot to tell you. Out of an abundance of caution, the police decided to close the Capitol Visitor Center due to the murder. They wanted to make sure the situation was under control," said Jill.

It made sense. If Bev had been killed recently, there could be a murderer in the vicinity, ready to strike again. However, I had a feeling whomever was responsible for Bev's death had covered his or her tracks last night and didn't pose an immediate threat. This was no random killing. Bev had been targeted and the murder was planned carefully. Disabling the security cameras had been a dead giveaway.

"How are we going to get in?" I sized up the police officers who were blocking the entrance.

"They have our names, silly," said Meg.

Sure enough, after we'd flashed our badges and our names were verified, we proceeded through the metal detectors and walked inside. "Where are we going?" I asked.

"Downstairs. On the lower level of Emancipation Hall by the Statue of Freedom," said Jill, who was busy studying her phone. Thankfully, one of us knew what was going on.

After descending on the escalator, I spotted our group across the way, standing in front of the statue. The full-size plaster model, now on display inside Emancipation Hall, was used to cast the bronze statue on top of the United States Capitol dome and had been restored for display. Almost twenty feet in height, the statue's right hand holds a sword while her left hand grasps a victory wreath. On her head is a helmet of stars, an eagle's head, and feathers. Normally, I would have enjoyed seeing my colleagues gathered by the impressive statue and probably insisted on a group photo for Twitter. Given the circumstances, it wasn't appropriate.

James Bennett was joined by House of Representatives staffer Chase Wintergreen, historians Mila Cunningham and Edgar Beaufort, and of course, Trevor. Meg walked over to Trevor and put her arm around his waist, giving him a gentle squeeze. Trevor said nothing but smiled weakly at Meg. His silence was noteworthy. Trevor was usually the first to ask a question or demand that someone take action.

Bennett spoke first. "I'm glad everyone is safe, and we have been able to gather to discuss next steps."

Everyone stood awkwardly, listening to Bennett. "James, might we consider sitting at one of the tables over there?" I pointed to the empty cafeteria, usually swamped by tourists looking for a place to get off their feet and rest.

Bennett looked at his watch. "Sure. I don't think the CVC will open up for another thirty minutes or so."

As we walked over to the adjacent cafeteria, I glanced at the other statues that lined Emancipation Hall, which had been named in honor of the enslaved people who had built the United States Capitol. My favorite was Kamehameha from Hawaii, one of the largest and apparently the heaviest statue in the entire collection. His golden cloak and sword showed he was a warrior, yet his right hand was outstretched in a traditional *Aloha* greeting. I also liked Jeannette Rankin from Montana, the first woman elected to Congress in 1916 and an ardent suffragist. A young Helen Keller from Alabama rounded out my personal favorites. The entire Capitol collection included two statues from each state, and I found it fascinating to discover which famous residents were chosen for the memorials.

"I'd treat you all to a cup of coffee, but they're not opening until the public is allowed in," said James Bennett.

"Let's discuss moving forward," I said in a businesslike tone. This wasn't a social gathering. One of our colleagues had been killed.

"Did you and Meg discover the body?" asked Trevor.

I nodded and explained the details of this morning. Everyone listened in rapt attention.

"Have the police spoken with you yet?" Meg's question was directed to Trevor.

"No, but I'm sure it won't take long for them to show up," he said.

"And why would the police want to speak with *you*, Trevor?" asked James Bennett pointedly.

Only in Washington, D.C. would someone get jealous about a murder investigation. In our nation's capital, if you didn't figure out a way to stay in the news, it meant that your star was fading. James Bennett wanted the police to focus on him because he was the Chief Administrative Officer of the House of Representatives, not his underling Trevor.

Trevor shifted in his seat uncomfortably. "I was at the tent last night after hours. I dropped off a box of programs that Kit gave me."

"Did you see anyone inside the tent?" I asked.

Trevor shook his head vigorously. "No. It was already dark. I spoke to the police officer who was on guard and showed him my badge. He let me enter the tent and I dropped off the box. I took a quick glance around and left."

"Did you pass the police officer again when you exited?" I asked. This was an important detail and we needed to find out what happened. Precisely.

Trevor must have understood why I asked. "Unfortunately, I did not. I ducked out through an open flap in the tent and went on my way."

"That means anyone could have entered the tent and murdered Bev!" exclaimed Meg.

"It's certainly plausible, but it also means that Trevor could have waited around for the opportunity to kill Bev. No one saw him leave the tent," I said.

James Bennett looked uncomfortable. "You'll have to speak with the police soon, Trevor. The Chief Administrative Officer must be viewed as cooperating with law enforcement."

"Of course. I will be happy to tell my story. It's the *truth*." Trevor emphasized the last word in the sentence.

"Well, now that's settled, we can now discuss how to handle the remainder of the day's planned events," said Bennett.

"Obviously, everything we had scheduled inside the tent today must be cancelled," I said.

"Is that absolutely necessary?" asked James Bennett.

I narrowed my eyes. "Yes, it is. The tent is a crime scene, including the Lincoln catafalque. Even if that wasn't a problem, Bev Taylor was murdered. I'm not sure it makes sense to continue like nothing has happened."

Bennett sat up straight in his chair. "There are members of Congress who were planning to attend."

"I'm sure they will understand. I can speak for my boss, the chair of the relevant committee in charge. Maeve Dixon would not want us to proceed like nothing happened." There was an edge to the tone of my voice. As the Chief Administrative Officer of the House, James Bennett certainly outranked me. But I couldn't let his zealotry override good sense.

"I will have to check with my boss," said Chase Wintergreen. "With Chairwoman Dixon on the campaign trail, she entrusted him to provide leadership of the House Administration Committee in her absence."

What a self-important jerk. There was no reason to check with his boss. Before moving crooked, his boss would check with my boss. And we'd be right back where we started.

Edgar Beaufort cleared his throat. "Perhaps I may offer a suggestion?" Edgar straightened his bowtie after speaking.

Bennett gestured for Edgar to proceed.

"I agree that today's events on Capitol Hill must remain cancelled." He bowed his head slightly in my direction. "However, we do have an evening reception at Georgetown University and my lecture."

"I think we can proceed with your lecture and the accompanying reception," said Meg. "You will need to say some kind words about Bev Taylor."

"You'd better start thinking about it right now," said Mila Cunningham. "You'll need all the time you can get to figure out what you can say that's nice about Bev and not a total lie."

Edgar smiled nervously. "I'm sure I will be able to come up something."

Jill interjected. "I can help you draft some talking points if you need it," she said. Jill's eagerness was frequently an asset, although this time, her offer to assist felt a little out of place.

"Perhaps a consultation with the English Department would be beneficial," said Mila. "Since they specialize in *fiction*."

"That's enough," said James Bennett. "Bev was . . ." He paused, searching for the right words. "An acquired taste. Nevertheless, she was talented and served as the director of the Capitol Visitor Center." He took a breath. "A very important position."

"Maeve Dixon will support going ahead with the Georgetown event tonight," I said, looking directly at Chase Wintergreen. "No need to check with your boss."

Chase said nothing. But if looks could kill, I would be floating in the Potomac River by now.

"Then we're settled. We'll reconvene this evening at Georgetown." He looked around the table at all of us. "I expect *everyone* will have something appropriate to say about Bev."

We had our marching orders. It was impressive how quickly James Bennett had taken control of the situation. He had quite a reputation on Capitol Hill, and I was finally experiencing it firsthand. He made it his business to know what was going on.

Our merry band broke up with everyone headed separate ways. I motioned for Meg, Trevor, and Jill to huddle next to the statue of Mother Joseph, a Pacific Northwest missionary representing the great state of Washington.

"What do you think?" I asked to our tight circle.

Meg looked left and right. James Bennett had taken off, likely in pursuit of solving the next crisis. Mila and Edgar were deep in conversation. Chase was lingering, studying his iPhone while clearly trying to eavesdrop.

Meg came to the same conclusion as me. "Let's get out of here. In a few minutes, the Capitol Visitor Center will open to the public and it's going to be chaos inside."

We were in the middle of the spring break season, signaling the beginning of the summer tourist crunch. Between families visiting the Capitol and school groups, it was one of the busiest times of the year. Emancipation Hall was like Grand Central station during rush hour.

"How about an early lunch?" I asked.

Never one to turn down food, Meg responded enthusiastically. "I'm in the mood for a good burger. How about Good Stuff?"

"James will be busy dealing with the fallout from the murder," said Trevor, glancing at his watch. "I probably have an hour before he'll realize I'm missing from the office."

"Jill, would you like to join us?" I asked. In the training I took before participating in this internship program, we were encouraged to ask our mentees to join us for appropriate social interactions. In other words, happy hours were out. Lunch seemed fine. Everyone had to eat, right? I didn't really know when we would have another chance to talk, given today's events. Lunch would have to suffice as the chat I promised Jill.

She nodded in agreement. "I was supposed to be at the tent all morning and afternoon, so I'm free. I like Good Stuff."

"Let's go. I didn't have time for a proper breakfast this morning," I said.

We exited the Capitol Visitor Center just in time. The police had just started admitting the long line of visitors into the building. After a short walk on Independence Avenue that turned into Pennsylvania, we arrived at Good Stuff Eatery.

"Who owns this place? I know it's someone famous, but I always forget the name," said Jill.

"Celebrity chef Spike Mendelsohn," said Meg. "He has a number of restaurants, but the Capitol Hill location was the original."

We walked inside and scanned the menu on the wall. Yes, Good Stuff Eatery had salads, and they were yummy. However, unless your diet prohibited it, the reason to eat at Good Stuff was the burgers. The fries and milkshakes were a close second.

I really wanted the Farmhouse cheeseburger, Spike's signature creation and most popular selection. However, the waistband of my pantsuits wasn't getting any looser, and there were many more receptions and dinners to come with *Spring Into History*. Instead, I opted for the Free-Range Turkey burger.

Meg, however, felt no guilt when it came to food. She ate what she pleased and never gained an ounce. I'd suggested several times she offer herself as a case study for the Mayo Clinic. She ordered the Good Stuff Melt, a side of fries, and a soda.

She saw me looking at her as she placed her order. "I didn't get a milkshake, okay? I'm trying to restrain myself."

Trevor, who was always conscious about his diet, opted for a Farmhouse Chopped Salad. Jill chose the Fried Green Tomato Veg, one of the vegetarian options on the menu. Since we were early for lunch, there were plenty of tables available. We sat down while we waited for our orders.

"Have the police contacted you?" I asked Trevor.

"Not yet. I suspect it won't be long before they do, however. Once they talk to the police officer who was stationed at the tent last night, I'm sure I will be at the top on their list."

I couldn't disagree with Trevor's assessment of his status as a suspect. "Let's talk about the police officer. If the officer was at the tent entrance when you dropped off the box of programs, what happened afterwards? Why didn't he or she see anything?"

Trevor shrugged his shoulders. "I don't know. Like I said, I left the tent at the opposite end. I didn't see anyone, including Bev."

Our orders were ready, and Jill offered to retrieve them for us. She came back with a full tray of food that smelled delicious. My stomach rumbled in response. It was bad to skip breakfast, particularly when I had to deal with a murder. It might be wishful thinking, but I thought that sleuthing burned extra calories.

After distributing our orders, the group conversation came to a halt as everyone dug into their lunches. Meg offered me a French fry and I didn't turn her down, dipping it in the famous Old Bay sauce.

Trevor finally broke the silence. "We don't know why Bev was inside the tent last night."

"Good point, Trevor. She gave me the programs to deliver, which you brought to the tent instead. There wasn't a reason for her to be there," I said.

"We also don't know when she was there," said Meg. "Trevor, do you remember when you dropped off the box?"

"I didn't do it immediately after leaving the reception at the Belmont-Paul House. Instead, I went back to my office and finished up some work. I pulled my car up on First Street, as close as I could get to the tent and unloaded the box from my trunk," he said.

I helped myself to another French fry. Meg was so focused on Trevor's answer, she didn't seem to mind. "You don't know what time it was?" I asked.

"Pretty late. Maybe around eight or nine o'clock," he said.

"It was dark outside?" asked Meg.

"It was," said Trevor. "When I went inside the tent, I had to use my cellphone as a light so I could see where I was going."

Meg and I exchanged glances. Great minds think alike, or at least great detective minds do.

"I wonder if Bev had already been murdered by the time you dropped off the box," I said.

"Did you look at the Lincoln catafalque?" asked Meg.

Trevor slowly shook his head back and forth. "I didn't. Quite frankly, being inside the tent with the catafalque was sort of creepy. I didn't stick around."

Since Trevor didn't see anyone inside or outside the tent and didn't look closely at the catafalque, it was impossible to know whether the murder had already happened when he was there. After all, in broad daylight, it had taken Meg and I several minutes to observe that something was underneath the black cloth that covered the catafalque.

"Maybe Sergeant O'Halloran will have more details soon," Meg said, munching on her burger.

"Trevor, your boss certainly assumed charge this morning," I observed.

He rested his fork next to his salad. "That's James Bennett for you. Always bossing someone around."

"You don't like him?" I asked. Trevor had worked inside the office of the Chief Administrative Officer for a couple years now as a senior advisor, but James Bennett had only been in the lead role for a short period of time.

Trevor considered my question for several moments before answering. Always deliberate and formal, Trevor never rushed his response to tricky questions. It was part of the reason why he'd done well for himself in Washington, D.C.

"I wouldn't say that," said Trevor diplomatically. "It's been a period of adjustment. His leadership style isn't the same as mine."

"Meaning?" I wasn't going to let Trevor off the hook so easily.

"Upon occasion, James reminds me of a stereotypical character in television political drama. He can be ruthless and cunning, yet also your best friend at the same time."

"Sounds like Machiavelli," I said.

"As you might recall, Machiavelli stated that it's better to be feared than loved. Ideally, it's best if the prince is both feared *and* loved," said Trevor. "That is James Bennett in a nutshell."

I suddenly remembered we hadn't spoken to Jill during the lunch. There was no point in taking an intern to lunch if you didn't speak to her the entire time. If I didn't watch it, Jill would give me failing marks as a mentor and I'd never participate in the leadership development program again. Of course, how many other mentors provided career advice during a murder investigation?

"Jill, I'm sorry we've forgotten you in our conversation. How are you doing?" I asked. "I imagine this must be quite confusing for you. We've helped to solve murders before, so it's not entirely new to us."

She put down her sandwich. "I'm fine. Just taking it all in, I suppose." Then she added, "I know that you're an amateur sleuth. I read about it in the newspapers after I asked you to serve as my mentor in the program."

Trevor looked at her like he'd never seen her before. He pushed his salad aside and adjusted his glasses. "Are you learning a great deal in your internship?"

Jill's face brightened. "I certainly am. I'm accomplishing all my goals. There's been a few unexpected obstacles, like what happened today, but everything is on track."

"Good for you," said Meg. "How do you like working with Kit?" She winked playfully at Jill and lowered her voice. "You can tell me what you *really* think."

"It's been exactly what I hoped for. I asked to work with her and I'm thrilled she agreed," said Jill.

"Certainly not a dull moment with Ms. Marshall," said Trevor. "You probably are getting more than you bargained for. Why did you decide to accept this specific assignment for your internship?"

"I'm ambitious, but if I didn't have the support from this internship, my family situation would have prevented me from working on Capitol Hill." The table fell silent as Jill sat straight in her chair. "I knew what I was getting into when I requested Kit as a mentor. Like I said, everything is working out the way I planned it. Despite what happened today, I don't have any regrets."

Jill hadn't really answered Trevor's question, but I was impressed by her drive and dedication. I pointed at Trevor and Meg. "Don't listen to these two. They're just trying to cause trouble."

"That's like the pot calling the kettle black," said Trevor.

As usual, Trevor's words rang truer than I would ever admit.

Chapter Five

AFTER FINISHING OUR LUNCHES, the members of our merry band each went their separate ways. Jill left for Georgetown University to oversee setup for this evening's lecture. Meg headed to the Library of Congress, no doubt saddled with the task of explaining to the powers-that-be about what had happened this morning at the debut event of *Spring Into History*. Trevor returned to his office, likely to face additional questions from his boss and eventually the police.

I decided to take a detour before heading to Representative Dixon's suite located inside the Cannon House Office Building. Sergeant O'Halloran had more time to process the crime scene, and I wondered whether he might share additional details with me, especially if the chief of the Capitol Hill police had let him know about my boss's instructions.

The police had the entire area surrounding the tent blocked off with yellow police tape. Luckily, I saw O'Halloran in the distance and called out to him. He motioned for the officer to allow me through. I trotted over to the beefy sergeant.

"Ms. Marshall, why am I not surprised to see you again at the scene of the crime?" He snapped his chewing gum. At least he was sticking to his diet and not munching on chocolate and candy as he previously did.

"I figured I would stop by before heading back to my office," I said. "Are there any updates about the investigation?"

O'Halloran pulled out his notebook from his back pocket and consulted it. "Well, let's see. I got a phone call from the big boss saying that I was supposed to keep you informed about the investigation. I don't suppose you had something do with that, did you?"

"Actually, it was Chairwoman Dixon who made that decision. She's running for the Senate, as you might know, so she's campaigning in North Carolina presently. I'm her eyes and ears on the ground."

"That's such a nice way of putting it," said O'Halloran. I knew him well enough now to understand he was teasing me. As long as I shared information with him, we made a pretty effective team.

"Anything I should know about?" I asked.

"A few things, Ms. Marshall. First, I think you heard the medical examiner when you and Blondie were eavesdropping earlier. The time of death is the late evening, around eight or nine o'clock."

I nodded. "You're right. I did *overhear* that detail."

"What a polite euphemism." O'Halloran raised his eyebrow.

"Where was the police officer at that time?" I asked. "The one supposedly guarding the tent and the catafalque."

O'Halloran wiped the sweat off his brow. "Unfortunately, the cop assigned to watch the tent wasn't as diligent as you might have hoped. After a stern interrogation by yours truly, he confessed that he walked away from the posted location several times, potentially during the time period in question." O'Halloran flipped through the pages in his notebook. "He used the bathroom inside the Library of Congress, and on his way back, he stopped to talk to his buddy who was working the late shift inside the parking booth in front of the Jefferson Building."

I sighed. "Plenty of time for Bev to appear, the killer to strike, and place her body on top of the Lincoln catafalque."

"I'm afraid so, Ms. Marshall. And, of course, the cop in question didn't see or hear anything that might be helpful. In case your boss is wondering, we're placing him on administrative leave for now, and disciplinary charges will likely be forthcoming."

Maeve Dixon would care about that detail, but right now, I was focused on learning as much as possible from O'Halloran about the murder of Bev Taylor.

"Bev was killed last night. Did the murder take place inside the tent?" I asked.

"We don't know for sure, but it appears as such. There was no trail of blood to indicate she was moved. The ground around the catafalque didn't appear disturbed."

That made sense, since we knew the cameras had been disabled. The killer seemed to know the victim would be inside the tent and took advantage of the cop who had left his post.

"And the manner of death," I said. "You can confirm she was stabbed?"

"I suppose that's another example of *overhearing*, huh?"

"Well, you did mention blood. And when I saw the body briefly earlier today, it didn't appear she'd suffered a severe blow to the head."

O'Halloran narrowed his eyes. "A fair deduction, Ms. Marshall. I'll give you that one." He flipped through the pages of his trusty notebook again. "Stabbing was the likely cause of death. We'll have to wait for the formal autopsy, but that's a reasonably safe conclusion to make. We even found what we believe was the murder weapon."

"Really?" That was important news.

"I had police officers scour the area around the tent. In a garbage can a few blocks away, we found a bloody letter opener," he said.

"A letter opener?" I repeated back.

"You know, one of those thingamajigs that are sharp at the end and open envelopes." O'Halloran looked at me skeptically.

"I know what a letter opener is, but it's certainly an odd weapon," I said. "Has it already been sent for processing?"

"Yep," said O'Halloran, chomping his gum. "But I did take a photo of it with my smartphone." O'Halloran proudly pulled a brand-new phone out of his back pocket.

I was impressed but couldn't resist a gentle tease. "Joining the twenty-first century, huh?"

"I still don't trust these devices for keeping track of all my details. I won't give up my notebook for that." He took a deep breath. "But I have to admit these phones do come in handy for those of us who fight crime." O'Halloran stared at the device held in his thick right hand.

"Do you think I could see the digital image of the supposed murder weapon?" Perhaps I was pushing my luck, but after all, he'd mentioned the photo he'd taken of it.

O'Halloran pursed his lips and remained silent for several seconds. He spoke slowly. "I can show you, but no tweeting or posting or snapping about it."

I suppressed a giggle. "Do you mean Snapchat?"

"Whatever it is." O'Halloran took a deep breath. "I don't want to read about this online, either on the Washington Post's website or Tik Tok's app."

I patted O'Halloran gently on the shoulder. "Congratulations. You got that last one right. But you don't have to worry. I don't spend much time on social media. It takes enough of my energy to make sure Maeve Dixon's profiles are managed well. I don't have the energy for my own."

O'Halloran nodded and swiped across his phone until he found the photo. He handed the phone to me. "Here it is."

I expanded the photo with my fingers so I could see the detail better. Almost immediately, I knew where the killer had gotten the letter opener.

"I'm sure you know this already, Sergeant, but that letter opener was purchased inside the Capitol Visitor Center," I said.

"And how are you so sure?" asked O'Halloran.

"The seal of the United States House of Representatives is on it," I said. "Furthermore, I recognize the type of letter opener. Occasionally, Congresswoman Dixon needs to have small gifts on hand. For example, we provide tokens of appreciation to departing staff members and interns. As you know, campaign funds can be used to purchase nominal value gifts sold by the House gift store, located inside the Capitol Visitor Center. We've definitely purchased this letter opener several times for that purpose."

O'Halloran raised his eyebrows. "So, you knew where to buy a souvenir that could be used as a murder weapon?"

I waved my hand to dismiss O'Halloran's thinly veiled accusation. "You shouldn't be focused on me. I have a solid alibi during the time in question. However, what I'm trying to tell you is that this item is a popular one. Anyone had access to buy it. I bet the gift shop sells hundreds of these letter openers each week. It will be impossible to figure out who purchased the one used to kill Bev Taylor."

"That's helpful information, Ms. Marshall," said O'Halloran. "I have to admit, sometimes your inside knowledge is insightful."

I felt my face flush. This was probably the most effusive compliment I'd ever received from Sergeant O'Halloran. We'd come a long way from the days when he pursued me as a prime suspect in the death of my former boss, Senator Lyndon Langsford.

"I'm glad I could help," I said. "As always." I figured this was the last piece of information that O'Halloran was going to provide, so I turned to leave.

"Wait one moment, Ms. Marshall," said the sergeant.

I spun back around. "Was there something else?"

O'Halloran nodded. "Your friend Trevor who works for the Chief Administrative Officer. He was present at the scene of the crime last night. Do you know why?"

"I do." I tried to keep my voice light as I explained Trevor's task of dropping off the programs.

O'Halloran was scrubbing in his notebook. "Do you know if he saw anything inside the tent?"

"You'll have to speak to him directly, but I just had lunch with him and asked the same question. He said he did not see anything noteworthy."

O'Halloran touched the tip of his pencil to his temple. "Did Trevor know the victim?"

"He did. Remember, they were both on the organizing committee for *Spring Into History*."

"Yes, that's right. You mentioned that earlier when we spoke," he said. "So, were they friends?"

Uh-oh. I didn't like where this conversation was headed. It was time to invoke my inner politician. I'd never been elected to office, but I'd spent plenty of time around people who had. Many of their habits had rubbed off on me. One of the most common behaviors was the "deflect and redirect," which I was about to implement.

"They definitely knew each other," I said vaguely. "Capitol Hill is really like a small town, especially if you've worked here as long as they have."

O'Halloran squinted. "Perhaps I need to be more direct, Ms. Marshall. Did they like each other?"

Now it was time to employ another tactic, popularly known as "delay and scatter."

"You'd really have to ask Trevor that question. I wouldn't want to speculate in the middle of a murder investigation." I grabbed my phone out of my purse and glanced at it. "Wow, look at the time. I haven't made an appearance at our office today. I'd better do that right now. I wouldn't want to lose my day job. It pays the bills!"

Before O'Halloran could ask me another difficult question I didn't want to answer, I wagged my fingers in a "see you later" goodbye wave and headed off in the direction of the Cannon House Office Building, located adjacent to the United States Capitol.

Once I was out of earshot, I punched in Trevor's landline office number on my cellphone. I didn't want to text him. For all I knew, the police had gained access to his cell phone and were monitoring his texts and communications. I guessed that O'Halloran already knew that Bev and Trevor weren't besties. Instead, he'd asked me about it to affirm a hunch he already had.

There was an empty outdoor table on the plaza of the Library of Congress's Madison Building, tucked alongside the eastern edge of the structure. It was a hidden spot away from the public and potential eavesdroppers. It takes one to know one.

The call connected and rang twice before Trevor picked up.

"Kit, is that you?"

Leave it to Trevor to forego common pleasantries like "hello" or "good afternoon."

"Yes, it is. How did you know?"

"There's caller ID that provides the phone number calling. I recognized your number."

I couldn't remember any phone numbers if my life depended on it, but Trevor was certainly an unusual character. He took great pride in eschewing typical conventions, both social and work-related. I'd grown to appreciate Trevor's quirks. Others were not so forgiving, such as the recently departed Bev Taylor.

"I called because I just finished speaking with Sergeant O'Halloran at the crime scene. He asked why you were onsite during the approximate time of the murder."

"That's easily explained, Kit." There was a tinge of annoyance in Trevor's voice. He wasn't one for small talk.

"That's not why I'm calling," I said, not bothering to hide the annoyance in *my* voice. After all, I was a busy person, too. "The sergeant pressed me about your relationship with Bev."

"My relationship? There wasn't one to speak of," said Trevor.

"I tap danced like Ginger Rogers and then told him I had to get back to work," I said. "I didn't tell him you were at odds with her."

The line was silent for several seconds. Finally, Trevor spoke. "Thank you. I appreciate your discretion."

"Not a problem. After all, it's the better part of valor." I laughed weakly at my half-baked attempt at a joke.

"I assume that the police will contact me imminently. Because of your phone call, I will be prepared for their visit," said Trevor, a tone of finality in his voice.

"Don't get too worried. It's only a police interview. You're not being accused of anything or arrested."

"Not yet," said Trevor.

"Oh, I almost forgot one more detail," I said. "The murder weapon is a letter opener from the gift shop inside the Capitol Visitor Center. You haven't bought a letter opener from there recently, have you?"

"Of course, I have," said Trevor. "The CAO gives them out as gifts for foreign visitors. You can't imagine how many visiting heads of parliament we get there. Everyone wants to know how the United States Congress functions, although sometimes I wonder why."

Well, that wasn't good news. "Hopefully you can account for the items you've bought for your boss. I bet they'll ask you about it."

"Another helpful tip. This conversation has been most enlightening, Ms. Marshall. However, now I must return to my work and preparations."

"You're welcome, Trevor."

The dial tone came on the line, indicating the end of the call. Of course, with Trevor, there were no pleasantries to end a conversation, either. I'd grown to look past Trevor's irascible nature, yet I had the benefit of knowing him better than most. My only hope was that my friend's boorish behavior didn't turn into a one-way ticket to the D.C. jail.

Chapter Six

—⚬—

I LEFT MY PRIVATE outdoor table near the Madison Building and walked the block and a half west to the Cannon House Office Building. As I flashed my badge at the congressional staff screening door, I wondered whether my days entering the building this way were numbered. If Maeve Dixon lost her Senate bid, I could try to make a play for the staff director job at the committee. But if that gambit didn't work, I would be on the outside looking in. Not a great feeling of reassurance, especially after the murder of a close associate like Bev Taylor.

Five minutes later, I strode into my compact, private office inside our congressional office suite. As I sat down, I sighed. We weren't involving ourselves in too many legislative battles these days, but there were co-sponsorship memos to review, constituent meetings to prioritize, and budgets to balance. We were running both at half-speed and full-speed, and now I had a murder to top everything off, like a bright red cherry on a hot fudge sundae. Thinking of ice cream made me hungry, in addition to feeling overwhelmed and stressed.

I didn't have much time to ponder my state of discontent. My phone line buzzed, and I picked it up. It was Patsy, the congresswoman's trusted and inviolable scheduler.

"Kit, Maeve is on the line for you. Can I patch her in?"

"Of course, please do."

The line beeped a few times, and then I heard my boss's familiar voice.

"Kit, are you there?"

"Yes, Patsy connected us. How was the meeting with voters in Raleigh?"

I could hear Maeve's deep intake of breath. "Not as productive as I planned, I'm afraid. Chester Nuggets is making an issue of my voting record in Congress."

"On what issue?" I asked. Was it the environment? LBGTQ rights? Immigration? On most issues, like defense, the budget, foreign policy, and social security, Dixon was squarely in line with North Carolina voters. There were a few issues, however, that put my boss slightly askew from the average voter in the state.

"He says that I've missed too many votes during my tenure," said Dixon flatly.

Maeve Dixon didn't miss votes, so such rhetoric made no sense to me. "How many times is he claiming?" I asked.

"Three times," she said. "He said that's three strikes against me and I should be out. He vows he'll never miss a vote as a senator."

"Missing three votes is hardly derelict. Surely the voters of North Carolina will realize how ridiculous this claim is."

Maeve sighed. "I'm sure they will. But right now, it's the crisis of moment."

"Well, speaking of crisis . . ."

Maeve cut me off. "That's why I called you. Has the police sergeant gotten the message you're supposed to be included in the murder investigation?"

"He did, and I appreciate your intervention earlier today."

"Are there any leads? I hope Ms. Taylor's killer can be apprehended quickly."

"None to speak of, except . . ." My voice trailed off.

I could hear the skepticism in Maeve Dixon's voice. "What aren't you telling me, Kit?"

Ah, my boss knew me too well. If she lost her Senate race and we no longer worked together, I would miss our rapport.

"It's Trevor, Congresswoman. The police consider him a suspect.

He was at the scene of the crime near the time Bev was killed, and they didn't like each other much."

"That is unfortunate, Kit. You've known Trevor for a long time. However, he's not affiliated with *my* congressional office in any way. Correct?"

I admired Maeve Dixon for a lot of reasons, such as her work ethic, sense of fairness, and decisiveness. But when it came down to it, she was a politician running for higher office. She was concerned about the impact on her brand, her name, her persona. Everyone else was collateral damage.

"He's *my* friend, but you're right. He's not affiliated with *your* office."

Maeve must have picked up on the slight annoyance in my tone. "I understand why you're concerned, Kit. I'm sure you're confident in Trevor's innocence."

"Of course," I said abruptly. "He's simply a victim of circumstance."

"The sooner the guilty person is apprehended, the better for all involved. Otherwise, I'm afraid it will cast a dark shadow over the history program you've planned."

"By the way, we've cancelled the daytime proceedings, but we're moving ahead with the evening event tonight at Georgetown University."

"That seems reasonable," said Dixon. "Before I forget, you need to touch base with Amos Duncan."

I took a deep breath before answering. My yoga training was still helping. "And why would I need to meet with Representative Duncan?" I asked, in my sweetest possible fake voice.

"Kit, he's next in charge for the committee. You know that the chain of command is important."

Dixon was a veteran, and she never forgot her military training.

"Ma'am, I don't disagree, but I'm staying in contact with you as the chairwoman."

Dixon's voice grew softer. "Not for long, Kit. It's either up or out for me. Amos needs to know what's going on with the murder investigation."

I swallowed hard. "I understand. I'll make an appointment with him as soon as possible."

"And I will let him know that you will be calling for a time to meet," said Dixon.

"Roger that," I said. "Is there anything else?"

"No, but I need to run. The campaign staff want me back on the hustings. Keep me informed, Kit." Before she hung up, she added hurriedly, "And I wish Trevor the best."

That made two of us.

Chapter Seven

━━∽∽━━

I LET PATSY KNOW THAT I NEEDED AN APPOINTMENT with Congressman Amos Duncan to discuss the investigation surrounding Bev Taylor's death. Five minutes later, my phone rang. It was Chase Wintergreen, Duncan's chief of staff and my immediate competitor for future employment in the House of Representatives.

"Hello, Chase," I said with as much cheer as I could muster for my would-be political rival.

"Our scheduler says that you need time with Amos," he replied. "He's completely booked today."

I pinched the top of my nose in frustration. Nothing was ever easy. However, I had an idea.

"Are you both going to the *Spring Into History* event at Georgetown tonight?" I asked.

"We are," said Chase. "My boss is speaking for the House of Representatives."

He never ceased to remind me that Maeve Dixon was absent these days for many of these ceremonial events. It couldn't be avoided. When Congress wasn't in session, Maeve was campaigning for the Senate seat. It was more important for her to be there than here, although dealing with Chase Wintergreen daily was an unfortunate consequence.

"It's a bit of a drive over to Georgetown, especially during rush hour. Perhaps I could ride with you and Representative Duncan," I said.

Chase was silent on the other end of the line. He didn't like me spending time around Duncan. After all, it was an opportunity to get to know him better and perhaps seal the deal on the committee staff director job, if that was the job I pursued after the election. On the other hand, he undoubtedly wanted to insert Duncan into the investigation of Bev Taylor. There would be endless media opportunities in the coming days, and without Maeve Dixon in town, this would be a chance for Duncan to shine.

He must have been weighing the options. Finally, after almost ten seconds, he spoke. "That might work," he said. "Just to clarify, this is about Bev Taylor's murder, right?"

"I spoke to Chairwoman Dixon on the phone this afternoon and she asked that I brief Congressman Duncan about the investigation. As you might imagine, my boss instructed the police to share information with me. I will keep both her and your boss informed."

"You could just tell me what's going on," said Chase. "Then I can relay it to my boss."

I figured Chase would try something like this, and I was ready. "That's not acceptable. Maeve Dixon specifically told me to speak with Amos Duncan about this."

It was a slight stretch of the truth, but I doubted Dixon wanted me to discuss the murder with a third-hand party like Chase. Besides, Chase was a suspect. I wasn't sure about motive yet, but he would have known how to disable the security cameras inside the tent.

"Very well," said Chase. "I will text you and let you know when our car will be leaving Capitol Hill. We will pick you up at the garage exit. Please don't be late."

Chase hung up. He and Trevor had something in common. Neither of them believed in saying "hello" or "goodbye."

I used the afternoon to catch up on email, reviewing documents, and meeting with Dixon staff. Even though our boss was running for the Senate, we still had a congressional office to operate and run. I was determined to let nothing slide on my watch.

It was almost five o'clock and I knew Chase would be texting me soon about leaving. I hadn't let Meg know that I would be riding with Congressman Duncan to the event. She might have thought we would share a ride over.

I tried Meg's extension at her Library of Congress office, and to my surprise, she picked up on the first ring.

"Kit, I was just about to call you," she said.

"Maeve Dixon wants me to brief Amos Duncan about Bev's death and the investigation," I said. "So, I can't share a ride to Georgetown tonight."

"That's fine," she said quickly. "I'm going with Trevor."

I realized I hadn't heard from him recently. "Did the police interview him?"

"Yes. They showed up this afternoon and asked a lot of questions," she said.

Even though I couldn't see Meg, I recognized the concern in her voice. "About his relationship with Bev?"

"Of course, plus everything else. Why was he at the scene of the crime last night? Did he know Bev was going to be there? Did he see anyone else? Has he ever purchased a letter opener from the Capitol Visitor Center gift shop?"

I knew Trevor's answers to those questions. From the police perspective, he was definitely a suspect.

"But they didn't ask him to go to the station?" I asked.

"Not today. They would have, though. For fingerprinting."

"But they already had his fingerprints on record, correct?"

"Yes, they have all of our fingerprints on file."

Federal employment required fingerprinting these days. The Capitol Police handled the process for staff who worked on Capitol Hill in the legislative branch of government.

"Trevor's fingerprints will be all over the scene, just like ours. We were there earlier in the day and inspected everything, including the Lincoln catafalque," I said.

"He told them that," said Meg. "But I'm not sure they are trying to exonerate Trevor. It seems more like they are looking for ways to implicate him."

Meg's impression was likely accurate. Sergeant O'Halloran

wanted to find the person who killed Bev, and Trevor was his best lead so far.

"Don't worry, Meg," I said. "We've dealt with these types of accusations before, and we've always found the person actually responsible for the crime."

Meg sighed. "I know. This is going to cause Trevor a world of trouble. Things were already rocky with his boss. Now, they're much worse."

"Why is that?" I asked.

"James Bennett is considering whether to place Trevor on administrative leave while the investigation is pending," said Meg. "Do you know how embarrassing it would be for Trevor if that happened?"

"Is it *paid* administrative leave?" I asked.

"Yes, Kit, but that's not the point. Being placed on leave will be a permanent blot on Trevor's federal employment record. How would you feel if that was you?"

When I was a suspect in Senator Lyndon Langsford's murder, I hadn't been placed on leave. However, my immediate boss, the legislative director in the Senate office, had believed in my innocence. I wasn't so sure that Trevor enjoyed the same benefit.

"I understand, Meg. Trevor is in a tough spot." I glanced at my phone. Chase had texted me. It was time for me to head to the garage for my ride.

"Hopefully we can brainstorm about the case tonight," said Meg. "The sooner we clear Trevor, the better."

She was right, but I had to run, or I would be late. Chase Wintergreen wouldn't wait one extra second for me.

"We'll talk about it more after the event tonight," I said quickly. "Right now, I have to go. See you there."

I hung up the phone, grabbed my purse, waved goodbye to Patsy, and hustled out of the building like my life depended on it. I reached the rendezvous point in five minutes flat. Not bad for someone who had recently neglected her jogging routine.

Not a moment after I situated myself outside the parking garage, I heard Chase's voice.

"The backdoor of the car is open for you."

I climbed inside the car. Chase was behind the wheel and Congressman Amos Duncan sat in the front passenger seat. He was middle aged, perhaps forty-five years old, and African American. Duncan represented the congressional district that included Newark, New Jersey. Although Duncan and Dixon belonged to the same party, they adopted considerably different political personas. Duncan represented an urban district while my boss's constituency included a sizable share of suburban and rural voters. Duncan was liberal and Dixon was a die-hard centrist. Duncan appeared frequently on MSNBC, and Maeve only accepted cable television invitations when absolutely necessary. Fellow partisans didn't mean they were two peas in a pod.

After buckling my seat belt, Duncan turned around and offered his hand.

"Kit, I've heard your name often from Chairwoman Dixon, yet I don't think we have had the pleasure of meeting before." He flashed a welcoming smile.

We shook hands warmly. "It's an honor, sir," I said. "Did Chase tell you why I asked for an opportunity to chat?"

Chase didn't give his boss time to answer. "I told him what you said on the phone."

Duncan ignored the abruptness of his chief of staff. "It's about the murder, correct?"

I nodded. "Maeve Dixon asked that I brief you about it, since you are acting in her stead when she's on the campaign trail. As you know, our committee has jurisdiction over the Capitol Visitor Center and the police."

Duncan rubbed his chin. "It does put us right in the crosshairs, doesn't it? Especially not terribly long after our security concerns at the Capitol."

"You are correct," I said. "I serve as the liaison between the police and the committee. The chairwoman made sure that this arrangement would be honored with this investigation."

Chase cleared his throat. "Since Congressman Duncan is serving as interim chair when Dixon is absent, perhaps I should have the same arrangement with the police?"

Duncan waved his hand dismissively in Chase's direction. "From what I understand, Kit has considerable experience dealing with criminal matters. I've read about your other exploits on Capitol Hill. You've had a run of good luck in helping the police solve other serious cases. Do you think you will be able to repeat your performance with Bev Taylor's murder?"

I glanced at Chase's expression, which I could see clearly in the car's rearview mirror. If looks could kill, I would be drafting the text of my headstone.

"Yes, I believe so." I spoke confidently, perhaps with more bravado than I actually felt. "There are certain clues at the crime scene which indicate only those people involved with the planning of *Spring Into History* are credible suspects. That narrows down the list considerably."

Duncan's eyes grew wide. "How interesting. I'm sure you can't share all the details with us, but I am intrigued that considerable progress has already been made."

"Of course, we need to think about motive," I said. "People are murdered for a reason."

"There was no love lost between Chase and Bev Taylor." Duncan lightly patted Chase on the shoulder. "Isn't that right?"

Again, through the rearview mirror, I could see Chase's jaw tighten. I hadn't pegged Chase as a prime suspect, but Amos Duncan's remark piqued my curiosity.

"I didn't share Bev's view of running the CVC," said Chase. "She was making some changes, but they weren't fast enough."

Amos Duncan shook his head. "Chase is frustrated because many of our suggestions fell on deaf ears. We wanted more cultural diversity in the exhibits and a more aggressive outreach to schoolchildren from economically challenged areas, both urban and rural."

"And Bev didn't want to do this?" I asked. It didn't seem like initiatives that Bev would have opposed as the director of the Capitol Visitor Center.

Chase's grip around the steering wheel tightened, his white knuckles practically popping out of his hands. "There was never enough money. Security was her top priority, and then everything else got the scraps that were left."

Managing the visitor experience at the United States Capitol was not an easy job. Bev had always seemed uptight to me but keeping five hundred forty-one members of Congress happy was nearly impossible. Even though I wasn't close friends with Bev, I felt the urge to defend her, especially since she couldn't defend herself.

"I'm sure she did her best. Competing interests can be hard to juggle," I said.

"Chase might be interested in the job now that it's available," said Amos Duncan. "Didn't you mention it earlier?"

Chase's face turned bright red. "I haven't given it much thought," he stammered.

Duncan patted Chase on the shoulder. "I'd hate to lose my chief of staff, but I think Chase would be an excellent candidate to fill Bev's shoes. What do you think, Kit?"

I laughed nervously. "Sure. But I thought Chase wanted to become the committee staff director if you become the next chair?"

Duncan grinned. "We'll have to see how all of this plays out. We want the best people in the right jobs. Don't we, Chase?"

Chase nodded and remained mute. Certainly not music to his ears. Did Chase know that Amos Duncan was looking elsewhere to fill the top committee job? If so, would Chase consider killing Bev so he could take her position? I'd been around Washington, D.C. long enough to know it wasn't a crazy proposition.

We'd entered the Georgetown campus, and Chase maneuvered into a spot inside the parking garage. I consulted the schedule on my iPhone. As expected, reliable intern Jill had provided the location of the event.

"We need to head to Healy Hall," I said. "It's located at the center of campus."

"I'm glad you know where to go, because I certainly don't," said Duncan. "I'm not familiar with Georgetown's campus."

Situated several miles away from Capitol Hill, Georgetown was not easily accessible by public transportation. The lack of a subway station near campus prevented those without cars from visiting the campus cheaply and efficiently. Most people believed that the rich, upper-crust residents of Georgetown stopped the building of a Metro station near the campus to preserve the exclusive ambiance of the neighborhood. Doug had shared with me that the history was more complicated than that. Although there had been residential resistance to extending the subway to Georgetown, the real problem was geology. Georgetown was located right next to the Potomac River, which made digging an underground subway stop expensive and difficult.

I texted Doug, who was planning to attend the event.

Arrived. With Amos Duncan & Chase.

Three dots showed he was writing back.

Walking over now. See you there.

I was relieved Doug wasn't delayed. Hopefully the uncomfortable discussion about future career opportunities would end when we arrived for the academic lecture.

We walked towards the Lauinger Library and then made a left to walk alongside the main campus quad. With the promise of warmer weather right around the corner, students were making the most of the pleasant evening. Studying or socializing, many were sitting outside on benches and outstretched blankets. Others were playing frisbee or tossing a football lazily back and forth. The lawn was a bright shade of green and the smell of recently mowed grass was heavy in the evening air.

"It's refreshing to be back on a college campus," said Amos Duncan. "Almost idyllic."

His comment reminded me of Doug, who had recently left his position as the head of the scholarly center at the Library of Congress to return to this setting. Scenes like today drew him back. Just like Capitol Hill remained my comfort zone, Doug's natural habitat was the university. He'd made the right decision and I was thrilled for him.

"The main gate is just across the quad, but we're headed in this direction to Healy Hall." I motioned in the opposite direction.

"Now, this looks familiar," said Duncan.

The congressman was referring to the flagship building on the Georgetown campus, the image that is usually advertised on brochures, websites, or television. It was an imposing, Gothic style building complete with a tall clocktower.

"It looks familiar because the same architects who designed the Library of Congress's Jefferson Building also designed Healy Hall," I said.

Duncan nodded. "I'm not knowledgeable about architecture, but I see the resemblance." He looked at me and smiled. "Kit, you are chock-full of helpful information this evening."

Even though I avoided eye contact with Chase, I could practically feel the daggers he was shooting in my direction. However, I had to admit I was enjoying my time with Amos Duncan more than I thought I would. Perhaps working for him as the committee staff director wouldn't be such a bad option after all.

"To be perfectly honest, my husband is an academic dean at Georgetown," I said. "So that's why I know my way around the campus."

Duncan nodded appreciatively. "I hope he's able to join us tonight."

"Of course," I said. "His former colleague in the History Department, Professor Edgar Beauford, will be our lecturer this evening." I motioned for the congressman to follow me up the steps of the building and inside. We ascended to the third floor of the building and entered Gaston Hall, the ornate auditorium inside Healy.

Members of Congress see their fair share of beautiful landscapes, decorated rooms, and historic sites. Nonetheless, Amos Duncan's rapid intake of breath was audible as we strode inside Gaston.

"What a treasure," he muttered, looking up at the coat of arms of Jesuit universities that lined the ceiling along with the allegorical painted scene that adorned the adjacent walls.

A man's voice responded behind us. "We refer to it as the crown jewel, actually."

I turned around and gave Doug a peck on the cheek. "This is my husband who I told you about."

He stuck out his hand. "Doug Hollingsworth."

Amos Duncan shook it heartily. "Correction. Isn't it *Dean* Hollingsworth?"

Doug smiled. "We're amongst friends, not students. Please call me Doug."

Never one to be ignored, Chase interjected himself into the conversation. "Can you tell us more about Gaston Hall and its history?"

Doug smiled politely. He was a dean, not a tour guide. But he knew that it was oftentimes much better to appease than to offend.

"Certainly. I'm not an expert on campus architecture, but I can tell you the basics. The auditorium was completed in 1901. It is named after the first student at Georgetown, William Gaston, who incidentally went on to become a member of Congress from North Carolina. There were sixty Jesuit universities at the time of construction, and the coat of arms of each are displayed at the edge of the ceiling around the hall. There are also several paintings on the walls, as I'm sure you've noticed. Behind the stage is Athena, the goddess of wisdom."

Doug took a breath, which gave Amos Duncan the opportunity to ask a question.

"How many seats in the auditorium and who has spoken here?" he asked, his gaze transfixed on the empty stage before him.

"Over seven hundred people when it's completely full," said Doug. "To answer your second question, it's almost impossible to list everyone who has lectured here. In recent years, Georgetown has hosted Barack Obama, Bill Clinton, Prime Minister Tony Blair, Speaker of the House Newt Gingrich, First Lady Laura Bush, and even Bradley Cooper."

Chase raised his right eyebrow. "Bradley Cooper spoke here?"

"Yes. He's a Georgetown alum. Class of 1997, I believe," said Doug.

"I wasn't aware of that," said Chase. He was clearly intrigued by Bradley Cooper's status. Then again, who wasn't?

"Tonight's lecture will be another example of a prominent guest taking the stage," said Doug. "My colleague from the History Department, Professor Edgar Beauford, will be speaking as part of the terrific series of events sponsored by Congress and other prominent cultural institutions and historical societies around town."

"Congressman Duncan will introduce Edgar this evening," I said.

Doug nodded. "As I understand it, Edgar is giving an overview of our project on the role that slavery played in Georgetown's history. It's ongoing research, but Edgar has been front and center for us."

"Of course, it is a somber occasion tonight," said Duncan. "Due to the untimely murder of Bev Taylor. I will laud her government service in my opening remarks."

People had begun to file into the auditorium. We weren't expecting a sellout crowd tonight but hoped for several hundred attendees. Of course, the murder in the news undoubtedly drew attention to the *Spring Into History* programming.

Out of the corner of my eye, I saw Meg enter with Trevor. Even from across the room, I could spot the worry lines on Meg's face, which was normally free of blemishes, wrinkles, and any other facial imperfection. Also, uncharacteristically, Meg guided Trevor to a seat near the rear of the auditorium. Usually, Meg liked to see and be seen. Given the dark cloud that hung over the event due to Bev's death, she'd wisely decided to remain out of sight. There was no way I could leave my seat in the front row to speak with them now. I'd have to catch up with them at the reception afterwards.

Thankfully, Amos Duncan's introduction and Edgar Beauford's lecture both went off without a hitch. In typical politician fashion, Duncan gave an artful and poignant eulogy in tribute of Bev. I wasn't sure anyone who actually knew Bev when she was alive recognized her in Duncan's memorializing rhetoric, but it's never a good idea to speak ill of the dead.

For his part, Edgar explained the difficult history of Georgetown and the role Jesuits played in the sale of two hundred seventy-two enslaved people for the university's profit. The slave trade ensured the viability of then-struggling Georgetown in 1838, and the university community was now working to discover the descendants to learn additional details. When Edgar stated that

Georgetown University owed its existence to the sale of enslaved people, I could have heard a pin drop inside the august auditorium.

After Edgar took questions from the audience and gave his concluding thoughts, Doug squeezed my hand.

"What did you think?" he asked.

"I wonder how many people know about the relationship between slavery and Georgetown," I said. "I suppose I don't really know the full history of our most cherished institutions."

"Don't despair. Even historians don't have all the answers," he said, with a half-smile. "Martin Luther King, Jr. said that injustice anywhere is a threat to justice everywhere."

I gripped Doug's hand tightly in response. Being married to a historian had its benefits.

Chapter Eight

W**E WALKED OUTSIDE** the main Georgetown gate for the short
stroll to the famous nearby restaurant, 1789. On a quaint street
a few blocks away from the university, 1789 was located inside
a federal-style townhouse. Named for the year Georgetown was
founded, the inside decor matched the outside, complete with
cozy fireplaces, antiques, exposed wooden beams, intimate dining
rooms, and low lighting. We had reserved the Middleburg Room
on the third floor for an invite-only reception after the lecture.
A bit extravagant, but a generous Georgetown donor who loved
American history generously underwrote it. As Doug commented,
it certainly beat the catering at the university's faculty club, which
is where we would have ended up otherwise.

The room had a built-in bar, and the drinks were already flowing
by time we arrived. We hadn't dawdled after the lecture was over,
but obviously others were more motivated by free cocktails than
us. I spotted Trevor and Meg, who were chatting with historian
Mila Cunningham. I tugged on Doug's suit jacket. "Let's go over
there so I can find out how Trevor is doing."

"Okay," said Doug with less enthusiasm than a turkey before
Thanksgiving. Mila was too much for Doug. Although they had
never been colleagues, Washington, D.C. was, in some ways, a small
town and all the historians knew each other. She was always working
an angle and I suppose it exhausted him. When James Madison

wrote that "ambition must be made to counteract ambition" in the Federalist Papers, he had the future Mila Cunningham in mind.

"Hello, everyone," I said in my most cheery voice. "Did you enjoy the lecture?"

Trevor and Meg nodded and didn't say anything. Mila, of course, had an opinion. "Edgar did well. He covered the subject *adequately*."

Doug defended his former History Department colleague. "I'd say it was better than adequate, Mila." The edges of his mouth tweaked upwards. "At least *above average*."

Mila waved her hand dismissively and muttered, "That's what's wrong with the world today."

Doug wouldn't let her off the hook. "What do you mean, Mila?"

"Everyone accepts mediocrity," she snapped. "No one can handle criticism." She looked Doug in the eye. "It's pathetic." Then she stomped away.

I shook my head in disbelief. "Someone certainly isn't having a good day."

"She's always like that," said Doug. "But she might consider listening to her own advice."

"What do you mean?" asked Trevor.

If I was being honest, Trevor didn't look too good. His fair complexion had somehow become paler, if that was humanly possible. Normally, there wasn't a hair or stitch out of place on Trevor. This evening, his suit looked rumpled, and his short brown hair was sticking up in all the wrong places.

"As I understand it, Bev Taylor was threatening to fire Mila as a consultant," said Doug. "In fact, she wasn't happy with Edgar's work, either."

"Did Edgar or Mila care about getting canned?" asked Meg. "After all, they both have full-time positions. They were only doing the work for *Spring Into History* as a side gig."

"Working as a consultant can really boost your income as a historian," said Doug. "Also, it's prestigious and can help your career. If *Spring Into History* is a resounding success, then maybe an even bigger opportunity would present itself. Like the History Channel or helping with a major exhibit at a museum."

Meg sipped her drink. "Makes sense. I never thought of it that way."

Trevor's eyes lit up. "Doesn't this mean that both Mila and Edgar had a motive to kill Bev?"

"Definitely," I said. "Especially Mila. Her personality makes me think she wouldn't let anyone stand in her way."

I grabbed a stuffed mushroom from an appetizer tray passing by. Lunch seemed like a long time ago.

Doug wandered off to find glasses of wine for us. I turned my attention to Trevor. "How are you doing?"

Trevor managed a weak smile. "I'm doing okay. Did Meg tell you about the police interrogation this afternoon?"

I placed my hand gently on Trevor's lower arm and gave it a gentle squeeze. "The good news is that you survived."

"Barely. And the *really* bad news is that my boss might put me on administrative leave."

Only Trevor would think that being put on paid leave was worse than being a prime suspect in a murder investigation.

"Has he decided about it yet?" I asked.

"No, but it doesn't look good. If the police show up again, I'm sure Bennett will view me as a liability and I'll be out," said Trevor.

Trevor was typically an unruffled sort of guy. He existed independently of external opinions and lived according to his own impeccable standards. It upset me to observe Trevor in this vexed state of mind.

"Kit, we need to solve this murder quickly. Trevor's reputation is on the line," said Meg.

Some might describe Meg as a ne'er-do-well, but I knew she was much more substantive than what people gave her credit for. Her attractive looks and fashionable style encouraged others to view her less than substantial. She was thin (especially given her appetite for tasty food and wine) but she was no lightweight.

Even though Meg and Trevor were polar opposites on the surface, perhaps this is what brought them together: the fact that they were both victims of formidable public misperceptions. Trevor was considered snobbish and a prude, yet he was caring and sensitive once you got to know him. Meg was viewed as superficial and flighty, yet she was as smart as a whip and benefited enormously from a routine underestimation of her talents and abilities.

"I agree, Meg," I said. "We need to clear Trevor and remove any questions about *Spring Into History*. We worked too hard to have our program sullied by an unsolved murder."

Meg nodded solemnly. "We'll get to the bottom of this."

"You have my word," I said.

Doug returned with two glasses of wine. I took a sip as my phone buzzed. It was Sebastian, my (slightly) younger brother. He was a tech wizard for a local nonprofit by day and an ambitious social activist by night. We shared some of the same politics, but not the preferred approach to solving the world's problems.

"Who is it?" asked Doug.

"Sebastian," I said. "He read about the murder this morning and got worried because he knew I was involved with the Lincoln catafalque display. The press reports are emphasizing that Bev's body was found on top of it. That was the one detail about the crime which was released." I texted my brother back and explained I was involved but safe and sound.

"Of course, they are," said Trevor dryly. "The murderer literally put her on display. Who does something like that?"

Trevor's question went unanswered as intern Jill approached our coterie. "What did you think of the lecture tonight?" she asked. Probably all this talk of murder freaked her out. Even while claiming she was unaffected, Jill was dealing with more than a typical intern bargained for.

"Great job, Jill," said Meg. "Well executed."

Doug chimed in. "Everyone thinks it was a home run. Especially after the tragedy earlier today."

Jill beamed. "I'm glad it was a success."

I put my hand gently on Jill's shoulder. "You're doing excellent work. *Spring Into History* wouldn't be the same without you."

"I hope you'll think that in a few days, too," said Jill.

"Good point," said Doug. "This is only the first day. What's on the schedule for tomorrow?"

Jill smiled. "We move from the legislative branch to the executive branch. We're headed to the White House!"

The gloom on Meg's face disappeared for a moment. "That's right. I almost forgot. It's going to be amazing."

"As legislative branch employees, we don't get too many opportunities to go inside the most famous building in Washington," I said. "I'm really looking forward to our special tour tomorrow."

My phone buzzed again, and I glanced at the text message. Sebastian had written back. After reading the text, I tugged on Doug's shirtsleeve.

"Sebastian wants to meet us for a late dinner in Arlington," I said. "Do you want to go?"

Doug lowered his voice. "If you think your work is done here tonight."

"Trevor is stable," I said. Then I added under my breath, "For now, at least."

"Then, let's go. We haven't seen your brother in a while."

Doug was correct. Sebastian didn't live far away from us but had been in a bit of a funk lately. His girlfriend Lisa, a former Capitol Hill police officer, had been accepted at the FBI Academy, along with her dog, Murphy. They were away at K-9 training and Sebastian seemed lost without her.

I spoke up to the rest of the group. "We're going to meet Sebastian," I said. "I'll see everyone tomorrow. Jill, do you need our help with anything?"

Jill was busy texting on her smartphone. She looked up, clearly distracted. "Everything is fine here. See you tomorrow." Then her eyes went back to phone.

Meg gave me a quick hug. "Text me if anything happens with Trevor," I said. "But I have a lot of confidence in the police. They won't make any rash decisions."

Meg bit her lip. "Let's hope so."

We walked to the parking garage, where Doug had parked our Prius. I sank down in the passenger seat and took a deep breath.

Doug patted my hand as he began the short drive over the Key Bridge to Arlington. "Tough day?"

"I feel like I've lived three days in the past twelve hours," I said.

"Are you sure you want to meet Sebastian? You could always call him and reschedule," said Doug. "After all, you must be exhausted."

I ticked off the day's trials and tribulations on my fingers. "Get up early for the event, discover a dead body of the CVC Director, meet with the police, confer with the other organizers of our symposium, talk with Maeve Dixon, console Meg as Trevor becomes a suspect, deal with a passive-aggressive chief of staff and his boss, acclimate the intern to our sleuthing, and then attend a university lecture."

"Wow," said Doug. "Maybe you should decompress with Sebastian for dinner."

"Besides, who knows what tomorrow will bring?" I pondered. "Better see him tonight when the opportunity presents itself."

"Where are we meeting him, by the way?" asked Doug as he sped west on Wilson Boulevard in the densely populated neighborhood of Rosslyn.

"Ambar," I said. "You're headed in the right direction."

Doug nodded and we got lucky. There was street parking available not far from the restaurant, which featured Balkan cuisine served in small plates. The food was tasty, and the ambiance was upbeat and unpretentious.

"Let's see if Sebastian has already been seated," I said.

We walked to the restaurant and saw that Sebastian had scored an outside table. Even after the pandemic, several restaurants had kept their copious sidewalk dining, which was appreciated by many. Since the temperature was a cool-but-comfortable sixty degrees, we readily agreed to the arrangement.

Sebastian's face lit up when he saw us. We exchanged hugs and pleasantries before taking our seats.

"It's been a while since we've seen you, Sebastian," said Doug.

"I'm surprised you made it out," he said. "Given the murder on Capitol Hill today."

Since moving to Washington, Sebastian had assisted in the investigation of three murders. Most significantly, he'd become the prime suspect in a murder that occurred during our beach vacation on the Outer Banks. At this point, Sebastian was no stranger to capital crimes.

I placed my napkin on my lap. "As you know, it's only going to get busier and crazier until the killer is caught. We figured tonight was the best opportunity to get together."

Our waiter delivered a chilled bottle of wine and several small plates of food.

"What's all this?" I asked.

"While I was waiting for you to arrive, I ordered a bottle of Sancerre. I know it's your favorite wine, besides Prosecco, of course." Sebastian grinned. "And I ordered the Ambar experience for us."

The "Ambar experience" was an unlimited assortment of small plates shared by the table. It enabled diners to enjoy the full array of cuisine, much like tapas at a Spanish restaurant.

"I suppose that makes it easy," I said. "Thank you, Sebastian."

The waiter poured us glasses of wine, and Sebastian raised his glass and clinked it to both of ours. Something had changed. Sebastian had been down in the dumps for weeks due to Lisa and Murphy's departure for FBI training. Now, he was ordering Sancerre for the table and raising his glass in an unprovoked toast?

"You seem like you're in a pleasant mood all of a sudden," I said innocently.

Sebastian passed me the hummus and other spreads to sample. The garlic yogurt paste was particularly delectable.

Sebastian's eyes sparkled. "You know me too well, Kit Kat."

I groaned inwardly. Sebastian knew I hated it when he used the nickname my father had given me when I was little. Doug knew I disliked, it too. He patted my leg under the table in a futile attempt to make me forget it.

Doug scooped up more pepper dip with his pita. "We can't be detectives all the time, Sebastian. Tell us what has put such a spring in your step. We'd appreciate some good news, wouldn't we, Kit?"

"Certainly," I said as the waiter arrived with more small plates, these ones featuring an assortment of vegetables and spicy grilled meats.

Sebastian leaned across the table. "Lisa is coming for a visit this weekend. They have an extra day off from training so she can leave campus."

I smiled. "Now I know why you're happy. I'm glad you'll have an opportunity to spend time with her soon."

"It's not just that she's coming for visit," said Sebastian. He reached into the pocket of his blazer and produced a velvet ring box.

Always quick on the draw, Doug reacted first. "You're going to propose!"

Sebastian's face was flush with excitement. "That's right. Here's the ring." He flipped open the box. It was a stunning ring, although much different than most conventional engagement rings. A slim gold band with round sapphires, it was simple yet elegant.

"Do you think Lisa will like it?" asked Sebastian. He took another big sip of his wine.

I reached across the table and gave my brother's hand a squeeze. "It looks exactly like the type of ring Lisa would love. Congratulations."

Relief washed over Sebastian's face. "I went to a jeweler who specializes in ethical engagement rings for socially conscious couples. The gold is recycled, and the stones are conflict-free. The ring comes with a green certification."

Doug blinked several times. "Wow. That's very impressive, Sebastian. I'm glad you were able to find a beautiful ring consistent with the beliefs shared by you and Lisa."

Sebastian went back to the plates of food in front of us. Like me, he didn't let something like a marriage proposal get in the way of eating.

"It's not as hard as you might think these days," said Sebastian in between bites. "There's even eco-friendly wedding attire."

"Have you talked about getting engaged?" I asked. Maybe that was a nosy question, but I never let that stop me before.

Sebastian's eyes narrowed. "We've discussed the future, if that's what you mean."

"She doesn't know you're going to propose?" asked Doug, more as a statement than a question.

"No, it's going to be a surprise," said Sebastian quickly. The flush appearance returned to his face.

"Don't worry," I said. "You have a solid relationship. Everything will work out." In these situations, it was better to reassure than pressure. I gave Doug the high sign to cease any further interrogation.

"Well, I'll be sure to let you know how it goes," said Sebastian as more plates of food arrived. This time, it was baked cheese pie, meatballs, chicken skewers, and goulash. After eating all this rich food, I wondered whether I would be able to get up tomorrow morning to make it to the White House. Somehow, I'd have to roll out of bed to make it happen.

"I'll be busy the next couple of days," I said. "The multi-site history conference I helped organize is still moving forward."

"Despite the murder?" asked Sebastian.

"Yes, since there are so many events planned at different venues, we figured we could press on," I said.

"Do you have any suspects in mind?" asked Sebastian. More plates arrived, including a stuffed cabbage, short rib, fried chicken, and salmon. I hoped this was the last round. Even if it wasn't, I was calling it quits. The Lycra in my pants provided a limited amount of give, after all.

Doug spoke up. "Actually, our friend Trevor may be the primary suspect."

Sebastian's eyes widened. "You mean Meg's boyfriend? The uptight guy?"

"The one and only," I said. "He had a public fight with the victim right before her death. And he was at the scene of the crime around the time of the murder."

Sebastian whistled softly. "Doesn't sound good."

"It doesn't, but we know that Trevor didn't kill Bev Taylor, so we just need to figure out who did," I said. "Or the police need to figure it out."

"They'll need your help, as always." Sebastian pointed his fork at me. "However, I have to ask you a serious question, big sister."

"Go ahead. I'm listening," I said. Sebastian had a flair for the dramatic. His relationship with Lisa, a law enforcement officer, had calmed him down considerably, but old habits die hard.

He lowered his voice and leaned closer, moving the plates of food out of the way so he didn't get goulash on his cream-colored henley. "Did you ever consider that Trevor might have done it?"

Sebastian's words caught me off guard. I sat back in my seat and said nothing for several seconds.

Doug spoke first. "I don't think that crossed Kit's mind. Why do you consider that a possibility, Sebastian?"

My brother ran his hands through his sandy locks. Despite his relocation to northern Virginia from California a few years ago, there were still remnants of his former surfer persona, such as his frequently disheveled dishwater blond hair and blasé attitude.

"I mean, I don't know the guy *that* well," he said. "But he is pretty weird. Not the warmest person in the world. And he has that habit of appearing and disappearing without a trace."

Sebastian was right. I'd known Trevor for so long, it didn't faze me anymore. One moment he would be there, and the next second, poof! He'd be gone. I didn't know how he did it, and I didn't have the courage to ask Meg if she knew, either.

"Trevor is an odd duck. Certainly, that doesn't make him a murderer," I said in an even voice.

"True," said Sebastian. "I mean, I know what it's like to be accused of a murder I didn't commit."

Doug tittered. "Sebastian, all of us know what that's like." My husband was referring to previous murder investigations in which we had each suffered through police scrutiny and public accusations until the real culprit was caught.

The waiter brought three plates filled with baklava. I didn't know how I was going to eat it, but the warm, buttery smell told me that I was going to figure out a way to do it. We paused our conversation as we enjoyed our wonderful dessert. The flaky crust practically melted in my mouth. Maybe after Maeve Dixon's campaign was over, I could convince Doug to take a trip to Eastern Europe? I'd heard great things about Prague and Budapest. If the food at Ambar was this good, I could only imagine what the authentic version was like.

Sebastian smacked his lips together and took a final sip of wine. "Not to beat a dead horse, but you're missing the point. Trevor is an unusual guy. He's unpredictable. You just told me he had a solid motive and opportunity. You can't dismiss those facts."

I smiled at my brother. "What I love about you is that your passion about the environment and other social causes doesn't prevent the rational side of your brain from working."

Sebastian threw down a credit card, holding up a hand when we protested his payment of the bill. "No, no, no," he said. "I invited you to hear my good news. The least I could do is buy you dinner."

We got up from the table and said our goodbyes. Sebastian gave me a tight squeeze and whispered in my ear. "Don't forget, Kit. You have a rational side of the brain, too. Make sure you use it."

Chapter Nine

"THAT WAS A MORE EVENTFUL DINNER than I bargained for." I inhaled deeply as I fastened my seat belt.

Doug put the car in gear. "But good news, right?"

"I'm certainly happy about Lisa. I hope she says yes."

"Yes to the dress!" said Doug, laughing. He liked it when he could inject cultural references to our conversation that didn't involve dead white men from the eighteenth century.

"Nice call, but first, she needs to say yes to the ring."

"I'm sure she'll love it," said Doug. "He picked an enviro-friendly style, which fits them perfectly as a couple."

"A socially conscious couple," I said. "I can already see the *New York Times* headline in the wedding section."

"That might be a little ambitious," said Doug. He was still sore that the *Times* hadn't included our wedding. To be fair, we got married in a very unusual setting. If we had stuck to the Continental Club, as my mother-in-law had wanted, I'm sure the *New York Times* would have put us on speed dial.

Doug pulled into the parking garage underneath our condo building. After maneuvering into a compact car spot (one of the many advantages of owning a Prius), we exited our vehicle and walked towards the elevator.

"The engagement news was the best part of the evening," I said. "But Sebastian's suspicion of Trevor . . ." I didn't finish the sentence.

As we traveled upward to our condo, Doug looked at me with obvious concern. "You aren't taking Sebastian's supposition seriously, are you?"

The elevator door opened, and we made the turn down the hallway to the entrance of our home. "No, I suppose not. I can't imagine Trevor hurting anyone." I paused for a beat. "Although Sebastian does have a point. He can be rather odd."

Doug unlocked the door and out of habit, I braced myself for Clarence's typical onslaught of canine exuberance. However, much to our chagrin, it didn't come. We entered the apartment and found our beagle mutt lying on the couch. His tail thumped when he saw us, but he didn't even get up to greet us.

I went over and patted Clarence on the head. "Aren't you happy to see us, buddy?"

His tail thumping increased, and he licked my hand, but I could tell his heart wasn't in it.

Doug scrutinized our depressed pup. "Kit, when did Clarence's behavior change?"

I counted backwards in my head. "I think it's been almost two months."

Doug snapped his fingers. "I never put it together until now. Having dinner with Sebastian made me think of it. Clarence misses Murphy!"

Lisa and her dog Murphy had departed for FBI training right around that time. During the pandemic, Clarence and Murphy had spent considerable time together, since Sebastian and Lisa were some of the few people we had seen regularly. But Clarence didn't always seem happy to share the spotlight with Murphy.

"Clarence and Murphy used to get into fights," I said. "Remember what happened in the back of Sebastian's car?"

I was referring to an incident a while ago in which Clarence and Murphy decided to tussle over leftover barbecue chicken. The spat got out of hand, and the chicken (including the red, sticky sauce) ended up all over me.

Doug smiled at me and put his arm around my shoulder. "The problem is you're thinking like a human and not a dog," he said. "I bet Clarence liked his spats with Murphy. Now, he's lost his friend suddenly. Would you become depressed if you lost your best friend?"

I stared at Clarence. Could that be the answer?

"If that's the case, I'm not sure what we can do. Murphy has joined the FBI. He's not coming back."

"Maybe Lisa can bring him over this weekend," said Doug. "You know, if the engagement goes well."

I giggled. "I'll be sure to tell Sebastian that we need Murphy. Sorry to interrupt your romantic weekend. Can you bring over the dog?"

Doug shrugged his shoulders. "Can't hurt to ask."

After we fed Clarence his dinner (the depression didn't affect his appetite), we settled down to watch a show on Netflix. Even though it was a funny sitcom I normally enjoyed binge-watching with Doug when the opportunity presented itself, I couldn't focus on it. All I could see was Bev Taylor's dead body. Why would someone murder her and then arrange her lifeless corpse on the catafalque? When I'd investigated other murders, motive had driven the killer. Many of the crimes had been carefully plotted, yet the objective was crystal clear. The victims died for a reason. Bev Taylor's murder bothered me because the perpetrator had chosen to put her body on display, almost as if he or she wanted to tell us something. Unfortunately, at this moment in time, I couldn't figure out the message.

Doug must have sensed my unease. "Kit, why don't you go to bed? I'll take Clarence out for his nighttime walk."

I nodded and grabbed my phone. "I have a long day tomorrow. Getting some rest is a smart idea."

After I got ready for bed, I swiped open my phone. All the websites said not to use electronic devices before bedtime because of the disruption to sleep they cause. Easier said than done, especially for those of us who were running a multi-venue history conference, monitoring a close Senate race in North Carolina, and trying to solve a murder. Given the level of stress I was currently experiencing, I doubted a peek at my iPhone would really hurt much.

I felt vindicated when I spotted a text from Meg.

Meet for breakfast tomorrow?

I quickly consulted my schedule, which was packed. I had to spend time in the office in the morning before heading to the White House for a special tour with top donors who made *Spring Into History* possible. Then there was a program and reception at nearby Decatur House on Lafayette Square. If I got up early, I could squeeze in a quick tete-a-tete with Meg. Besides, I'd need to have a hearty breakfast before facing such a crazy day. I typed a reply.

Can do if early.

Three dots appeared, indicating that Meg was writing back. She was obviously not concerned about staying away from electronic devices before bedtime, either. Of course, birds of a feather flock together.

8am @Le Bon?

Ah, now Meg had me hook, line, and sinker. Le Bon Cafe was one of our favorite Capitol Hill restaurants. It would be worth the early alarm. Besides, I knew my best friend was worried about Trevor. Making time for her was the least I could do. Well, besides finding the person responsible for killing Bev.

After texting her back in the affirmative, I set my alarm for earlier than I liked and closed my eyes. I must have been more exhausted than I wanted to admit because I didn't wake until the sing-song alarm from my Alexa device signaled that it was time to get up. Doug was still sound asleep and per usual, Clarence had burrowed himself between us in a tight ball. When I got out of bed, he raised his head half-heartedly. Due to his depression, Clarence had been less enthusiastic about morning jogs. I was pressed for time, but I could squeeze in a quick twenty-minute jaunt around the neighborhood. Hopefully, it would offset the indulgent breakfast I would enjoy with Meg.

I cajoled a reluctant Clarence out of bed and ten minutes later, we were cruising down one of the busy streets in our suburban neighborhood of Arlington, Virginia. Besides burning a few extra calories, I had an ulterior motive. My jogs with Clarence usually allowed me to think about the current mystery I was trying to solve. Yesterday had been a blur, although the general contours of the murder had begun to reveal themselves. What did I know?

Bev Taylor died in the late evening hours. There was no sign her body was moved any considerable distance, so she was likely killed inside the outdoor tent. The murderer stabbed her with an unadorned letter opener sold at the nearby Capitol Visitor Center gift shop. The killer placed her body on the Lincoln catafalque, staging it for discovery.

That detail was worth exploring more. If this was an inside job, then it was common knowledge amongst the *Spring Into History* team that Meg and I planned to show up early the next morning as attendees began to queue. Was the body planted on the catafalque for me to find? Meg? Both of us?

Bev hadn't exactly won a Ms. Popularity contest on Capitol Hill. Undoubtedly, if I poked into her personal and professional life, I was bound to find a coterie of people who strongly disliked her. However, the evidence pointed to a member of our working group, since the guilty party disabled the cameras before committing the crime. He or she must have known where we had placed them to secure the Lincoln catafalque. Given that fact, I was limited to the following suspects: Chase Wintergreen, James Bennett, Mila Cunningham, Edgar Beaufort, and Trevor.

Chase seemed to want everyone's job in Washington. Did he kill Bev so he could become the next director of the Capitol Visitor Center? James Bennett wanted everything his way. I hadn't discerned a motive yet, but it might exist. After all, Bennett was a cantankerous character; he must have crossed paths with Bev at some point. Lastly, Mila and Edgar both clashed with Bev. From what I learned last night, Bev even threatened to terminate their status as historical consultants. That certainly constituted a motive. I had no idea about Mila and Edgar's whereabouts at the time of the murder. Fortunately, I would see both today and I could interrogate them about alibis.

And then, there was Trevor. Clarence and I had finished our loop and we were outside our condo building. As my beagle mutt sniffed the newly planted landscaped flowers, I allowed my mind to drift. I'd brushed off Sebastian's suggestion last night that Trevor could have killed Bev. I still didn't believe Trevor was the murderer. But if the facts continued to mount, did I need to reconsider my assumptions? Was I letting my emotions get the best of my reason, as Sebastian had suggested? I shrugged off the question, yet I knew that niggling scrap of doubt had been implanted in my brain.

Unfortunately, recreation time was over. I was no closer to knowing the identity of Bev's killer, but at least my thoughts were better organized. I had high hopes that today's activities might reveal helpful clues to bring this investigation to a conclusion. The sooner, the better.

Thirty minutes later, I was back outside. This time, I was walking with purpose to our nearby neighborhood Metro stop. There was no sense in taking the car today. Part of my day would be spent in the area surrounding the White House, and parking was impossible anywhere near the most famous residence in the United States.

After arriving at the Capitol South subway station, I glanced at my phone. It was three minutes before eight. Perfect timing. I took a hard right, walked past the rear entrance of the Library of Congress's Madison Building, and then headed north on Second Street. Le Bon Cafe was next to Pete's Diner, another breakfast favorite. Meg preferred the ambiance of Le Bon Cafe. If the Netflix show "Emily in Paris" filmed in Washington, D.C., then Le Bon Cafe would play a starring role.

As soon as I walked inside, I took a deep breath. The ambiance of Le Bon Cafe was pleasant enough. The real sell was the intoxicating, distinctive fragrance that mixed freshly baked cookies, quiche, waffles, espresso, and bread. It was heavenly.

Even though I was right on time, Meg had beat me to the punch. She was seated at a cozy table by the bay window. She waved to flag me down, although the place was so small, I couldn't miss her. Especially since she was wearing a red beret. *Très française.*

"Kit, you don't have to stand in line to order. I already did it."

I sat down opposite Meg. "You already ordered? What did you get for me?"

"Oat bran fruit crisp," she said. "What else?"

The promise of apples, peaches, and strawberries baked with a crunched oat bran almost made my mouth water. Meg knew me so well. Still, I couldn't let her off the hook that easily.

"I also like quiche," I said.

"Every time we come here for breakfast, you pretend to scrutinize the menu, yet you always order the oat bran fruit crisp."

"I give up," I said. "I can't argue with that logic."

My best friend had already secured two cups of steaming coffee. I picked mine up and took a long sip. Even more important than sumptuous breakfast goodies was coffee. Nothing could proceed without it.

"How is Sebastian?" asked Meg.

"I have news," I said. Then I told her about Sebastian's intention to propose.

Meg clapped her hands together. "Lisa will be so pleased!"

"Let's hope so," I said. "I don't think Sebastian could handle life without Lisa."

The woman behind the counter indicated that our breakfast was ready, so we stood and grabbed our plates from the counter. Meg had selected the baked French toast, topped with cinnamon, maple syrup, and fresh fruit.

As soon as we sat down, I dove into my warm oat bran. I'd already enjoyed several mouthfuls before I noticed that Meg had hardly touched her French toast. That wasn't normal behavior for my best friend, who usually exhibited an appetite heartier than my own.

I put my spoon down. "Meg, what's wrong?"

Meg blinked several times. "I'm not hungry, I guess."

I took a wild guess. "You're worried about Trevor."

She nodded silently.

"Meg, we've been down this road before. You know that between our sleuthing and the official police investigation, we always uncover the identity of the guilty party."

"Trevor is convinced that James Bennett will use this against him. Even if he's cleared of any wrongdoing, his career will be ruined."

"People on Capitol Hill have short memories, Meg. They can't remember what happened at last week's hearing, let alone the intrigue inside a place as obscure as the Chief Administrative Officer's workplace." I didn't mean to sound harsh, but sometimes as staff, we took ourselves a little too seriously.

"I can't go with you today to the White House, but I hope you're going to interrogate suspects to figure this out," said Meg.

"I'm already planning to make some inquiries," I said.

Meg began to eat her breakfast. The delicious smell of cinnamon and sugar must have finally overcome any angst she felt about Trevor's situation. "Some inquiries? Surely, you can do better than that."

Meg's demanding attitude was a bit too much to process this early in the morning. "Well, I have to be careful. After all, Trevor is a prime suspect. I can't go around accusing other people of murder."

Meg put her fork down. "What are you trying to say, Kit?"

Uh-oh. I inhaled deeply before speaking to steady my nerves. "I'm only stating the obvious. Trevor had a motive for wanting Bev dead. He was at the scene of the crime right around the time she was killed. It casts a cloud of suspicion over him."

Meg's chin trembled. "He needs our help to make that cloud go away."

"You have my word I will get to the bottom of this, no matter what happens." I paused for a moment. "I don't always know how I'm going to solve the murder when I start investigating, but we always manage to figure it out."

"Clearing Trevor needs to the number one priority," said Meg.

I didn't want to tell Meg she was being unreasonable. "Finding the killer is the top priority," I said. "That should solve Trevor's problems."

Meg's flawless complexion reddened. "*Should*?"

I kept my voice even. "Of course. If the real killer is exposed, Trevor will be in the clear."

Meg tapped her long, red fingernails on the table. "You seem to be hedging, Kit."

I put down my spoon and suppressed an inward groan. "Come on, Meg." I sighed. "You're getting upset for no reason."

"I hope not." Her eyes narrowed. "And I hope you interrogate as many people as possible today to figure out who *really* did this."

"Meg, I'll do my best." I reached across the table and grabbed her hand and gave it a squeeze.

"I've got to go. I have a meeting in ten minutes." She pulled her hand back.

"Thanks for breakfast," I said, trying to smooth things over.

"No problem," she said curtly as she stood to leave.

"I'll call you later and let you know if I uncover any clues or leads."

"I have a busy day so I might not be able to talk." She put on her lightweight jacket and turned to leave.

"Wait, Meg!" I placed my hand on her arm. "Are you upset with me?"

She didn't answer my question. "Just figure out who killed Bev Taylor." Then she turned around and left the cafe.

Chapter Ten

I SAT BACK DOWN AND FINISHED MY OAT BRAN. Even the scrumptious taste of one of my favorite breakfast foods couldn't buoy my spirits. Meg was temperamental. I'd gotten used to her mini tantrums throughout the years and didn't pay them much heed. Usually, she made a snarky comment, and all was forgotten. If I was honest with myself, I'd have to admit this time felt differently.

I didn't believe that Trevor killed Bev Taylor, but I needed to approach this investigation carefully. Meg was so distraught by Trevor's predicament, she wasn't thinking rationally. Hopefully, my instincts would guide me, and the identity of the real killer would be revealed sooner rather than later.

Right now, I had a few hours to focus on my actual job, which was serving as chief of staff to a member of Congress and committee chair who was currently MIA. Well, she wasn't truly missing in action, but given that she was focused on running for Senate, it was my job to make sure the trains kept running on time in her current position.

I wasn't at my desk for more than five minutes when my phone buzzed. It was Patsy, our scheduler. "Maeve Dixon is on the line. Can I forward the call?"

"Of course," I said.

I heard a click and then Maeve Dixon's voice. "Kit, are you there?"

"Yes, ma'am."

"Any updates on the murder investigation?"

"I caught up with Amos Duncan and his chief of staff, Chase Wintergreen, yesterday evening."

"And you briefed Amos?"

"I did. You should know that Wintergreen is a suspect. He was part of our planning committee, and it seems as though he's interested in Bev's job as head of the Capitol Visitor Center."

Maeve huffed. "Tread lightly. I don't want Amos Duncan complaining to me that we're fingering one of his own staffers without cause."

"Understood. I'm headed to the White House later today for a tour with some VIP donors that helped bankroll the events. I should have the chance to poke around more."

"Check in with Sergeant O'Halloran," said Dixon. "Perhaps he has a lead, and you can combine forces."

He'll be over the moon. "Certainly. I will call him before I leave."

"Do I need to come off the campaign trail to attend a memorial service later this week?"

"I don't think so," I said. "I'm sure something will be planned for Bev, but this is Congress, remember? Things move slowly. Next week at the earliest."

"For once, I'm relieved to hear about Congress dragging its feet," said Dixon. "I don't think I can leave North Carolina right now."

"Why? Is something wrong?" I could hear the strain in her voice.

"I ignored Chester Nuggets and his stupid monster truck duel," she said. "Even though my campaign manager said that voters in certain parts of the state have a hard time relating to me."

"Hopefully it will go away," I said. "Gimmicks don't last long, even on political campaigns."

"This one seems to have a second life," said Maeve flatly.

Not that I didn't think my boss cared about catching Bev's killer; I knew she did. However, in my heart of hearts, I also knew this was the real reason why she called. She wanted to talk about her campaign woes.

"What happened?" I asked. Best not to delay the inevitable. Maeve Dixon wanted to vent, and I was on the receiving end.

"Chester Nuggets ran a television ad on it," she said. "He appeared with a monster truck superstar who lives in North Carolina."

My fingers hit the keyboard as I searched the internet to find the ad. Sure enough, it popped up immediately. I bet the Nuggets campaign purchased minimal television time but was betting on getting a ton of social media and viral traffic on it.

"I'm watching it now," I said. "Give me a minute."

The name of the famous monster truck star was the "Crypt Crasher." Standing next to his huge truck with the biggest tires I've ever seen, Crypt Crasher shook Chester Nuggets' hand.

"When I compete for a monster truck championship, I want to know that my team has my back," said Crypt Crasher. "That's why I'm supporting Chester Nuggets for the United States Senate."

"I've got the guts to go head-to-head with the toughest guys in the business," said Nuggets, pointing to Crypt Crasher. "But my opponent, Maeve Dixon, likes to hide behind Washington lobbyists and other rich and powerful D.C. elites."

Crypt Crasher motioned to his mammoth truck. "Are you ready to take this baby for a ride?"

Nuggets and Crypt Crasher climbed into the twelve-foot vehicle and took off. The shot panned out to capture the action. Before I knew it, they were airborne as the truck jumped over an obstacle on the track. The ad ended with "Vote Nuggets" flashing on the screen in the signature Crypt Crasher green font.

Well, that was something. I took a moment to process what I'd seen before responding to my boss.

After several seconds, she spoke first. "Did you see it?"

I took a deep breath. "Yes, I watched it."

Silence on the line. A beat later, Dixon broke it. "Kit, what do you think?"

"I don't know how popular the Crypt Crasher is in North Carolina." Before my boss could interrupt with the latest public opinion poll (her campaign team had definitely run the numbers on Crypt Crasher) I kept talking. "However, I do know something about the voters in North Carolina. They won't be duped by a political ad that says nothing relevant about Chester Nuggets and what he stands for. Have a little faith in the system, Congresswoman."

Silence again. I waited a long five seconds before speaking. "Are you still there?"

"I'm here," said Maeve, her voice softer. "I guess I needed to hear that from someone I trust. Everyone here . . ."

I finished the sentence for her. "They're freaking out."

I'd worked on congressional campaigns before. Every day presented a new crisis. It was an emotional roller coaster. For someone like Maeve Dixon, it was hard to tune out the nonsense. I'd remained in Washington, D.C. to make sure her duties as a member of Congress and chair of a committee received the attention they deserved. My absence on the campaign trail had consequences, though. My boss was surrounded by political operatives whose only job was to get her elected to the United States Senate. They meant well, but I didn't think Dixon had established a trusting relationship that resembled how we worked together. Occasionally, my boss needed to press the reset button, so she didn't get lost in the craziness of the campaign bubble. More often than not, I provided it for her.

"Of course, they are," said Dixon. "It has them worried I'll lose the rural vote badly and turnout in the urban areas won't make up for it."

"You're not going to cut a monster truck ad, so what can you do?"

Dixon paused for a beat before answering. "I'm going to do what you suggested. I'm sticking to the issues I'm running on, which are commonsense solutions to our problems. And I'm not going to deviate from that message."

"Good for you," I said. "Remember, it's your name on the ballot. Not the name of the campaign consultants."

"Yes, that's right," said Dixon, her voice now sounding more like the confident woman I worked for. "I'll remind them."

"Is there anything else you'd like to talk about?" I asked. Maeve Dixon never liked to belabor a point. She appreciated prompts to move the conversation along.

"Not now. Call the police sergeant and find out if he's uncovered more information about Bev's murder."

"I'll do that," I said.

"One more thing," said Dixon.

"Yes, Congresswoman." I braced myself. It was always the "one more thing" assignments that ended up being the most difficult.

"Thank you, Kit. I needed to hear what you had to say."

"Of course, Congresswoman. My pleasure. Have a good day."

As I clicked the icon on my phone to end the call, I smiled.

Chapter Eleven

~~~

AFTER MEETING WITH SEVERAL MEMBERS of the Dixon staff to make sure their ongoing projects and work were on the right track, it was time to call Sergeant O'Halloran. As my boss said, perhaps he had a lead, and the murder would be solved soon. I hoped to reach him before it was time to leave for the White House. No need to interrogate would-be suspects if the police already had a solid lead. Luckily, the sergeant picked up my call on the second ring.

"O'Halloran here."

"Sergeant, it's Kit Marshall. I'm at my desk at work. I talked to my boss today and she suggested I check in with you about Bev Taylor's murder. Do you have any updates?"

I heard the flipping of notebook pages. O'Halloran was old school. He used pen and paper to keep track of clues and information when working a case. Some days, I envied his ability to eschew technology. I had more devices than I could keep track of, and when I heard a ring or a ding, I rarely knew which phone, computer, watch, or tablet to answer.

"Not too much to report. Still trying to see if we can find any eyewitnesses who might be able to place the guilty party at the scene of the crime. Unfortunately, the one person we can place inside the tent is your friend Trevor."

Drat. Trevor again. "Did the autopsy yield any interesting results?"

More flipping of papers. "Nothing you didn't know. Stab wound in the back which damaged the lungs, causing death."

Before O'Halloran could continue, I cut him off. "Bev Taylor was stabbed from behind?"

"Yes, she was. Does that matter?"

"Does it mean Bev was trying to run away from her murderer?"

"It's a possibility. Perhaps there was an altercation and Bev saw the weapon. She might have turned to escape and that's when the killer struck."

"The other possibility is that the murderer snuck up on Bev."

"Yes, certainly. Does this detail mean something significant to you, Ms. Marshall?"

"Not at this point," I said. "Although if Bev and her killer argued, wouldn't someone have heard the ruckus?"

"Like I said, we're still searching for a potential witness. Perhaps someone walking by the tent who might have heard something that could crack this case wide open."

That gave me some hope. O'Halloran and his team weren't simply settling on Trevor as the guilty party.

"I'm headed to the White House today with several of the people involved in *Spring Into History*," I said.

"Well, la-di-da," chuckled O'Halloran. "Isn't Capitol Hill fancy enough for you anymore?"

"We have a donor tour. You know, the people who pay the bills for things like history lectures."

"Must be nice," said O'Halloran. "I'll be hitting the pavement near our crime scene. I feel like we're missing something big here, but I don't know what. We have the time of death and the murder weapon. But a nagging voice inside my head tells me that something isn't adding up."

"We still don't know why Bev was inside the tent," I said.

"I can shed some light on that," said O'Halloran. "As you know, her phone was with her and we gained access to it yesterday. She texted her boyfriend that she would be home soon but was stopping by the site to take one last look to make sure everything was in order for the following day."

"Her boyfriend?" I said, a bit surprised. Bev had never mentioned anyone special in her life to me, although I had to admit, she didn't have the warmest personality in the world.

"Yeah, they lived together. Don't get your hopes up. We checked out his alibi. It's airtight. He was hosting a group of pals for a poker night at their apartment across town. He never left the game, even for ten minutes."

That was a dead end, no pun intended. At least we knew why Bev was at the tent. It made sense now that I thought of it. Bev was a micro-manager, which was why she generated so much ire from the people she worked with on projects like *Spring Into History*. Even though we were sure everything was ready for the next morning, it was consistent with Bev's obsessive personality that she decided to stop by the tent for one last walk through before going home.

"So, we're back to the people who worked on the event," I said.

O'Halloran sighed. "We are."

"Let's think about this for a minute. Did the killer arrive to the scene before Bev and disable the security cameras?" I asked.

"That's how it had to go down. We don't have any video footage of the crime. That means the cameras weren't functioning when the killer encountered Bev."

"If that's the case, how did the murderer know that Bev was going to be at the site?" I asked. "You said she texted her boyfriend about it. Did she tell anyone else?"

"Let me check," said the sergeant. I heard the shuffling of papers. He must be consulting the phone records the police were able to obtain.

"Nada," he said. "The only message was to the boyfriend. She didn't tell anyone else on your team she'd decided to take one last look at the setup for the next day, at least via text. I don't have any record of it from the interviews I conducted yesterday."

"Then how did the killer know she'd be inside the tent? She didn't mention it when we were together earlier in the day," I said.

"Maybe at the reception you had at the women's suffrage house," said O'Halloran.

"You mean the Belmont-Paul House," I said absently.

"Yeah, that's it. You were all there for a fancy soirée immediately before the murder, right?"

"Bev might have mentioned it to someone there," I said. "I was only with her for a short time. I don't know everyone she talked to that evening."

"Or the killer might have followed her from the reception to the tent and took the opportunity to commit the crime," said O'Halloran.

I shook my head. "That sequence of events doesn't make sense. The killer needed to arrive at the tent *before* Bev, remember? He or she disabled the security cameras so there would be no evidence of what happened."

"Good point," said O'Halloran.

"We need to find out if anyone knew about Bev's decision to visit the tent last night," I said. "She might have told the killer, or the killer might have overheard her mention it."

"Or the perp might have seen her text the boyfriend," said O'Halloran. "Someone could have been looking over her shoulder as she typed the message. After all, there were a lot of people at that reception, right?"

"It's a possibility, but Bev wasn't really the type to allow someone to look over her shoulder," I said. "At least we're making progress about last night's timeline and what transpired."

"If you find anything out today at your fancy White House get together, Ms. Marshall, do I need to remind you that you must contact me immediately?"

"No, you don't. I understand this working relationship goes both ways," I said. "If I uncover important evidence or have any great revelations, don't worry. You're on my speed dial."

O'Halloran made a grunting sound, which I took as affirmation of my commitment to share any forthcoming information. The phone clicked and I hung up the receiver. So much for a fond farewell.

I thought about calling my boss and giving her an update, and then decided against it. She had other problems to deal with right now. Besides, maybe the day would produce an answer to who knew Bev was stopping by the tent for a final walkthrough. If we could figure that out, we'd be much closer to identifying the killer.

After finishing up paperwork and answering as many emails as I could, I let Patsy know that I was leaving for the White House.

"How exciting," she said. "In my entire congressional career, I've only gotten to go to the White House once. It was during the holidays and all of the state rooms were decorated beautifully."

"There's not many opportunities to visit the White House as a legislative branch employee," I said. "Separation of powers in the Constitution, you know."

"A minor and inconvenient detail," said Patsy with a wink. "Have fun and take a lot of photos."

I hopped on the subway and got off at McPherson Square, the station closest to the White House. I walked briskly a few blocks south until I reached Lafayette Square, the park situated directly adjacent to the White House complex. From my cursory knowledge of women's history, I knew that suffragists petitioned for the right to vote in this park over a hundred years ago. They were the first Americans to protest in front of the White House, and since their social activism, Lafayette Park had become one of the most popular places for peaceful demonstration in the entire city. Even today, a small protest made its way through the park, its participants carrying signs and headed towards the White House perimeter, where they would argue for their cause in front of the residence of the most powerful elected leader in the world. Nothing like seeing democracy in action.

I consulted the instructions for entrance. I was scheduled to enter through the East Wing, where I would meet Mila Cunningham and the select donors scheduled for our tour. Now that Bev was dead and Meg couldn't attend, I was the only member of the *Spring Into History* organizing committee to join the group.

After passing through two Secret Service identification checks and security screening, I approached the entrance to the East Wing of the White House. I'd planned to read more about the history of the White House before my special tour, but Bev's murder had interrupted my plans. Last week, I had squeezed in a few minutes and learned that the East Wing as it appears today was constructed in the 1940s by Franklin Roosevelt to cover up the underground bunker he built for top-secret wartime meetings. Now, of course, it housed the office of the first lady. Someday, it would become the office of the first gentleman. With a woman serving as vice president, anything was possible, right?

I spotted Mila Cunningham standing right outside the entrance along with a small group of guests, our top donors for *Spring Into History*. I hustled over and introduced myself to everyone. Bev had handled the fundraising component of our project, which covered invited receptions and the modest stipends we paid our historian consultants Mila and Edgar. It wasn't much, since most of the program was supported by the federal cultural institutions we worked for. However, as I'd learned quickly, there were certain aspects of our weeklong program which required private support, and we were lucky that Bev had secured philanthropic funds to make everything possible.

After the introductions and a brief discussion about Bev's murder, we were ready to enter the White House. Mila led the way. "Please follow me," she said. "There are no guided tours of the White House for the public, so our group will be a little unusual."

I spoke to a gray-haired woman who I believe had introduced herself as Lucinda. "We're quite lucky to have Mila take us through the White House. She's an expert on the history of the executive mansion."

Lucinda nodded. "Such a shame about Beverly, though. Such a sweet young woman. I really enjoyed getting to know her."

I guess Bev could turn on the charm when necessary. Previously, I'd thought that her feud with Trevor was par for the course. Bev seemed like a challenging personality, and Trevor had simply crossed paths with her at an inopportune time. Was that the right assumption to make? Or would the police discover that Trevor's animosity towards her was an outlier? If the latter turned out to be true, Trevor's status as a suspect would only become more serious.

As we walked along a wood paneled East Wing entrance hallway, Mila chatted amiably with the guests on our tour. We turned left and headed down the colonnade to the Family Theater, which I imagined was a popular stop on the tour. Mila explained that the White House staff had allowed our tour to enter the small theater, which is frequently popularized by the press when the president and first family screen a popular film or host a movie night. Lush red armchairs filled the first row. I wouldn't mind watching a movie here. Maybe the executive branch had its advantages.

As the donors explored the theater, I took the opportunity to approach Mila.

"Have you recovered from yesterday's events?" I asked.

Mila shrugged. "Not much to recover from. You and Meg discovered the body. I didn't know Bev that well. We certainly weren't friends."

Mila certainly had a way with words. Of course, indifference might serve as an attempt to cover up guilt. I remembered the brief conversation with Doug last night at the reception after the Georgetown lecture. Time to find out if Mila had a motive to want Bev dead.

"I heard through the grapevine that Bev was threatening to fire you as a historical consultant," I said.

That caught Mila's attention. Her eyebrows shot up faster than a speeding ticket.

"Where did you hear that?" Her blue eyes sparkled with rage.

I never give up my sources. "Oh, just around. Small talk at the Georgetown reception last night."

"It's a lie. Bev would have never fired me. She needed me." Mila pointed at her chest emphatically.

We had to end our conversation because it was time to move everyone along to the next part of the tour. One of our VIPs had a question for Mila, and I receded into the background. I'd wait for another break to continue my interrogation.

After passing through the East Garden Room which featured a large sculpture of Abraham Lincoln, we entered the Ground Floor Corridor. Large red carpets blanketed the floor, giving it a regal appearance. We were able to peer into the China Room, the Vermeil Room, and the library. China and fancy silver didn't really excite me, but books were a different story. I drifted towards the library for a closer look and eavesdropped on Mila's commentary about the room.

"Before it was a library, it served as a laundry facility and servants' quarters. Franklin Roosevelt renovated the room to make it a library in 1935," said Mila. "The collection of books specializes in American history and heritage. It is a functional library with over twenty-seven hundred books currently. Those who live and work at the White House have borrowing privileges."

Although stately, the room seemed a little less formal than the other rooms on the ground floor. There was something inviting and cozy about it. Maybe it was the books, or perhaps it was the Georgia O'Keefe painting over the fireplace?

We walked up a marble staircase to the White House's state floor. After an immediate right, we were inside the grand East Room. Mila clapped her hands to get everyone's attention.

"This is the largest reception room in the mansion. It was designed by White House architect James Hoban for that purpose. In addition to social gatherings, it also served as the place of mourning for Abraham Lincoln after his assassination in 1865. Notice the portrait of George Washington. This is the painting saved in 1814 when the British attacked the White House and set it on fire."

"Wasn't Dolley Madison responsible for saving the portrait of Washington?" asked one of our donors. I remember hearing that story in a history class during my public education.

Mila shifted her weight back and forth. "Yes and no. Dolley Madison likely gave the order to save the Washington portrait. But she didn't pull the painting down and sequester it to safety single-handedly. According to a firsthand account from an enslaved teenager named Paul Jennings, she had help from servants who worked at the White House. They were the ones who actually removed the painting and made sure it was safely secured in a departing wagon."

Our donors stared at Mila. I could tell she'd burst their bubble about Dolley Madison. I spoke quickly to change the subject. "Can you tell us about what this room is used for today?"

Mila seemed to sense she'd lost the room. She recovered almost instantly, smiling from ear to ear. "I'd be delighted, Kit." Then, she launched into a lengthy exposition about the East Room serving as a multi-purpose space for diverse events such as press conferences, concerts, dances, funerals, and even weddings.

I wandered quickly from the East Room, through the Green Room, and into the oval shaped Blue Room. This room was extraordinary in its beautiful decor, restored furnishings, and most importantly, the stunning view overlooking the South Portico and the perfectly manicured White House lawn. On a clear day like today, the view of the Washington Monument was spectacular. The rest of the group caught up with me, and I noticed we were joined by a slight woman in her late twenties.

Mila brought her over to me. "This is Jennifer, and she works in the White House Curator's Office. She's an expert in the history and restoration of this room, so she agreed to show everyone the highlights."

"How delightful," I said, shaking her hand. "We appreciate it."

"It's not a problem," she said. "I'm new here, and this is good practice for me."

To give Jennifer adequate space to give her presentation, Mila and I moved to the corner of the room. Mila had apparently not forgotten the abrupt ending to our conversation inside the Family Theater.

She leaned closer to keep her voice low. "Bev needed me on this project."

Her words resembled a hiss. She stared at me with her blazing blue eyes, which moderately freaked me out.

I inhaled deeply to steady myself before responding. Keeping this conversation under control was a priority. We were in the White House, for goodness' sake. I might not be an executive branch employee, but I was an American. Though I was partial to the United States Capitol, was there any more prominent structure in our entire country than 1600 Pennsylvania Avenue? I think not.

"She wasn't going to fire me. If she did, it would have been her funeral." She narrowed her stare. "Before her murder, of course."

Chapter Twelve

IT TOOK ME A MOMENT TO RECOVER from Mila's comment. Gosh, she was a cold customer. Doug had been right. He said that there was something that bothered him about her. Perhaps it was the ice that ran through her veins?

"Mila, I was only telling you what I'd heard. Obviously, you had a disagreement with Bev. What was it?"

Mila motioned for me to follow her into the adjacent parlor, which was outfitted in red from ceiling to floor.

I couldn't resist. "The Red Room, I presume."

Mila looked at me. "You're a regular Sherlock Holmes."

"I try to live up to my reputation."

Mila rolled her eyes. "The Red Room has been used as a music room, a family living room, and Eleanor Roosevelt met with the press here."

"Who is that woman?" I pointed to a distinctive portrait above the fireplace mantle of a young woman dressed in a white dress and a fancy feather headpiece. She was quite attractive and looked almost too *avant garde* for the White House.

"That's Angelica Singleton Van Buren," said Mila. "She was the daughter-in-law of Martin Van Buren, who was a widower when he became president. She took over the chief hostess duties. In other words, she was the substitute first lady during the Van Buren presidency."

"Well, Angelica struck quite a figure," I said. "But we've gotten off track. I know you were at odds with Bev. What was the source of your disagreement?"

Just as Mila was about to answer, our guests moved into the Red Room, and she was overtaken by questions. Why red? What was the room used for previously? What famous events had taken place inside the parlor? I was glad that our donors were enjoying the personalized tour of the White House, but they had more questions than Bob Woodward.

Finally, we moved into the State Dining Room, which served as Thomas Jefferson's private office during his presidency. Teddy Roosevelt had the room enlarged during a renovation and hung a moose head over the fireplace. I couldn't quite see how that would match today's decor. These days, the only portrait in the room was the famous painting of Abraham Lincoln deep in thought, with his chin resting on his hand. With a maximum capacity of a hundred forty guests, the State Dining Room is used for ceremonial functions and official events, including official diplomatic dinners.

We moved into the hallway and the surrounding area near the exit, which was ironically called the entrance hall since the president and first lady previously welcomed guests to the White House from its North Portico. Today, it's more common to receive guests from the South Portico on the opposite side.

Mila pointed to the long hallway that connected the East Room to the State Dining Room. "This is called the Cross Hall. It allows entrance to the parlor rooms we have visited. There are some famous presidential portraits along the Cross Hall, including this one of John F. Kennedy."

The painting of Kennedy was unusual. His eyes were downcast, which obscured part of his face. I knew next to nothing about art history, yet even I could observe this was not a typical example of portraiture. Sure enough, one of our inquisitive donors asked why Kennedy had been painted in this way.

"The artist's name was Aaron Shikler, and he painted JFK in a different way at the request of Jacqueline Kennedy. She looked at several sketches and chose the one that Shikler painted for the portrait," explained Mila. "Later, the artist explained that the pose depicted Kennedy deep in thought. He also thought it highlighted Kennedy's humility."

The rest of the Cross Hall and Entrance Hall displayed other presidential portraits, featuring the most recent occupants of the White House prominently. The group fanned out over the area, examining the various paintings, architecture, and furnishings.

Mila was standing in the entrance vestibule, near the Grand Staircase where the president and first lady often descended to greet their guests for a formal event. I didn't want her to make a fast escape after the tour was over. I'd barely had a chance to speak with her. But before I could continue our conversation, a tall middle-aged man dressed impeccably in a fashionable suit beat me to the punch. Mila became quite engaged in the conversation. She clapped her hands to signal for everyone's attention and motioned for them to gather near her.

"We have a special treat this afternoon. The Chief Usher of the White House, Gordon McHale, has joined us to say hello. He holds a very important position and will briefly tell us about it." She stepped aside so that Gordon had the floor.

As Gordon launched into a description of his duties as the head of the household staff at the White House, I moved closer to Mila and nudged her.

"Can we continue our chat?" I whispered.

"Not now," she hissed. "We'll go somewhere after this is over."

Gordon finished his speech and agreed to pose for photos with those who wanted them. I wasn't quite sure why our donors were so keen on getting their photo with him, but who was I to judge? I attributed it to the cache of the White House. Even though the Capitol was grand and impressive (and likewise filled with priceless artwork), it somehow didn't have the same effect on people as 1600 Pennsylvania Avenue.

Gordon finally excused himself and we said our goodbyes to our supporters. They seemed tickled pink by the special experience. Bev would have been proud. Thinking about her reminded me I had to focus on Mila as a suspect. Who knows when I would have another opportunity to speak with her?

"Mila, are you still willing to finish our chat?" I asked. My stomach grumbled. There was a tour this afternoon at nearby Decatur House on Lafayette Square and then a reception following it. I'd never make it without a snack.

She was scrolling through the messages on her iPhone and didn't bother to look up to answer my question. "Sure. I need to run back to my office now and check on a few things about the event we're hosting later today. Can I meet you at Teaism?"

Washington, D.C. wasn't a big city. However, almost all my time was spent on Capitol Hill. This neighborhood was entirely foreign to me.

"Teaism? I don't know where that is."

Mila kept her gaze focused on her phone. "Just look it up. It's north of here, right off Lafayette Square on H Street. You can't miss it."

I didn't want to push my luck with Mila, who appeared just as mercurial as the departed Bev Taylor. Perhaps that's why they clashed so much?

"I'll figure it out. See you there in thirty minutes?"

Mila nodded and then abruptly walked away. What a strange character. She certainly behaved oddly. Was that due to guilt? Had Bev Taylor threatened to terminate her consulting gig and Mila decided to beat Bev to the punch?

I wandered into Lafayette Square, the public park north of the White House. I stood before the statue of the Marquis de Lafayette. From reading the exhibits at the Belmont-Paul House, I knew this was one of the locations where the suffragists demonstrated peacefully to draw attention to their cause. They believed Lafayette, a revolutionary and lover of freedom, would have supported their cause. For their activism, many suffragists were arrested and then imprisoned. It was hard to believe such inspirational history had taken place right where I was walking. Of course, the same could be said for Capitol Hill, where I worked every day. Every so often, it felt satisfying to leave a familiar environment and experience something new. I looked back at the White House to the North Portico. When would a woman ever walk though those doors as President of the United States? Who knows? Maybe it would be Maeve Dixon. First the Senate, then 1600 Pennsylvania Avenue. Stranger things had happened, after all.

A helpful wayside marker explained that the statues in Lafayette Park commemorated the foreign generals who fought alongside the American colonists in the Revolutionary War. In the center stood an impressive equestrian statue of Andrew Jackson, certainly a controversial figure in history. What surprised me was that an enslaved apprentice to the sculptor, Phillip Reid, helped to construct the statue of Jackson. There were endless stories that needed to be told, and I hoped that in some small way, our *Spring Into History* project was helping to tell them. That's why Bev was so obsessed with getting everything right about our week of activities. She had told me once that she felt an incredible pressure to share the rich and diverse history of the United States Capitol with as many visitors as possible. Even though I wasn't sure what Bev had thought of Andrew Jackson, in a strange way I was inspired by the sculpture. There are more stories like the one of Phillip Reid in American history, and we needed to make sure they saw the light of day. Our carefully planned week of history-related activities would operate under a shroud of darkness until Bev's killer was caught.

I pulled out my phone to figure out where I was meeting Mila. She hadn't lied. Teaism was a short walk outside the park, across H Street. I still had about ten minutes to kill before meeting her. The spring day was pleasant, with both a hint of chill and warmth in the air. The shoulder seasons were the most tolerable in Washington, D.C., which was, after all, built literally and figuratively on a swamp.

I found an empty park bench, sat down, and decided to check my messages, wondering if Meg had gotten in contact with me. Nada. Not a good sign. She rarely went a few hours without a text or call. I decided to reach out proactively and find out how she was doing. I typed a message and hit send.

White House was AMAZING today. Sorry u missed it.

The infamous three dots appeared, indicating she was replying.

Update on Bev's murder?

Geesh. I guess I wouldn't forward her any of the photos I took during the tour.

Meeting w/ Mila soon.

That should satisfy her. I wasn't blowing it off. Trevor or not, we needed to figure out who killed Bev pronto. But then I noticed Meg had replied.

Taking your sweet time.

I didn't want to explain to Meg that we had donors to placate during the tour, and, on top of that, we were inside the White House. I couldn't exactly pull Mila into the Rose Garden, sit her on a bench, and shine a bright light in her face. I don't think Jackie Kennedy would have appreciated such aggressive tactics in the space she worked so hard to create.

Instead, I simply typed a "smiley face" emoji and swiped my iPhone shut. Meg excelled at riling people up. I'd seen it enough times. I wasn't about to fall victim to her oldest trick in the book. When she calmed down and thought about the situation rationally for a moment, she'd return to her senses.

My phone buzzed. Now what did Meg want? But it wasn't her. Instead, it was a text from intern Jill.

Did everything go well at the White House?

Shoot. I should have pushed for Jill to join me for the tour. I'm sure she would have appreciated it. Bev's murder had drawn my attention away from my responsibility as Jill's mentor. I responded and let her know it went well. She replied immediately.

See you at Decatur House for the reception.

At least Jill was coming to this afternoon's event. Once this murder was solved and Trevor was in the clear, I vowed to spend more time with Jill so she would have a better internship experience. Quite frankly, I don't think I would have been able to pull off *Spring Into History* without her.

I didn't want to keep Mila waiting. She seemed like the type of person who refused to tolerate tardiness. I got up from my comfortable seat on the bench and walked the short distance across the park. I looked up and down H Street and spotted Teaism across the way.

I pulled open the door and looked around. The cafe was beautifully adorned, with numerous tables and a counter for ordering. Although I wasn't a tea drinker, I was open to trying new caffeinated beverages. After all, what if there was suddenly a coffee or espresso shortage in the United States? A woman needs options.

I spotted Mila, who had apparently already ordered since she had a cup of tea in front of her. I motioned that I would place my order and join her.

As I studied the menu, the young woman behind the counter, replete with a nose ring and several piercings in each ear, must have sensed I was perplexed by the options.

"Would you like a recommendation?" she offered.

"I would. I'm not normally a tea drinker."

"Try a chai. It's an Indian blend with cardamom, cinnamon, ginger, cloves, and pepper. We boil it with milk and sugar."

"That sounds lovely," I said.

"It's made from black tea, so it has caffeine. Is that okay?"

"Absolutely. I wouldn't have it any other way."

She must have spied me eyeing the cookies displayed on the counter. They looked and smelled absolutely delicious.

"Would you like to try one of our famous salty oat cookies?"

My stomach rumbled. A reception awaited me, but it would likely be finger food and nothing *that* substantial. I had skipped lunch. A cookie seemed like the perfect snack. Besides, if I was going to interrogate Mila, I needed to fortify myself.

"Sure. I love chocolate. Can I have one of those?" I pointed to indicate which one I wanted.

"Yes, of course. Chunky chocolate pecan. That's a popular one."

She plunked the cookie on a plate. I noticed it was about the size of a hockey puck.

"Thank you. The cookie is my lunch."

"There's a lot of people who come in here and eat our cookies for lunch." She handed me the plate. "Enjoy. I'll bring your chai to your table when it's ready."

I could smell the delicious sweet and salty aroma of the cookie as I walked to Mila's table. If nothing else, at least I'd enjoy my dessert.

Mila eyed my cookie suspiciously. "There's a reception at Decatur House in less than an hour."

"I know, but I haven't had lunch and I can't wait." I took a knife and split the cookie in half. "Would you like to share?"

Mila vigorously shook her head back and north. "No, thank you. I limit my refined sugars. Plus, that's too many carbohydrates for this late in the day."

Should I tell Mila my diet was mostly carbs? It might blow her mind and then we wouldn't be able to talk about Bev's murder. Instead, after shrugging my shoulders, I plopped a piece of the cookie in my mouth. Now I understood why people chose to eat these cookies for lunch.

The helpful server brought my tea to the table. "Are you enjoying the dessert?"

I finished chewing before answering. "Heavenly," I said. "I may need to make the trip from Capitol Hill over here more often."

Mila smiled politely and glanced at her watch. "I'm glad you're enjoying the snack, but I didn't come over here for pleasantries."

Mila sure could ruin a sugar rush. After taking a sip of the milky tea, with earthy spices that perfectly complemented the sweetness of my cookie, I leaned forward in my chair.

"I don't know if Bev was going to fire you or not. She never confided in me about such details," I said. "However, too many people have told me that you didn't get along with her. What was the nature of the problem?"

Mila took a long sip of her tea before answering. "Bev had a lot of constituencies to keep happy in her job. Congressional leadership was always in her business as the director of the Capitol Visitor Center. That translated into pressure on the historians."

Now I was getting somewhere, although I didn't fully understand what she was trying to tell me. "You mean she pressured you and Edgar?"

Mila nodded. "Most of the time, she thought our interpretations of history were too far to the left. She kept saying she wanted us to become more mainstream." When she said "mainstream" she used her hands to make the sign for quotes.

"What does that mean?" I asked, as I took another bite of my cookie.

"You know, more traditional interpretations of history. Staying away from what she thought as controversial topics, like slavery or the oppression of women."

Now I understood. Mila's explanation helped me appreciate the difficulty of Bev's position at the Capitol Visitor Center. The CVC served as the tourist conduit for the United States Capitol, but more precisely, it was the place that all members of Congress sent their constituents when they came to Washington, D.C. for vacation or a visit. It must have been an almost impossible task to satisfy the preferences of all those elected officials.

"But you and Edgar didn't shy away from those topics. In fact, Edgar's lecture last night at Georgetown focused on the history of slavery," I said.

"That's right, but only after Edgar had a long fight with Bev about it. She didn't threaten to fire us as historians. She threatened to cancel the events she thought were too controversial."

An interesting distinction, but Mila's comment opened another line of inquiry for me. "You weren't the only one drawing ire from Bev. Edgar, too?"

"Absolutely. In fact, Edgar was more antagonistic with her than me."

"Why was that?" I asked.

"First, Edgar is African American, and her criticisms personally offended him. Second, his research focuses on the historical topics of greater controversy than my own." She motioned in the direction of Lafayette Park and the White House. "I'm a political historian and I concentrate on the history of the presidency, the White House, and other related topics. I support what Edgar works on, but it's not my particular area of specialty."

"Why did Edgar care so much about what Bev thought? He's tenured at Georgetown." I wasn't a university employee, but Doug had made me aware of the politics in academia. Once a professor was tenured, he or she had a lot more freedom for expression since tenure confers an indefinite appointment, which can only be revoked in extraordinary circumstances. In other words, Edgar didn't need this consulting gig with the Capitol Visitor Center.

Mila shrugged. "You'd have to ask Edgar. He did, though. Maybe he just wanted to make sure *Spring Into History* was an inclusive event."

"Fair point," I said. Edgar might not have cared professionally if he got fired as a consultant by Bev. However, he may have wanted to make sure the programs were the best they could be for the public who would attend them.

"When did Bev and Edgar have these heated discussions?" I asked.

"They were fighting the day before the symposium was scheduled to start. I remember because Edgar called me after he spoke with her. She'd looked at the final description of events and thought she would be criticized by her congressional bosses."

Edgar's status as a suspect had definitely risen. If Edgar had gone rounds with Bev when Mila said he did, then it meant Trevor wasn't the only suspect to exchange heated words with our victim on the day she died. This new information gave me a great deal to think about. However, I wasn't quite ready to let Mila off the hook. At least not yet.

"Mila, the police are pretty sure they can pinpoint the time of Bev's death. She likely died between eight and nine o'clock in the evening," I said. "Can you tell me where you were at that time?"

Mila crossed her arms. "I've already talked to the police about this. I don't suppose it hurts to tell you. I was already at home at that time, inside my apartment."

"Did you take an Uber home from the reception at the Paul-Belmont House?" If that was the case, there would be a record of it.

She shook her head. "I live on the H Street corridor in Northeast," she said. "It was only a twenty-minute walk home."

"Did anyone see you?" I asked.

"No, as a woman walking home at dusk, I did not stop and chat with anyone." Her face tightened.

"And you live alone?"

"Yes. I hope that's not a crime," she said. "If you must know, after I got home, I watched a history program on my DVR, read a book, and then went to bed."

It wasn't a crime to live alone, but it certainly didn't help confirm her alibi. Best not to point that out to Mila, who was likely one step away from ending our conversation.

Neither of us said anything. I took advantage of the lull in the conversation to polish off the cookie. Mila's loss was my gain. If she did kill Bev and I figured it out, she would be sorry in prison that she passed up the opportunity to have a bite of such a delicious dessert.

Mila must have gotten tired of watching me eat. She took a final sip of her tea and stood. "I'm headed back to Decatur House. The reception will start soon, and I'd better make sure everything is ready."

"I've forgotten. Is there a formal speaking program tonight, in addition to the reception?" Bev had planned the entire day, since it was geared towards the generous donors who had supported our program.

"Not a lecture," said Mila. "However, I will give brief remarks inside Decatur House in about thirty minutes. After that, our guests can explore the house. Then, we will adjourn to the courtyard for the reception."

"I can see you're busy," I said. "Thank you again for making the time to speak with me this afternoon. As you may know, Trevor is a suspect, and I don't think he killed Bev." I cleared my throat. "I *know* he didn't kill Bev, I mean."

Mila smirked. "You'd better watch yourself, Kit. People will start to think you're trying to convince yourself that Trevor is innocent."

I concentrated on maintaining a neutral expression on my face. But there was no way to stop the heated flush of embarrassment that overcame me.

Chapter Thirteen

~~~

I SIPPED MY CHAI TEA WHILE REPLAYING the conversation with Mila in my head. She was certainly an intelligent woman, so if she was the murderer, it wasn't going to be easy to prove it. Mila did not strike me as the type of person who acted on a whim. If she killed Bev, I had no doubt she'd plotted it meticulously, waiting for the right opportunity to present itself. The destruction of the security cameras at the scene of the crime seemed like something Mila would have done. She was a control freak, and that type of obsessive personality would certainly inform her *modus operandi* as a criminal.

The other critical revelation from our conversation was Edgar Beaufort and his disagreement with Bev. Mila had revealed that Bev was prepared to cancel the events she didn't agree with. If Mila's depiction of the contentious relationship was accurate, then Edgar's lecture would have been on the chopping block. I wondered if Bev told Edgar she was thinking about pulling the plug on his event. If so, it would have given him a perfect motive for murder.

I wasn't sure if Edgar was going to show up at tonight's event. He and Mila seemed tied at the hip, so I hoped he would come out in a show of support. Furthermore, if he did kill Bev, he might want to act normally. Avoiding a reception could draw suspicion. Either way, if Edgar made an appearance, I needed to find a way to speak to him, preferably alone.

Another possibility, which I had to think about more, was that Edgar and Mila teamed up to kill Bev. Perhaps one of them surprised her while the other killer stabbed her in the back. It was a gruesome thought, yet that was the problem with trying to solve murders. A successful sleuth must *think* like a killer, and most sane people found such musings quite disturbing.

I hoped Meg was on her way over to the reception so I might be able to give her an update about my progress. I didn't know who killed Bev, yet the conversation with Mila had certainly uncovered new possibilities.

I texted Meg and asked her where she was. A few seconds later, a reply appeared on my phone.

At work. Can't make it.

That was too bad. Telling Meg about my conversation with Mila would surely cheer her up.

Want update on case?

Her response appeared almost immediately.

Tell Trevor. He'll be there.

I frowned.

Don't u want to know?

Three dots, then Meg's answer.

Gotta run.

I sighed and put my phone back in my purse. Meg still had a bee in her bonnet. There was nothing I could do about it now. I'd have to sort it out later. Right now, I needed to focus on the task at hand.

After finishing my chai, I walked across the street and found the right address for Decatur House. After passing through a corridor next to the White House Historical Association's boutique gift shop, I was inside a private outdoor red-brick courtyard adjacent to the northwest corner of Lafayette Square. The new Executive Office Building loomed in the corner, which housed many career executive branch bureaucrats.

A tent covered most of the courtyard for the reception. I peeked around the corner and recognized a few people from the White House tour who had already availed themselves of refreshments. The mammoth cookie had done the trick, so I was no longer famished. I was about to reintroduce myself to one of the donors when someone tapped me the shoulder. I spun around and was pleasantly surprised to find intern Jill standing before me. Dressed in a pantsuit with her hair neatly styled in a bun, Jill looked like a quintessential Washington, D.C. intern.

"Jill, it's good to see you," I said. "I hope you were able to find this place without too much trouble. We're not in Capitol Hill anymore."

Jill smiled. "I was glad to have the opportunity to see a different part of the city."

"Yes, working for Congress tends to be consuming. You forget there's a lot more to Washington than the three or four blocks surrounding the Capitol."

"Have you seen Decatur House yet?" asked Jill.

I shook my head. "Just got here. I think Mila is doing a presentation soon."

"She'll speak briefly about the house inside the parlor and then provide a tour."

I glanced around the tent. "Is Edgar Beaufort scheduled to attend this event?"

Jill pulled out a piece of paper from the leather portfolio she was carrying. "He's supposed to be here. Maybe he's inside with Mila?"

Hopefully not plotting how to pin Bev's murder on Trevor. As if on cue, I noticed Trevor had entered the tent, along with his boss James Bennett.

I'd have to keep my eye out for Edgar. In the meantime, I turned my attention to Jill. "Given the circumstances, how are you holding up?" I asked.

Jill blinked rapidly. "It's unsettling, but nothing I can't handle."

Jill was a woman of few words. While I appreciated her brevity most of the time, it could be a challenge if we weren't talking about the immediate task at hand.

"Have you caught the history bug?" I asked. "Perhaps it might be something you'd like to pursue in your career?"

That got a reaction. Her face brightened considerably. "Once I'm done with this internship, I might like that."

I moved immediately into operational mode. "I can help you with that. I have some contacts around town at the Smithsonian, National Archives, Library of Congress, and Mount Vernon."

Jill hesitated for a moment. "Let me think about it. I'm not quite certain what my next step will be."

"That's normal for someone early in her career," I said. "Let's touch base when this is all over and hopefully the murder has been solved."

Jill smiled. "Sounds like a good plan."

"Excuse me, Jill," I said. "I need to speak with Trevor before the program begins." At least I'd made an honest attempt at my mentorship responsibilities. Interns were a vital part of the Washington, D.C. ecosystem and I was lucky Jill was such a hard worker. I would have to let her advisor know.

I hustled over to James and Trevor. Bennett's nose was buried in his phone. I wasn't sure why Trevor's boss bothered to attend these *Spring Into History* events. He didn't seem to enjoy learning about American history. Furthermore, he didn't appear to enjoy being around people. However, because Bennett's attention was focused elsewhere, it was easy to signal Trevor that we needed to chat in private.

After moving a safe distance away from James Bennett, I spoke in a low voice to Trevor. "I might have discovered another person who wanted Bev Taylor dead."

Trevor ran his fingers through his brown hair nervously. "In addition to Mila?"

I nodded. "Edgar Beaufort had a beef with her. She'd threatened to cancel the events he was planning for this week."

"Have you spoken with him yet? Does he have an alibi?"

"Not yet. He's supposed to attend this evening. I'll find a way to talk to him about it."

Trevor gently grabbed my arm and pulled me into the far corner of the tent. We looked suspicious huddled in the recesses since there were only a few other attendees inside with us.

"Do you need to tell me something important?" I asked. "We're drawing attention to ourselves."

"I can't risk my boss hearing me tell you this," he said. "But I think he should be considered a suspect, too."

"Why do you think that?"

"Bev complained about James Bennett to her boss, the Architect of the Capitol. She felt as though Bennett didn't treat her professionally."

"A formal complaint, you mean?"

Trevor nodded curtly. "Exactly. I don't have a copy of it, since it's privileged information, but I have it on good authority that she filed it last week. As you know, there's new procedures in place to handle these types of allegations."

Trevor was correct. After years without a centralized office to deal with issues of workplace or sexual harassment, the House of Representatives had adopted protocols and processes for evaluating and investigating such allegations. As a chief of staff, I attended mandatory training about it, although Maeve Dixon had made it clear from the beginning of her elected term that she wouldn't tolerate such behavior in her congressional office.

"Bennett knew about it?" I asked.

"He would have been notified," said Trevor.

"That certainly gives him a motive to eliminate Bev Taylor," I said.

"Especially since my boss helped put the harassment policy into place," said Trevor. "It could end his career."

I had to agree with Trevor. It was a volatile situation for Bennett, which had magically disappeared when Bev met her untimely death.

"Did you ask your boss where he was the night that Bev died?"

"That's not exactly the type of conversation I can have with him." Trevor rubbed his neck. "He's already hinted that he suspects I killed Bev. What am I supposed to say? Hey, I didn't kill Bev, but did you?"

"Something like that," I muttered. "Listen, you have a point. I'll try to speak to Bennett during the reception and find out if he has an alibi."

"I hope this can get cleared up soon," said Trevor. "In the past, I admit I've appeared unconcerned when others have been accused of crimes they didn't commit. Now that the shoe is on the other foot, I understand."

Trevor had come a long way from the socially inept guy I'd met when we both worked for Senator Lyndon Langsford. Meg had a positive influence on him.

"Anything else you have to report?" I asked.

He motioned toward the other side of the tent, where Chase Wintergreen had just entered. "What about him?"

I rubbed my chin thoughtfully. "I had a chance to chat with Chase and his boss last night, on the way to the lecture at Georgetown."

Trevor peered at me through his wire, horn-rimmed glasses. "And what did you conclude?"

I sighed. "Chase wants everyone's job. He's guilty of unfettered ambition. When Dixon turns over the reins of the committee chairmanship to Amos Duncan, he'd like to become the staff director."

Trevor interrupted me. "But if Dixon loses her bid for the Senate, isn't that job yours?"

I raised my hand to signal for Trevor to tone it down. Trevor's voice had risen, and there were now too many people around us who could overhear the delicate matters we were discussing. It was unlike Trevor to become excitable. Normally, he was so cool and collected, most people found him emotionally detached. I suppose the accusations about murdering Bev had gotten to him.

I gently pulled Trevor closer. "Let's keep it down, okay? Yes, he's in competition with me. But my job isn't the only one he wants. He's also interested in becoming the next director of the Capitol Visitor Center."

"Do you think he might have killed Bev to get her job?"

"It's certainly possible," I said. "Listen, I have to speak to Edgar Beaufort and James Bennett after the tour. Do you think you can handle speaking with Chase? See if he will tell you where he went after the event at the Belmont-Paul House."

Trevor saluted me with his right finger. "I can do that. Shall we try to catch up after everything is over?"

"I don't know if Doug has plans for us this evening, but we'll touch base somehow."

Our conversation was interrupted by Mila's voice. "Please, everyone. Join me inside Decatur House. In five minutes, I will provide you with a short tour, featuring a particularly interesting part of the house's history."

Trevor touched my shoulder lightly. "Thank you, Kit. I appreciate that you're trying to help clear my name." He paused briefly before continuing. "And, of course, finding out who killed Bev Taylor."

We exited the tent and walked toward the entrance of the house. "Meg seems to think I should be doing more to uncover Bev's killer."

"You know Meg. She's happy-go-lucky until things fall apart. Then she becomes a big worry wart."

"Thanks for understanding. You do know I'm trying to figure it out. There's no shortage of suspects. Bev certainly had her enemies."

Trevor averted his gaze as he held open the Decatur House door for me. "She did, but that doesn't mean she deserved what happened to her. There's something deranged about how her body was put on display . . ." Trevor's voice trailed off. "On the Lincoln catafalque."

I was about to agree with Trevor, who seemed to share my befuddlement about the crime. Murders were always messy and gruesome. Yet, something was off about this one, and once I put my finger on it, I knew the identity of Bev's killer would be revealed.

Before I could respond, Mila's voice rang out, loud and clear. "Please, gather around so I can provide you with a short history about the house we're inside."

There were about fifteen of us there, including all the murder suspects. I'd have to move quickly after the program was over so I wouldn't lose the opportunity to speak with James Bennett or Edgar Beaufort. I was counting on Trevor to take care of Chase Wintergreen for me. With his innocence on the line, Trevor wouldn't let me down.

I put aside thinking about the murder for a few minutes and listened to Mila's speech. She explained that Decatur House was one of the oldest buildings on Lafayette Square. Commodore Stephen Decatur, Jr. and his wife Susan purchased the land on the

northwestern corner of the square and then commissioned the
famous architect Benjamin Henry Latrobe to design and build
the house, a federal-style three-story townhouse constructed with
red brick. Decatur was a naval officer and hero, who served in the
Barbary Wars, the Quasi-War with France, and the War of 1812.

Unfortunately, the Decaturs occupied the house for only a little
over a year because Stephen Decatur lost his life in 1820 as the result
of a duel. Susan couldn't afford to keep the house on her own, so
she rented it to famous Washingtonians, including Henry Clay and
Martin Van Buren. Eventually, wealthy tavern owner John Gadsby
bought the house and brought members of his enslaved household
to live there. The Beale family bought the house in 1872 and it
became a prominent place for social gatherings and high society
parties in Washington. Descendant Marie Beale donated the house
to the National Trust for Historic Preservation in the 1950s and
now it was occupied by the White House Historical Association,
the nonprofit and nonpartisan organization that supports the
preservation and history of the executive mansion.

"Quite a storied history," I murmured.

"That is an understatement," said Trevor. "Decatur House is one
of the most important structures in this city's past."

Good to know that while Trevor remained a prime suspect
in a murder investigation, he hadn't lost his penchant for benign
condescension.

"If you'd like to look around on the first floor, feel free to do so.
We have displayed select items from the Decatur House collection
in each of the rooms," said Mila.

I drifted through the rooms, noticing a beautiful mahogany desk
that apparently belonged to Stephen Decatur, as well as a globe that
was over two hundred years old. Resting on a fireplace mantle was
an old sword and scabbard. The label indicated that Stephen Decatur
had been given the sword by the Commonwealth of Virginia after he
captured the British frigate *Macedonian* in 1812.

After ten minutes of perusing, Mila made an announcement. "If
anyone would like to see the second floor with me, I will provide a
brief tour of the slave quarters, which have been recently restored.

This is one of the few examples of urban slave quarters within Washington, D.C. still in existence."

I needed to speak with James and Edgar, but there was no way I was going to pass up the opportunity to observe a place so historically significant. If I'd known what we were going to see, I would have insisted that Doug join us. Luckily, as Mila moved toward the staircase, I noticed that James and Edgar followed. I wouldn't be losing track of them and could continue the tour. It was my lucky day. Unfortunately, Chase Wintergreen had peeled off from the group. Trevor spotted his exodus and followed Chase in hot pursuit. I silently congratulated myself. Trevor's assistance with my various investigations over the past several years had obviously taught him something.

After we climbed a flight of stairs, we entered an empty medium sized room, probably close to the size of a modest one-bedroom apartment. Along with a brick chimney, the wooden framing of the ceiling was exposed, likely restored to resemble its original appearance. There were also wooden vertical beams, indicating a hallway might have existed there. Mila asked for everyone's attention and then began.

"We are inside the slave quarters of Decatur House, built at a right angle to the original house in the early 1820s. Originally, it housed a domestic staff of servants. However, as a tenant in the late 1820s, Secretary of State Henry Clay lived in the house with his family and enslaved servants. When John Gadsby, a wealthy tavern and hotel owner, purchased the house in 1836, he also brought enslaved people with him. Although the room is open today and without walls, it was likely divided into three small bedrooms when it served as slave quarters." Mila took a breath and was immediately interrupted by one of the donors who had been on the White House tour earlier today.

"How many people lived in this space?" she asked.

I could tell from the annoyed look on her face that Mila didn't like being interrupted, but thankfully she took it in good stride. "We think up to twenty-one people lived here at a time, ranging from children to older adults. The numbers varied over the decades."

The donor didn't bother to hide her surprise at Mila's answer. Even with the space divided into three rooms, the living quarters would have been incredibly tight for that number of people.

Mila went on, "Many of the people who lived here worked in the kitchen and laundry, located directly beneath us on the first floor. Unlike today, the only exit from this part of the house led to an interior courtyard. This allowed the Gadsby family to restrict the movement of the enslaved people who lived here. Also, it kept them out of sight."

Another donor spoke up. "Because this residence is so close to the White House."

Mila nodded. "Yes. The enclosure kept the enslaved workers sequestered and away from public view. Staircases connected this part of the house, all the way from the basement to the attic. This way, elaborate parties and social occasions could be held while keeping the enslaved workers physically separated within the house itself."

"After slavery was abolished, what happened to this space?" asked an older gentleman.

"When the Beale family took possession of the property after the Civil War, it became a place to house domestic servants, including free African Americans and immigrants," said Mila. "It was a service wing to the house until the property was bequeathed to the National Trust for Historic Preservation."

Doug would have enjoyed Mila's fascinating tour of the space. I rarely had the opportunity to teach my historian husband something he didn't already know.

We retraced our path down the staircase and returned to the reception tent in the outside courtyard. Although I had thoroughly enjoyed the history lesson, it was time to return to my detecting. Edgar was busy helping himself to the considerable spread of food that was now arrayed on tables next to the bar. It always hard to have a conversation when the other person was stuffing his or her mouth. I knew, because as the chief of staff for a powerful member of Congress, I was often trying to eat while others chatted me up.

As it turned out, I didn't have to try to decide whether I'd pursue Edgar or James first, because the latter was headed straight for me.

"Kit, I need to speak with you," said James. He looked around furtively, scanning the growing crowd inside the tent.

"Sure, James. I'd like to talk to you, too."

He gently pulled me outside the tent. "There are too many people here," he said. "We can't talk privately."

"I can't leave right now, but if you like, we can speak after the reception is over," I said. "I don't think the organizing team should leave right in the middle of it, given that Bev is no longer with us."

"That's fine," said James quickly. "I'll email you with instructions where to meet once the event winds down." Once again, his eyes darted back and forth, as if he was expecting someone to interrupt our conversation.

"What's going on James?" I asked. "I hope this isn't about Trevor. I understand he's a suspect in Bev's murder, but he should be afforded all due process . . ."

James cut me off and grabbed my right arm, forcing me to move closer to him. "Listen, Kit. This isn't about Trevor."

Quite frankly, I'd had enough of being dragged outside the tent and now having my personal space invaded. This guy already had one harassment complaint lodged against him. He was about to have another. I placed my left hand on James's shoulder and pushed him back.

"That's a little too close for comfort, James. If you have something to tell me, we can talk after the reception somewhere." I headed back inside the reception, and then turned to face him. "Make sure it's a public place, too."

After stepping inside the tent and moving to an unoccupied corner, I inhaled slowly and deeply. I needed a moment to compose myself. What had gotten into James Bennett? Had he heard I'd been investigating and wanted to shut me up? Trevor had been right. His strong-arm tactics were exasperating. His behavior certainly substantiated the claims that Bev Taylor had apparently lodged against him before she was murdered. Hopefully I could catch up with Trevor before meeting up with James. Perhaps he could provide me with some additional background on him.

I spotted Edgar Beaufort across the room. He was standing by himself at a high-top table, and it appeared as though he had just finished his plate of food. Perfect timing. I hustled over to speak with him.

"Good to see you, Edgar," I said cheerily. I found it most effective to disarm suspects with pleasantries, at least initially.

"Hello, Kit." He stuffed a canapé into his mouth. "This reception had a really great spread."

I smiled. "It's too bad that Bev didn't get to enjoy the results of her hard work."

Edgar nodded politely but remained silent. I'd have to push a little harder.

"Did you have a good relationship with Bev?" I asked.

Edgar scrunched up his face and paused for a beat before answering.

"Define what you mean by good," he said.

I willfully suppressed an audible groan. So, this was the game we were going to play?

"What I mean to ask is whether you got along with her," I said. "I heard through the grapevine that you and Bev had your differences."

Edgar took a sip from his bottle of Perrier. "That's no state secret." He looked me straight in the eye. "*Everyone* on this organizing committee had disagreements with Bev."

Edgar might be an academic, but he certainly knew how to deflect suspicion like a real Washington, D.C. insider. Time for a new approach.

"Where did you go after the reception ended at the Belmont-Paul House?"

"Home, of course."

"Did you drive home? Take a car service?"

"I walked. I live in one of the newly constructed apartment buildings in the Navy Yard area."

That neighborhood was directly south of Capitol Hill, nearby the Washington Nationals ballpark. It was an easy walk, particularly in nicer weather. Sigh.

"And you live alone, I presume?"

"With my cat. Just so you know, I told all of this to the police."

"I understand that. We need to find Bev's killer. I feel like it's already cast a pall over *Spring Into History*."

Edgar motioned widely with his right hand. "I don't know about that. Seems like everyone is having a decent time at this event. And my lecture was a complete success."

His last comment left me with an excellent opening. "Was it even going to take place if Bev Taylor hadn't been killed? I heard you got into a big fight with her on the day she died. She threatened to cancel the events because she was worried the agenda had tilted too far toward the liberal end of the spectrum. Congressional bosses were giving her grief, and she might have been forced to take action."

The expression on Edgar's face didn't change. However, I suspected Edgar was working hard to make sure he didn't reveal his true reaction to my question.

"Bev had some concerns, but you're blowing it way out of proportion. We had a conversation, as you mentioned. There wasn't going to be any cancellation. She was dealing with the elected officials who were being uncooperative."

"She was dealing with them by promising to alter the agenda, which would have certainly meant some of the events you planned might have been scrapped."

This time, my insistence must have irritated Edgar. Several beads of sweat formed on his forehead. He grabbed a napkin on the table and wiped them away.

"If Bev planned to do that, I had nothing to do with it," said Edgar flatly.

"It seems to me that you had a credible reason for making sure Bev was out of the way," I said. "And you have no alibi, either."

Edgar pursed his lips. "If that's the case, how would I have even known Bev was going to be at the tent that evening? We didn't have a scheduled meeting there with the planning team."

Edgar had me there, but that was the case for any of the suspects. It seemed most likely that whoever killed Bev saw her leave the reception and followed her. Perhaps there was an altercation or disagreement and Bev decided to leave. The murderer killed her from behind and placed her body on the Lincoln catafalque. The main problem with my theory was that the killer disabled the security cameras before committing the crime, so I wasn't quite sure about the sequence of events. Something didn't quite fit my scenario.

"I'm not sure about every detail yet," I admitted. "Perhaps you had been looking for an opportunity to kill Bev for a while, and the fact that she was alone in the tent at night simply presented itself to you."

My latest accusation must have been too much for Edgar. He slammed his hand down on the high-top table. "I've heard enough from you. I know you want to make sure your friend Trevor isn't arrested for the murder, but you've gone too far." Behind his professorial glasses, his eyes were cold and piercing. "I would have expected more from Doug Hollingsworth's spouse. I may need to share my concerns with certain administrative officials at Georgetown."

With that threat, Edgar picked up his Perrier water and walked away, exiting the tent. No one likes being accused of murder, but Edgar's reaction was certainly cagey. On top of James Bennett's odd behavior, I'd say the suspects were piling up faster than I could keep up with them. Speaking of suspects, I wondered where Trevor had gone and whether he'd had any luck speaking with Chase Wintergreen. Neither of them was inside the tent.

I'd better let Doug know that Edgar Beaufort was unhappy and had made an oblique threat to transfer his anger with me onto him. I moved to the edge of the tent and pulled out my phone. The situation was too complex for a text. Instead, I dialed Doug's number and hoped he would answer.

Thankfully, Doug picked up. I caught him up on my day and explained that I might have pushed Edgar a bit too hard in my interrogation. After recounting the veiled jab directed at him, Doug responded with a hearty chuckle.

"What's he going to do? Tell the provost that my wife is investigating him for a murder? That doesn't sound like a conversation you'd want to have willingly."

My heart warmed. I could always count on Doug to look at the bright side.

"It's too bad I didn't think to invite you to this event," I said. I described the historic slave quarters we'd seen, along with as much of Mila's explanation as possible.

"I wasn't aware of a restored urban slavery living space in Washington," said Doug. "Did you happen to take any photos?"

Darn it. I should have thought to snap a few when I was on the brief tour. "No, but maybe I can slip back up there and get a few for you."

"If you can, that would be great, Kit," said Doug. "What are you doing for the rest of the evening?"

I explained that James Bennett had wanted to speak to me privately after the reception was over, and I was waiting to hear from him.

"After that, you don't have any other commitments?" asked Doug.

"Nothing else," I said.

"After I finish up work, I can meet you at the Hay Adams Hotel right off Lafayette Square," said Doug. "There's a hidden gem there, a pleasant place where we could enjoy a drink together to end the evening."

"That sounds perfect, Doug. After I get done with James Bennett, I'll be more than ready for a relaxing cocktail with you."

As it turned out, truer words had never been spoken.

Chapter Fourteen

I LOOKED AROUND THE TENT. Trevor was still nowhere in sight, and neither was James Bennett. It would take Doug at least thirty minutes to finish up his work and drive across town from Georgetown. That was plenty of time to touch base with Trevor about Chase Wintergreen and find out what was bothering James Bennett. Of course, if both magically disappeared, who knows how long it would take to locate them and speak with them.

Several donors to *Spring Into History* came over to chat and express satisfaction with the VIP experience they had today. Thankfully, Bev had set everything up perfectly and all we needed to do was follow through on her plan. Even though Bev and I hadn't become close friends, I still felt badly about her death. She'd been the catalyst for organizing a week full of activities devoted to American history and had initiated planning conversations with all the cultural institutions, museums, universities, and historical societies involved. It seemed particularly cruel she was murdered the day before her vision came to fruition.

I couldn't shake a guilty feeling I had about her death. The fact that I entertained a sense of remorse made absolutely no sense. I was in no way responsible for what happened to her. Meg and I discovered her body, yet we knew that she'd already been dead for hours. Then why did I feel *responsible* for what happened to Bev

Taylor? I didn't like it. Rationality was my strong suit, and these pangs of guilt were decidedly irrational.

I took another look around the reception. The crowd was starting to thin, yet there was still no sign of Trevor and James. In fact, no one from our organizing committee was there. Perhaps Mila had left after the tour, and I hadn't seen Chase Wintergreen since we were inside Decatur House earlier.

Maybe everyone had gathered back inside the stately mansion. Doug had wanted me to snap photos from the historic area we'd visited during the tour. I left the tent and went back inside the house, which was eerily quiet. If anyone was there, they weren't chatting or making any noise. I walked through the first-floor parlor and dining room. No one was here. I found the rear staircase that led upstairs and walked up. Was I allowed to be here unescorted? If I was careful not to touch or disturb anything, I couldn't see how it would matter. Besides, I didn't even know if Mila was still on the premises.

Before following the corridor to the restored enslaved living quarters, I looked around the corner at the top of the stairs, and I immediately understood Mila's explanation during the tour. The structure had been deliberately constructed to enable a division between the "fancy" part of the house, suitable for entertaining guests, and the service wing of the house, where enslaved people and domestic servants had lived and worked. We hadn't seen the other rooms on the second floor during our tour. Nothing was cordoned off, so I decided to explore. The main staircase was there, which enabled the invited guests and dignitaries to move from the first floor to the second. Past that was a small drawing room I walked by without entering.

The big room on this floor was the next one. No electrical lights were turned on, and the natural sunlight for the day was waning. The interior shutters on the tall windows had been closed, but if I had my geography correct, this large drawing room faced Lafayette Square. There was an enormous glass chandelier hanging from the ceiling, reminiscent of the ornate light fixtures that hung inside the grand dining room on the Titanic (or at least as I could recall from having watched the blockbuster movie numerous times in my youth). The room was almost completely empty, probably used as a space to hold contemporary receptions, dinners, or other elaborate events.

From the doorway, I spotted a sizable replica of the Lansdowne Gilbert Stuart painting of George Washington, certainly one of the most famous images of our first president. Hubert Vos, a Dutch artist, had painted this replica. The original painting was part of the Smithsonian's National Portrait Gallery collection, and I'd seen a Stuart copy earlier today in the East Room of the White House. Of course, I'd also learned on the tour that Dolley Madison didn't actually save the painting in the manner folklore had popularized. What a strange day. It was rare that I got to appreciate fine art in my daily job, and today, I'd seen not one but two copies of one of the most famous paintings in American history. The dimness of the room prevented me from getting a good look at the painting from the doorway. There was no stanchion to prevent me from walking right up to the large artwork. What the heck. If I could, perhaps I could use my flash and get a photo for Doug in addition to securing a few images of the historic service wing.

I stepped forward and my right foot skidded ahead of me. It was just my luck. The floor was wet. If I hadn't grabbed backwards for the doorframe, I would have ended up on my butt. Then, who knows? Such a commotion might have brought attention to my presence, and I probably shouldn't be walking around a two-hundred-year-old house without permission.

After steadying myself, I decided the photo of the painting wasn't worth it. If I hustled, I could snap a few photos of the service wing for Doug and try to find Trevor and James. If I was being completely honest, the empty house creeped me out.

But then I spotted something in the shadows. To the right of the George Washington painting was a small piano. Was there something underneath it? The light in the room was so dim, it was impossible to figure out what it might be.

I stepped forward again, cautiously so I wouldn't slip on the floor's wetness. There was no way I could find the light switch to turn on the chandelier. Should I try to open the interior shutters that covered the enormous windows facing the park? I walked quickly across the room and unhooked the shutters, allowing the fading daylight to stream into the room.

I turned around and looked at the piano. There was something underneath it, but without a closer look, I couldn't be sure what it was. While the light from the windows helped, it wasn't bright enough to illuminate the far recesses of such a large room.

My phone buzzed. I pulled it out of my purse and looked at it. It was a text from Trevor. He was ready to chat. I told him where I was and suggested that he should find me. There was no one else on this floor of the house, and if he had something juicy to tell me about Chase Wintergreen, we could exchange information privately.

After sending the text, it dawned on me that I had a light source at the ready. I switched on the flashlight function of my phone, turning the camera flash into a steady stream of light. Someone was coming up the stairs. Maybe I could find the light switch inside this room so I wouldn't have to talk to Trevor in the dark.

Using my newfound light source, I spotted the switch across the room and hustled over to turn it on. Trevor called out to make sure I was there. "Kit, are you here?"

"I'm here," I said loudly. "I just found the overhead lights and I'm turning them on."

A moment later, the large, empty room was illuminated by the glass chandelier overhead. Trevor appeared right next to me. "Why are you sneaking around inside this building?"

A fair question, but I didn't feel like explaining that in addition to the fact that I was a natural-born snoop, I also wanted to snap photos for Doug.

Instead, I kept it simple. "Just curious, I guess. The reception was wrapping up and you weren't around. Neither was your boss."

At that moment, Trevor's face drained itself of color. For someone with a pale complexion in the middle of summer, it was alarming.

"What's wrong? You look like you've seen a ghost," I said.

Trevor pushed past me and made a beeline for the piano in the corner of the room. With Trevor showing up, I'd temporarily forgotten I'd spotted something underneath it.

Now with the lights on, I looked down at my shoes. They were black flats, but some sort of colored substance covered the sides of them. I reached down and touched my finger lightly to my right shoe. My heart skipped a beat. Unfortunately, from previous experience, I knew exactly what it was, and it wasn't water. It was blood.

Chapter Fifteen

"**K**IT, WHAT ARE YOU DOING? Get over here!"

At this point, Trevor was on the floor, underneath the piano. He'd pushed the bench aside, grabbed the body with both hands, and dragged it to the edge of the room. There was no mystery about who it was. James Bennett, Trevor's boss, was the victim. A large stab wound in his chest appeared to be the source of his demise.

"I'm calling for an ambulance," I said. "Try to see if you can resuscitate him."

I pulled out my phone and punched in 9-1-1. I had no idea what the address of Decatur House was, but since it was a historic structure, the emergency operator had no problem locating it on a map. She promised help within minutes.

Trevor was crouched down on the floor, with his hands on Bennett's chest. He shook his head slowly. "It's no use. He's dead."

"Help is on the way now," I said. "I'm going to run downstairs and see if anyone here is a doctor or nurse."

I flew down the main staircase and took a fast look around the first-floor rooms. I couldn't see anyone, but I called out loudly for help, just in case. When I didn't get a response, I found the door that led to the interior courtyard. I spotted Mila, Edgar, and Chase immediately. They were standing right outside the tent, each with a beverage in hand.

"Help!" I exclaimed. Three heads swiveled in my direction.

"Kit, what were you doing inside the house?" asked Mila. "We were looking for you."

"It's James Bennett," I gasped. "He's been stabbed!"

Mila dropped her drink. Luckily, it was one of those clear, plastic cups typically used at outdoor receptions in lieu of actual wine glasses. Still, it hit the ground and spilled all over her feet. As she bent down to retrieve the empty glass, Edgar stuttered, "What did you say? Bennett has been stabbed?"

"That's what I said." I rushed over to join them. "Mila, do you know if there's a doctor or medical professional who can look at him? An ambulance should be arriving in the next couple of minutes."

Mila looked like she'd seen a ghost. She was surprisingly tongue-tied, which may have been a first for her. "Um . . . what did you say? A doctor?"

"Yes. Anyone who could treat James immediately?"

Mila looked around with a helpless expression of despair. "I don't think so. Not that I know of. Most of the guests have gone."

At that moment, we heard the familiar siren of the approaching ambulance. "Never mind," I said. "I'm going to meet the ambulance outside, so they know where to go."

I went back through the house and exited through the door facing Lafayette Square. The ambulance was headed down H Street, and I stepped cautiously into the busy roadway to flag it down. The EMTs parked directly in front of Decatur House, and I led them upstairs to the large drawing room. Trevor moved away from Bennett's still body when the first responders arrived. He shook his head slowly. "He's dead, Kit. There's no signs of life."

We moved into the hallway to give the EMTs some space. Trevor's white dress shirt had a smear of blood on the collar, and there were streaks of blood on his hands and shoes. I was about to point this out to him when one of the paramedics approached us.

"I'm sorry to be the bearer of bad news, but this man is dead," he said. "Did either of you know him?"

Trevor explained it was his boss, who served as the Chief Administrative Officer of the House of Representatives.

"The police are on the way," he said. "You'll need to stay here to provide a statement."

My mind began to click into investigation mode. "How did he die?" I asked. Obviously, I had an idea, but I wanted the paramedic to confirm it.

The EMT looked at me like I was an idiot. "He suffered a fatal stab wound."

"I meant the murder weapon. Have we located it?" I asked.

Trevor pointed to the piano. "Look on the top of the piano, Kit. We missed it earlier because we were so focused on James."

I walked toward the entrance of the large drawing room. The paramedic immediately thrust his hands outward, motioning for me to stop.

"You can't come inside this room," he said. "With a murder investigation, it's our job to preserve the crime scene as best as we can until the police arrive." Speaking of the police, I could hear the familiar siren in the distance. They were almost here.

"Okay, I understand." I wasn't going to argue with a first responder. I took a few steps back, but I was still able to look through the doorway. The historic sword from downstairs was sitting on top of the piano. It was difficult to determine from a distance, but it seemed as though the faint red sheen of blood shimmered on the tip of the blade.

I lowered my voice to speak with Trevor. "That's the sword we saw on the tour from downstairs," I said. "It's part of the collection here at the Decatur House."

Trevor nodded. "Stephen Decatur's sword. A beautiful, yet deadly, weapon."

"Beautiful, deadly, and *convenient*," I said. "Mila gave us plenty of time to wander from room-to-room downstairs. Everyone admired the sword on top of the fireplace mantle."

"That means anyone could have come back inside the house, picked up the sword, and killed James Bennett," said Trevor.

"And the killer didn't even try to hide the weapon afterwards," I said. "Instead, he or she put it on top of the piano."

"Almost like it was on display, similar to the way it was situated on the fireplace mantle," said Trevor. "Is that significant?"

I pursed my lips. "I don't know. But it reminds me of the way that Bev's body was put on display inside the tent, placed on top of the Lincoln catafalque."

"What do you think that means?" asked Trevor.

"I'm not a FBI criminal profiler. However, I think the murderer is showing bravado in these displays. There's not much opportunity for elaborate staging like with many serial killer murders. Yet he or she takes the time to draw attention to the crime scene."

The blue and red lights of a police car flashed through the tall windows inside the drawing room. My phone dinged just as I heard a barrage of footsteps coming up the staircase. I glanced at my device. It was a text message from Doug. He'd arrived at the Hay Adams Hotel and wanted to know where I was. He certainly wasn't going to like my answer. I shoved the phone back inside my purse. After I dealt with the initial police barrage, I'd have to call Doug back. He usually traveled most places with a book, so hopefully he was true to form this evening. That would keep him occupied for a while.

The troop of police officers was led up the stairs by a petite woman with brown hair pulled back into a neat, sleek ponytail. She was wearing a trim, stylish pantsuit that was fashionable, yet entirely functional for chasing down bad guys. I didn't have to wait for her to introduce herself. This was Detective Maggie Glass, D.C.P.D. From firsthand previous experience, I knew she meant business.

Detective Glass blew past us and walked directly into the parlor room. She conferred quietly with the paramedic, who I noticed gestured towards me and Trevor. Glass looked our way and shook her head slightly from side to side. She must have recognized me, too.

Glass appeared to give instructions to the police officers who joined her. Then she headed our way.

"It's been while since we've seen each other, Ms. Marshall," said Detective Glass. She wore tiny silver studs as earrings, giving just a hint of femininity. Underestimating her would be a rookie mistake, indeed.

"Not since the death of the lobbyist," I said. "Although there have been other murder cases. Just none that involved you."

Trevor shot me an exasperated look. At times, I offered too much information.

"What I'm concerned about is the dead man in this room." She gestured toward the doorframe. "Who discovered the body?"

Trevor spoke up. "We both did. We decided to meet here for a private chat. Kit had just located the switch for the chandelier and when the lights came on, I noticed James Bennett's body lying underneath the piano."

Glass tapped her pen on the side of her cheek. "You look familiar. Weren't you involved in those other murders? The lobbyist and those high society people at the Continental Club."

"Guilty." Trevor's face flushed red. "I wasn't guilty of the murders. But I did work with Kit to uncover the identity of the responsible party."

Glass raised her eyebrows, but ignored Trevor's commentary, which was quite uncharacteristic. Usually, Trevor was calm and collected, too cool for school. Bennett's death had him rattled. It didn't take a genius to figure out why. If the police determined Bev's murder was connected to this crime, Trevor was going to skyrocket to the top of the suspect list. It wouldn't take the cops long to figure out that Trevor and his boss weren't bosom buddies. He'd be the only logical person with obvious motives to kill both Bev Taylor and James Bennett.

Glass turned her head to look around. "Strange place for a meeting. Were you here for another reason?"

I explained the *Spring Into History* weeklong schedule of events. I hesitated before mentioning Bev's murder. That didn't stop Detective Glass from making the connection.

"Didn't I read that a woman involved with that history program got killed the other day in a tent outside the United States Capitol? And if my memory serves me right, she was stabbed, too."

I took a deep breath. "You're correct. Bev Taylor was her name. She was part of our planning committee."

Glass pointed her pen at me. "So, let me get this right, Ms. Marshall. This is the second body that's showed up at one of your history soirées?"

"Yes, although technically, Bev's body was discovered in the morning, not in the evening," I said.

"Why does that matter?" snapped Glass.

"Well, soirées are typically evening affairs," I said.

Glass pursed her lips. "I don't care what time of the day her body was discovered. What matters is that the man lying dead in the room next door isn't the first victim related to these events." She looked pointedly at me.

"I can't disagree with that statement," I said. "The deaths may be connected."

"You said *may* be connected," repeated Glass with an incredulous tone that rose an octave at the end of the sentence. "That is the understatement of the night."

Best to change the subject and try to help Maggie Glass. If I wasn't careful, she'd have Trevor and me in handcuffs. A perp walk on H Street during the bustle of the evening would do wonders for both of our careers.

"Detective, can I make a comment about the murder weapon?" I asked.

"Certainly, Ms. Marshall," she said, her voice dripping of sarcasm. "Why not? Please feel free to share your insight."

"Between the ambulance and police arrivals, Trevor and I noticed the likely weapon was on top of the piano. I thought you should know that the sword was on display downstairs during the tour of Decatur House that occurred earlier this evening."

"Was it secure?" asked Glass.

"I'm afraid not. One of the historians here arranged to have several items of the Decatur House collection on display for the tour," I explained. "It was a small group, and everyone in attendance were donors or VIP guests of ours."

I'd piqued Glass's interest. "Are you saying that anyone would have had access to the sword?"

"Absolutely. The historian in charge explained its significance and pointed it out. No one missed it," I said.

"I've heard enough for now," said Glass. "First, someone get the Capitol Hill police on the phone. Who's in charge of the first murder? Is it Sergeant O'Halloran?"

I nodded. If memory served me correctly, Glass and O'Halloran were acquainted with each other. My bet was that they'd be sharing notes within the hour. That wouldn't help Trevor, since once Glass learned he was a prime suspect in Bev's murder, she would question his role in discovering Bennett's body.

"You both need to give your statements to the officer over there." The detective pointed to a cop standing nearby. "Then check back with me. I'll decide what to do with you later."

Trevor whispered to me. "What does *that* mean?"

I shrugged my shoulders. "She's probably deciding whether we need to go with her to the police station for more questioning."

Trevor rubbed the back of his neck. "I can't believe James is dead." He paused for a moment. "This doesn't look good for me, does it?"

I didn't want to alarm Trevor. At least, not yet. "You joined me after I was already upstairs. But I couldn't find you after the tour. I waited for you at the reception. James Bennett came up to me and said he had something important to tell me. After that, I spoke with Edgar for several minutes. Finally, I had a phone call with Doug. Where were you during that time?"

Trevor squirmed. "I took a walk around the neighborhood."

"Around Lafayette Park?" I asked.

"No, the Secret Service had cleared the park. I guess there was something going on at the White House. Instead, I walked down H Street and wandered into St. John's Church."

"You mean the church of the presidents?" Even though I was a Congress geek, everyone knew that St. John's Church near the White House was famous for its lovely architecture and the fact that all presidents since James Madison had attended services there, either regularly or upon occasion.

"Yes. I thought the church might be open, and it was. So, I went inside."

"Did you sit in the president's pew?" I asked.

Trevor's lips parted. "I'm impressed you know these details, Kit."

"I try to read more than just public policy papers," I said.

"The answer is no. I did not sit in the president's pew. Instead, I took a seat in the back of the church, where Abraham Lincoln sat when he visited the church during the Civil War."

"Most importantly, did you see anyone when you were there?" I asked. "Someone who could corroborate your alibi?"

Trevor cast his gaze downward. "I'm afraid not. The church was empty."

Drat. There might be some type of security camera inside or around the church, but it would be a while before the police could pull those. And if they did, it meant they were seriously considering Trevor as a suspect for both murders. Without someone to confirm Trevor's whereabouts, he'd have to contend with Detective Glass and Sergeant O'Halloran's suspicions, at least for now.

I needed to contact Doug before I gave my statement to the police. I fingered my phone, trying to decide what to tell him. If I called and told him there had been another stabbing, he'd worry until I showed up. It was best to explain there had been a delay. When I made it over to the hotel, I'd let him know what had happened. After an evasive message to Doug letting him know that I would be late, I turned my attention back to Trevor.

"Now, what do we do?" I asked. It was more of an existential question than anything.

Trevor motioned toward the officer who was standing a few feet away from us. "I think we need to give him our statements."

"Of course." We walked over and spoke with the officer, who wrote everything down. He had a lot of questions for both of us, including why I had returned to the upstairs floor of Decatur House. But he focused more on Trevor and where he had been for the period of time between the tour and when he returned to Decatur House to meet me.

After the third degree, the officer asked us to stay put while he consulted with Detective Glass. Trevor and I huddled together in the corner of the hallway, near the formal staircase, while swarms of cops and crime scene investigators filled the adjoining rooms.

"I suppose someone told Mila and Edgar what happened," I said.

"I'm sure the police filled them in," said Trevor.

"Before they come back for us, there's two questions I want to ask you," I said. "First, were you able to speak with Chase Wintergreen? I saw you follow him after the tour downstairs was over."

"I wanted to join you to see the historic slave quarters that Mila talked about, but I figured I'd better talk to Chase," said Trevor. "I caught up with him and was able to talk to him for a few minutes. That guy is cagey."

"I agree, but cagey doesn't make him a murderer," I said.

"He definitely had a motive to eliminate Bev," said Trevor. "It only took me a few questions before he was asking me about James Bennett and how long he plans to remain in his current position as the Chief Administrative Officer."

I shook my head. "Do you think he might have killed James, too?"

"I'm not sure it would have been premeditated. I could see him asking James about a job, even the Capitol Visitor Center position. If my former boss was his usual self, he might have said something snarky and blew him off," said Trevor.

The gears in my head started churning. "If that happened, maybe he seized an opportunity to kill Bennett. He grabbed the sword from downstairs, which was a ready-made and available weapon, and then stabbed him."

"You know, I hadn't thought of this before, but I bet James was going to have a say in picking Bev's replacement," said Trevor.

"Now it's becoming clearer. Chase went to speak to James about the position, now conveniently vacant due to Bev's death. James picked up bad vibes from the conversation."

"And James might have told Chase that he had no chance at getting the job."

"Exactly," I said. "Chase reacted badly, and James got a weird feeling about the conversation. Maybe he put two and two together and fingered Chase as the killer."

"Chase had no choice but to kill James," said Trevor. "He suspected him of murder, and there was no way he was going to enable him to get that job."

"Now it all makes sense. Like I told the officer in my statement,

James found me in the courtyard after the tour was over. He seemed distraught or upset. He wanted to speak with me, and I was waiting for him to let me know when we could meet."

"He never got the chance to tell you what was bothering him," said Trevor.

I shook my head slowly. "No, but whatever it was, I'm positive it got him killed."

Chapter Sixteen

I KNEW THERE WAS TROUBLE when the police officer who took our statements didn't come back alone. Instead, Detective Glass accompanied him.

"I have good news and bad news," she said.

"Please tell us the good news first," said Trevor.

Glass motioned towards me. "You're free to go," she said. "We have your contact information and we'll be in touch so you can review and sign your formal statement."

I was relieved, yet I knew there was still bad news to come, and I had a hunch about what it was. Unfortunately, my intuition was correct.

She turned to face Trevor. "You need to come downtown with us. Sergeant O'Halloran is going to join us there. We have some more questions and want to review various timelines connected to both murders."

"Wait a second," I said. "Are you bringing Trevor in for formal questioning?"

"You can call it whatever you like. If he'd like to have a lawyer present, he can. However, we aren't making any arrests." Glass added, "At least, right now."

Trevor spoke in a strained voice. "Kit, it's perfectly fine. I have nothing to hide. I'll make a few phone calls and see if counsel can meet me at the police station."

"Do you want me to come with you?" I didn't want to abandon Trevor in his time of need.

Glass interrupted. "He can have a lawyer, but that's it, Ms. Marshall. As I said, we're done with you at this time. You can leave."

She might have said that I *could* leave, but it was more of a direct order than a suggestion.

"Let me confer with my friend and then I'll go," I said. Glass nodded and walked away with the officer who had accompanied her.

"Do you have someone you can call who can meet you there?" I asked.

Trevor nodded. "I might not win Mr. Congeniality, but I have held a number of jobs in Washington. I even wrote a book about it. My connections are strong." The corners of his mouth shifted upwards in a half-hearted smile.

"Should I call Meg?" I asked.

"No, I'll do it right after I call the lawyer. It's best she hears this information from me."

Trevor had always been a bit of a mystery, even though I've known him for years. Over time, he'd grown on me, and I'd learned to accept his quirky personality, abrasiveness, and lack of social graces. Now, of course, he was in a serious relationship with my best friend. Given what he was facing, I couldn't restrain myself. I reached out and gave him a hug.

Under normal circumstances, Trevor would have stiffly resisted and issued a snarky comment about unnecessary displays of affection. This time, he didn't. Instead, he gently squeezed me back.

After we moved apart, I placed my hand on his arm. "Don't worry about this, Trevor. They're not arresting you because there's no real evidence you did anything wrong. I'm going to try to put it all together and figure out who is responsible for these heinous capital crimes."

"I have no doubt you'll get to the bottom of this mystery," said Trevor. "I'll let you know when I get home tonight."

With that, I walked down the stairs and was back on the first floor of the house. There were a slew of cops milling about, particularly inside the room where Stephen Decatur's sword had been displayed.

I didn't see anyone from *Spring Into History*. I imagine the police had gotten statements and told everyone to go home.

I pulled out my phone and texted Doug that I could join him. He explained that he had a table at Off the Record, the bar at the Hay Adams Hotel located in its basement. I crossed H Street and entered the stately Hay Adams at the front of the hotel, situated on 16th Street. A stiff drink would be welcome and might even help me make sense of everything that had happened yesterday and today.

I walked into the hotel lobby and was immediately transported to a century ago. The plaster ceilings were intricately decorated, elaborate arches served as entryways, and dark oak finishing complemented the elaborate architectural design. Large vases filled with fresh flowers rested on every tabletop. The Hay Adams was certainly a five-star experience. Within five seconds, the concierge had undoubtedly identified me as someone who was not staying at the hotel that evening.

"Ma'am, can I help you find something?" he asked.

"Yes. I'm looking for the hotel bar. Is it downstairs?"

"Yes, ma'am. Follow me." He led me down a hallway to door with a small sign indicating that Off the Record was indeed downstairs.

"Sort of hidden, isn't it?" I said, almost to myself.

The concierge must have heard me. "We like to keep it that way, ma'am."

At the bottom of the stairway was the entrance to a dimly lit lounge almost entirely decked out in deep red furnishings and wallpaper. It was the classic, old-school throwback hotel bar. Sure enough, I spotted Doug sitting in a high-backed crimson armchair. To my surprise, my brother Sebastian sat opposite him.

I trotted up to the table and gave both of them hugs. "You didn't tell me you brought Sebastian along."

Doug grinned. "It was a surprise."

"Well, speaking of surprises. I have a doozy for you."

Both Sebastian and Doug leaned forward in anticipation.

"But first, I need a drink. Once you hear what I have to say, you'll understand."

Doug signaled for the waiter. I asked him if there were any drink specials, and he immediately produced a menu. Without hesitation, I picked "The Running Mate," which was a combination of rum, homemade apricot syrup, yellow chartreuse liqueur, and a lime.

"Anything to eat?" he asked. Doug and Sebastian were snacking on an array of assorted cheeses. Suddenly, I was famished. The cookie I ate while chatting with Mila seemed like a year ago. A cheese plate wasn't going to cut it.

"Do you have a recommendation?" I asked the waiter.

"Our sliders are excellent," he said. "I can offer you an assortment."

"Sounds delicious," I said. "But make sure to bring my drink first." I winked at the waiter, and he made a "perfect" sign with his fingers in response.

"Kit, enough of the delay. What happened today?" asked Sebastian.

I explained my conversation with Mila, which began at the White House and continued at Teaism. Then, I gave them a blow-by-blow of my conversations with Trevor, James Bennett, and Edgar Beaufort. For good measure, I also provided a summary of the conversation Trevor had with Chase Wintergreen.

Doug sat back in his red armchair. "You've had an extraordinarily busy day. No wonder you wanted a drink."

I chuckled and raised my index finger. "I'm not done yet. In fact, what I've told you is simply the warmup."

The waiter returned with my drink, which looked delightful in a fancy martini glass. Doug ordered another glass of Cabernet while Sebastian asked for a local IPA.

"I figured I'd need another beer," said my brother. "Obviously, you have something salacious to tell us."

"I suppose, but I would describe it as upsetting more than anything," I said.

I picked up my drink to take a sip and noticed that the coaster was actually a political cartoon depicting the current Speaker of the House.

"This is pretty cool," I said, pointing to the coaster.

"Off the Record has been printing original political cartoon coasters for a while," said Doug. "You can try to collect them all. I guess it encourages a loyal patron base."

I grabbed the coaster and put it in my purse. Then, I launched into the story of discovering James Bennett's body.

Doug's eyes grew wide as I explained the part about the sword on the top of the piano. "Wait a second, Kit. When do you think the murderer killed Bennett?"

"I didn't get a time of death, but it must have been soon before I climbed the stairs to the second floor," I said. "I suppose it could have been anytime between my last conversation with James Bennett and when I returned to the inside of Decatur House."

"And that was how long?" asked Sebastian.

The police had asked me the same question. "Maybe twenty or twenty-five minutes," I said. "Not long at all."

The waiter returned with Doug and Sebastian's drinks and my sliders. I bit into the first one, a crab cake. Delightful.

Doug took a sip of his wine and then reclined in his chair. "That means the killer likely tailed Bennett. The murderer knew what he or she wanted to do."

"I think so," I said. "Besides, remember that Bennett asked to speak with me. I believe he knew something about Bev Taylor's murder and wanted to tell me."

"But he was never able to let you know," said Sebastian, shaking his head.

"The murderer silenced him," said Doug. "Did anyone overhear your conversation with Bennett?"

I tried to think back to the scene when Bennett approached me. "James pulled me outside the tent to speak with me. I know Edgar was inside the tent at the time. He might have seen what happened and eavesdropped. I'm not sure where Mila or Chase was at the time. According to Trevor, after speaking with Chase, he went for a walk to nearby St. John's Church."

"He went to St. John's?" asked Doug, his eyes narrowed.

"That's what he told me," I said.

"I didn't realize your friend Trevor was religious," said Sebastian.

"Well, it's a historical church. People go to St. John's for a lot of reasons." I tried to keep my voice even and not defensive.

"For his sake, I hope someone saw him there," said Doug.

I shook my head back and forth as I chewed on my second slider, a traditional cheeseburger. It really hit the spot.

"The police are going to consider him a prime suspect," said Sebastian. "Knowing Trevor, I bet there was some reason to conclude that he didn't get along with his boss."

"Unfortunately, you're right on both counts," I said. "The police decided to bring him in for additional questioning. He's there now. And he wasn't on the best of terms with James Bennett."

Doug had a grave expression on his face. "Do you think they'll arrest him, Kit?"

"It's hard to say, but I don't think so," I said. "As far as I know, they don't have any hard evidence to tie him to either crime. He was at the scene near the time when Bev died, and he might not have an easily corroborated alibi for Bennett's murder. Those coincidences will cause serious suspicion, but it's not enough to hang a murder rap on him. Especially since we're dealing with a double homicide now."

Our conversation fell silent. As I took another sip of my drink, I looked around the establishment. This was an unusual place. It had the appearance of a cocktail bar from an earlier era with its sheltered tables, winged armchairs, and noir ambiance. To add to the overall experience, the walls were decorated with originally-drawn political cartoons, both contemporary and historical.

My quiet gaze around the room was interrupted by Sebastian. "Earth to Kit," he said, waving his hand in front of me. "Are you there?"

"Sorry. I must have drifted off there for a bit. I really like the lounge's decor."

"What I asked you was whether you have a plan for getting Trevor out of the mess he's in," said Sebastian. "It seems as though he needs you. Meg, too."

The mention of Meg's name made me wonder whether Trevor called her on his way to the police station. My phone was in my purse, and I hadn't checked it since I sat down. I grabbed it and checked for messages. Sure enough, Meg had texted ten minutes ago.

Call me.

"You're right," I said. "About Meg, at least. She wants me to call her. Please excuse me." I got up from the table after taking another sip of my drink. Somehow, I figured I would need it.

I stepped into the hallway outside the lounge and found a quiet corner where no one could hear our conversation. I punched Meg's number on my phone. She picked up during the first ring.

"Kit, where are you?" Meg's voice was breathless. I hoped she hadn't decided to try to join Trevor at the police station. There was nothing she could do for him there.

"I'm with Doug and Sebastian near the White House," I said.

"What are you doing there?"

"We're at a lounge in the basement of the Hay Adams Hotel," I said. "Doug was already here when . . ." I paused for a moment. "When Trevor and I discovered Bennett's body."

"Why didn't you go with Trevor to the police station?" I could sense the anger in my best friend's voice. Understandably, she wasn't thinking rationally right now.

"I couldn't, Meg. The police told me no one was allowed to accompany him but a lawyer."

There was silence on the line.

"Meg, are you still there?" I asked.

"I'm here," she said. "Are the police going to arrest Trevor?"

"I don't think so. There's no concrete evidence, just coincidences." I took a deep breath. "I know this is difficult for you, but the police will find the real killer. Now that two people have died, there will be more pressure than ever to find who is responsible."

"The police aren't spending time looking for the real killer, Kit. Instead, they're interrogating Trevor. He's going to become an easy scapegoat."

"You're not thinking clearly," I said. As soon as the words came out of my mouth, I regretted them.

"I'm not thinking clearly?" repeated Meg. "What about Kit Marshall, the great Capitol Hill sleuth? Do you have any idea who did this?"

"Meg, I'm working on it. In fact, when you texted, I was going over the details with Sebastian and Doug."

Meg interrupted me. "What good will that do? You need to be out there, finding clues or chasing down leads."

"You know well enough that it helps to talk about the details of an investigation to figure out the next steps. That's what I'm doing. I'm not abandoning you or Trevor." I sucked in a deep breath. "Have a little confidence in me, Meg. Have I ever let you down before?"

There was silence on the line for several seconds before Meg spoke. "Just figure out who the killer is," said Meg in a clipped voice. "I have to go. I don't want to miss Trevor's call when he's finished with the police."

Before I could remind her that all cell phones have a "call waiting" feature, she ended the conversation. A dial tone rang in my ear. I punched the button on the bottom of the screen to get rid of it.

Meg was my best friend, yet she could be infuriating at times. She was upset about what was happening to Trevor, but did I bear sole responsibility for the accusations leveled against him? I was trying my best. Perhaps this time, it wasn't enough. Along with my feelings of frustration, I also had a nagging feeling that I was missing a big piece of the puzzle.

I walked back inside the bar. Sebastian and Doug must have admired my sliders because they ordered more for themselves. I sat down and helped myself to another sandwich, which turned out to be a spicy mushroom burger.

"I just asked Sebastian if he can bring Murphy over to the house when Lisa visits," he said.

My mind went blank. "Murphy?"

Doug reached over a touched my hand lightly. "Remember, we think Clarence's depression might be linked to missing Murphy."

"Now I remember," I said, chuckling. "Obviously, I have too much on my plate if I've forgotten Clarence's plight."

"Completely understandable, given everything you have going on these days, Kit," said Sebastian, chomping on a burger. "Back to the murders. What did Meg have to say?"

"She's upset, of course. And in typical Meg fashion, she's highly emotional," I said. "She's worried about Trevor."

"Speaking of Trevor, what are you going to do to help him?" asked Doug.

I took the last sip of my drink and signaled to the waiter for another. I'd regret it tomorrow, but after Meg hanging up on me, I needed it.

"I'll speak with him tomorrow morning, and depending on what I find out, I might need to consult with Sergeant O'Halloran," I said. "Or even Maeve Dixon."

"Your boss can't interfere in a police investigation," said Sebastian. "As an elected member of Congress, it's not ethical." Sebastian's personal history as an ardent advocate of political reform still strongly influenced his thinking.

"No, she can't," I agreed. "On the other hand, I need to let her know what's happening with the investigation. If the police try to pin this on Trevor without much evidence, she might want to register her opinion privately with the chief."

My drink arrived, and we sipped and chewed in silence for a minute or two before Doug spoke. "I hope it doesn't come to that, Kit. You're the expert on Capitol Hill politics, but involving Dixon sounds thorny."

"Especially given her Senate race. You're right. I'll just have to see what happens. Who knows? Maybe I'll figure out who the real murderer is."

"If you come across an important clue, then you'd better let the police know immediately," said Sebastian. "If the killer was willing to stab James Bennett in a historic Lafayette Square house with a reception going on in the nearby courtyard only steps away from the White House, he or she will stop at nothing."

In less than twenty-four hours, my brother's conclusion would be proven dead right.

Chapter Seventeen

For another hour or so, we chatted amiably about topics other than the double homicide. Doug talked about the latest academic gossip at Georgetown, where there was never a day without intrigue. Sebastian gave us the blow-by-blow plans for his anticipated proposal to Lisa, who was scheduled to arrive on Friday for the long weekend. I hugged Sebastian goodbye when we parted ways and wished him well.

"The next time I see you, you'll be an engaged man," I said, almost wistfully. My little brother was growing up.

"Hopefully," said Sebastian, with a broad smile.

Doug shook Sebastian's hand and wished him good luck. "You'll do fine, man."

Doug had driven from Georgetown to the bar. The car was parked a few blocks away, and in less than five minutes, we were speeding back to Arlington.

"Quite an eventful day, Kit," said Doug.

"That's an understatement," I said, rubbing my forehead.

"Did Meg say something that upset you?" asked Doug. "I didn't want to press in front of Sebastian."

"Actually, she hung up on me," I confessed. "She doesn't think I'm doing enough to clear Trevor."

While keeping his gaze on the road, Doug reached over and squeezed my hand. "Kit, you're not a miracle worker. You've been amazing these past couple of years, solving murders and helping the police. That being said, it's not your job to put criminals in prison. Don't let Meg put a guilt trip on you."

"I've been able to help everyone else. When you were accused of murder, I found the killer. When Sebastian was a suspect, I figured out who did it. Even when Maeve Dixon was under suspicion, I cleared her name," I said. "You can understand how frustrated I am about what's going on with these murders."

Doug pulled into the underground parking garage at our condo building. "You're being too hard on yourself. After you get some rest tonight, perhaps tomorrow will bring clarity."

Quite frankly, I had no idea where to turn next. James Bennett clearly knew something important about the guilty party, yet I missed my opportunity to talk to him before he was killed. He was my one good lead, and now it was literally a dead end.

We took the elevator up to our floor and unlocked the door to our apartment. As a force of habit, we braced ourselves for Clarence's greeting. Instead of the enthusiastic welcome we were accustomed to receiving, Clarence merely thumped his tail when we entered. My dog's depression was another problem to solve, although a visit from Murphy would surely perk him up. I hoped the proposal would go as planned so we could celebrate the engagement.

I should really write down the suspects with Doug and methodically document each person's movement, motive, and opportunity. However, the thought of all that analytic thinking exhausted me. Instead, I watched a favorite television program and decided to call it a night. Perhaps a good night's sleep would help clear my mind.

Doug was still reading a book when I went to bed. Clarence ambled into the room with me and snuggled at the foot of the bed. He was content, yet I knew something was wrong with him. I'd turn my attention to Clarence once I had the double murderer in cuffs. That was a resolution I vowed to keep as I drifted off to sleep.

I woke up the next morning regretting the second martini. It took an extra ten minutes to get out of bed and drag myself to the kitchen for my espresso fix. I punched the correct buttons on our monster java machine and threw myself onto our overstuffed sofa. Thankfully, Doug always preloaded our espresso maker the night before, so all I had to do in the morning was choose the correct settings and power up the apparatus.

I'd planned to take Clarence for a jog, but he hadn't budged from the bed. He was snoring peacefully alongside Doug. It was yet another indicator of Clarence's doggie depression. Normally, he would have begged me to take him on a trot outside, especially with the springtime weather making a morning sojourn ideal.

My phone buzzed. It was Maeve Dixon. During the chaos last night, I had forgotten to update her about James Bennett. Even though it had been late, I should have definitely called her. By now, the news would have reached her, and I'm sure she didn't appreciate that she was caught off guard. I swiped open the phone and steeled myself for the tongue lashing I was about to receive.

"Good morning, Congresswoman," I said in my strongest voice.

"Is it true that James Bennett is dead and that you were at the scene of the crime?"

So much for hello.

"Yes, ma'am. That's correct. I apologize that I didn't call you last night. I had to give a statement to police. Unfortunately, Trevor was taken to the station for additional questioning, which complicated matters."

Dixon was silent. Obviously, the news about Trevor hadn't reached her.

"That sounds serious. Do you know what happened with him?" asked Dixon.

"Not yet. I plan to check with him this morning. I'm sure if he was . . ." I paused for a beat as I searched for the right word to finish the sentence. "Detained further, then I would have known about it."

"You're got your hands full, Kit," said Dixon. "Do you need me to pause campaigning and return to Washington?"

"Not yet," I said. "I'm sure you'll want to attend the memorial services that will take place at the Capitol, but nothing has been scheduled yet."

"I'm glad to hear you say that. I've got a lot to deal with here. Chester Nuggets is coming on strong."

"Is he still on the monster truck kick?" I asked. "Did Crypt Crasher cut another ad for him?"

"No, thankfully. He seems to have moved on from that one. But his radio program is popular, so he's able to use his show to discredit me."

Dixon had a point. Nuggets had a considerable platform, and he was going to use it.

"The more you can draw him into talking about the issues that North Carolinians care about, the better," I said. "Also, while he was busy talking for three hours a day, you were fighting the global war on terror. How's that for a comparison?"

I heard Dixon exhale. "Kit, that's a great idea. I'm going to speak with the campaign team about an ad to that effect."

"Happy to help." I silently congratulated myself that I had somehow managed to make Dixon forget that I had neglected to call her last night with the news of Bennett's death.

"Be sure to keep me up to date about what's going on with these murders," said Dixon. "I hope we don't have a serial killer on our hands."

The thought had crossed my mind, but why would a serial killer target congressional staff involved with planning history-related events? It made no sense.

"The key is figuring out the connection between the two deaths. I have a hunch that James Bennett may have unexpectedly discovered something out about the killer. Before he had a chance to speak with me, he was dead."

"Be careful, Kit," said Dixon. "If the killer was willing to silence Bennett, it's likely he or she won't stop if someone else comes close to solving the crimes."

"I won't be going too far out on a limb," I said. "If I discover anything meaningful, I'll speak to Detective O'Halloran or Maggie Glass from the D.C. police."

After saying our goodbyes, I ended the call. I meant what I said to my boss. I had a bad feeling that the violence hadn't ended.

I got ready for work and checked in on Doug and Clarence one last time before leaving. Doug was finally waking up, although Clarence was still buried underneath the covers.

"I'm headed to work," I said.

"Where are you off to today?" asked Doug, rubbing his eyes.

"We have an event at the Smithsonian African American Museum later this afternoon," I said.

"Let's keep in touch. Maybe I can meet you somewhere nearby when you're finished," he said.

"Sounds good." As I gave him a peck on the cheek, he placed his hand on my arm and pulled me closer.

"Keep your guard up, Kit. Two people are dead. You don't want to get caught in the crosshairs."

"I'll be extra cautious," I promised. "I'm checking in with Trevor and the police this morning to find out if there's been any breakthroughs overnight."

Doug nodded, and I gently moved the blanket to give Clarence a pat on the head.

On my short walk to the subway, I texted Trevor and asked him how his interview with the police had gone. By the time I had arrived on Capitol Hill, he'd responded and asked that we meet at the Capitol Visitor Center cafeteria for breakfast. There were better (and cheaper) places to eat, but with only tourists inside the cafeteria, it might be a good place to chat without the threat of being overheard by gossipy Hill insiders, journalists, and staff. I replied that I would meet him there in thirty minutes.

I made a brief stop at the office to speak with our staff. Congresswoman Dixon was lucky to have such talented self-starters working for her. Everyone was doing their jobs without much supervision these days. Between *Spring Into History* and two murders, I certainly wasn't spending much time in the office.

After speaking with my boss this morning, I wondered whether it made sense to remain at my post in Washington, D.C. while she battled Chester Nuggets in North Carolina. We had decided to allow the campaign professionals take over for the "Dixon for Senate" effort, but now I was having real doubts about the advice she was getting. My thoughts were interrupted by a knock on the door of my claustrophobic office. Jill the intern poked her head around the corner.

"Please come in," I said. "If you can find a space."

There was barely enough room for one chair opposite my desk. Jill squeezed through the door and maneuvered to sit down.

"Jill, I'm sorry I didn't follow up with you last night. You might have heard that I discovered James Bennett's body upstairs at Decatur House."

Jill nodded. "The police asked me if I'd seen anything unusual. I didn't have anything to report, so they let me go home."

"I'm glad to know you weren't detained for too long." I studied Jill's face, which was impassive. "Once again, I'm fully aware you didn't sign up for murders. If you'd like to move off *Spring Into History*, I can find other work for you within the Dixon congressional office. You shouldn't have to feel unsafe while you complete your internship."

Jill didn't hesitate. "I'd like to continue with the history events. It's the reason why I took this specific internship."

"Okay," I said slowly. "But if you see anything suspicious or out of the ordinary, you need to tell me immediately. Or a police officer."

"I will," she said. "Are you going to the African American History Museum this afternoon?"

"Certainly. I don't know who else will be there. Our ranks are dwindling."

"Did Trevor get arrested last night? I didn't see anything in the papers."

"No," I said. "But how did you know he was being questioned?"

"Everyone found out before the police told us to go home. People knew he was a suspect from the first murder, so it made sense."

"He wasn't arrested because he didn't kill those people," I said. "In fact, I'm going to meet him for breakfast now. Let me know if anything is out of place at the Smithsonian when you get there."

Jill nodded and scurried out of my office. I certainly hoped she took the threat seriously. I'd keep an eye out for her, but quite frankly, I was pretty busy keeping myself out of harm's way. When this was over, I'd make sure to introduce Jill to my valuable history contacts in town so she could parlay her internship into a full-time position at a good institution. I'd try to hire her at the Dixon office, but she had caught the history bug. Politics wasn't for everyone.

I got myself together and dashed out of the office so I wouldn't be too late for Trevor. He detested tardiness. I didn't know if his status as a murder suspect mellowed him. Quite frankly, I was doubtful.

As I hustled into the Capitol Visitor Center cafeteria, I spotted Trevor at a table in the corner, his head lowered. He was obviously trying to keep a low profile. Trevor always reminded me of Batman; he appeared and disappeared with drop-dead precision. Given such talent, he shouldn't have too much trouble staying out of sight.

Trevor had a steaming cup of coffee in front of him. I'd had my espresso this morning at home, but there had been no time for breakfast. My stomach grumbled.

"Good morning," I said. "Before we chat, do you mind if I grab food? I'm starving."

Trevor waved his hand indiscriminately. "I would never stand between Kit Marshall and breakfast. Be my guest."

Well, the interrogation couldn't have been that bad. Trevor seemed like his typical, sarcastic self. I really wanted pancakes, but I resisted and instead helped myself to a healthy scoop of scrambled eggs and an English muffin. Protein during a murder investigation was critical, and I needed all the help I could get.

Trevor raised an eyebrow when I returned to the table. "You resisted the chocolate chip pancakes? I thought for sure you'd have them for breakfast, slathered in maple syrup."

"A sugar high isn't going to help me today. Eggs are brain food." I tapped my head.

Trevor sighed. "I can't think of a more critical time when we needed everyone's mental focus."

"What happened last night after you went to the police station?" I asked.

"It wasn't that bad. A lawyer met me there, and she advised me when not to answer leading questions. There's no physical evidence that ties me to the murders, so they didn't keep me very long."

I looked closely at Trevor's face. He'd always looked younger than his thirty-some years. For the first time, I spotted fine lines framing his forehead and mouth. Being a double-murder suspect was wearing on Trevor.

"Are you still worried?" I asked.

Trevor pushed up his glasses, which had crept lower on his nose. "Of course, I'm worried, Kit. As far as I know, I'm the only person the police have brought in for official questioning. You and I both know that the Capitol Hill community isn't going to stand for *two* unsolved murders. Someone needs to be charged. Pronto."

Trevor spoke the truth. We'd both been around Congress long enough to understand that justice needed to be served— swiftly and definitively. At this moment in time, Trevor was the scapegoat, certainly not an enviable status.

"I'm going to call Sergeant O'Halloran as soon as I get back to my office. He'll tell me if they have any other leads."

"Do you have any idea who did this?" asked Trevor. "O'Halloran is a good cop, but I'm not sure many of those previous murders on Capitol Hill would have been solved if you weren't leading the way."

"*Leading* the way might be a bit of an exaggeration. I did manage to pick up several clues *along* the way, which made a difference."

"You're selling yourself short," said Trevor. "But that's not the matter at hand. We both know that I didn't do it. If not me, then who is responsible?"

"Trevor, I wish I knew. The remaining suspects are Chase Wintergreen, Mila Cunningham, and Edgar Beaufort. They all had their own reasons for disliking Bev Taylor, our first victim. James Bennett might have gotten killed because he knew too much."

"And they all had the opportunity to kill James last night?" asked Trevor.

"I didn't see Chase or Mila at the reception, so I assume they could have slipped back inside. I talked to Edgar for a while, but there was enough time between our conversation and when I returned to the second floor of Decatur House."

Trevor slumped in his seat as I finished off my eggs. "That doesn't narrow it down."

"No, but I feel like we're missing a big piece of the puzzle. Why was Bev's body displayed on the Lincoln catafalque? In the same vein, why did the killer leave the Decatur sword on the top of the piano, almost like it was on display?"

"Sounds like we need a forensic profiler," said Trevor glumly.

"Well, I don't have a degree in criminal psychology. I think the motive is something other than eliminating a rival. There's a real bravado associated with these crimes."

Trevor rubbed his chin. "Almost as if there was a desire for the murderer to show off."

"I think you're right. That's why he or she showcases what they've done. In the first murder, it was the body on the catafalque. The second time, maybe there wasn't enough time."

"Instead, the killer put the murder weapon on the top of the piano," said Trevor.

We sat in silence for a minute, thinking about what we discussed. Perhaps we were dealing with a serial killer. Could it be someone completely off our radar, maybe a person who worked in Congress but who wasn't on the *Spring Into History* planning team? If that was the case, then our only hope was that either Detective Glass or Sergeant O'Halloran would uncover a solid piece of physical evidence that could connect the murderer to the crimes.

"If your boss got killed because he discovered something about Bev's murder, it means we really need to focus on the first crime," I said.

Trevor leaned forward. "That makes sense. How can we do that?"

"Means, motive, and opportunity." I ticked the three items off my fingers. "The murder weapon was a generic letter opener from the U.S. Capitol gift shop. Anyone could have bought it. Since the tent was open, anyone could have followed Bev inside, watching closely for a moment when the police officer's attention was elsewhere. That takes care of means and opportunity."

"One second, Kit. Who knew that Bev was going to make an evening stop at the tent?" asked Trevor.

"That's a good question. I thought about this yesterday. She didn't tell me about it, and I didn't hear anyone mention it. Either the killer overheard her talking about it or the killer followed her there."

"It makes sense," said Trevor. "If the murderer really wanted Bev dead, then he or she might have been stalking her, waiting for an opportunity. Are there any more details we should consider?"

"Bev was stabbed from behind," I said. "That means she was trying to get away from her assailant or the killer snuck up on her."

"Surprise might be more likely. Think about it. If Bev was scurrying around the tent, trying to escape, wouldn't that have drawn attention? The police officer wasn't right outside, but if Bev had screamed, he might have heard her."

I considered Trevor's comment. He was right. We couldn't be sure, but the scenario he outlined made more sense.

"The other detail is the security cameras," I said. "The killer disabled them, likely before the murder."

"That means the murderer got there *before* Bev," said Trevor. "There's no way he or she could have turned off the cameras without attracting attention from Bev."

"You're right. That means the killer had to know that Bev was going to end up at the tent that night."

"If that's the case, then what we really need to figure out is who Bev told about her unplanned stop. If we can do that . . ."

I finished Trevor's sentence for him. "Then we'll know who truly had the opportunity to kill Bev Taylor."

Chapter Eighteen

———

M Y CONVERSATION WITH TREVOR helped focus my mind on such a baffling investigation. By thinking through the events logically, we'd made several plausible conclusions that at least pinpointed the crucial pieces of the puzzle.

After briefly discussing the motives to kill Bev (which were numerous, since she wasn't a particularly likable person), I ate the last bite of my breakfast and we parted ways. I promised to let Trevor know if I made any progress. We hadn't talked about Meg, although I could only hope that she was relieved that Trevor hadn't been detained overnight at the police station. I planned to speak with her in person at the Smithsonian African American History Museum later today.

I was marching through the byzantine underground tunnels that connected the Capitol Visitor Center with the congressional office buildings when I almost ran into Sergeant O'Halloran.

"You just saved me a phone call," I said.

"Good morning to you, too," he said grumpily.

"Do you have a minute to chat?" I asked.

"I was headed to grab a late breakfast," he said.

Now I understood why he was testy. We were steps away from the underground Dunkin' Donuts kiosk inside the Longworth House Office Building, and I was impeding his progress.

"Why don't you have a seat and I'll get you a doughnut?" I offered.

O'Halloran hesitated. "Are you sure that's allowed?"

A host of ethics rules and laws governed gifts ranging from meals to lavish presents. I was sensitive to the procedures because I never wanted to get Congresswoman Dixon in trouble, especially since she was the chair of the committee that had oversight over such matters.

"A doughnut is well under the $50 limit," I said. Then I lowered my voice and leaned closer. "I won't tell if you won't."

O'Halloran waved his hand at me. "Chocolate-glazed and sour cream, please."

I should have known that it would be *two* doughnuts, not one. I returned to the table with O'Halloran's breakfast and a fresh cup of steaming coffee for myself. It was my third cup today, yet something told me I was going to need the extra caffeine boost.

As my portly police colleague bit into the chocolate glazed, I began my interrogation. "Do you have anything on Trevor besides the fact that he was present at both crime scenes?"

O'Halloran grabbed and napkin and wiped chocolate from the corner of his mouth. "We've got motive, of course."

Rather than quibble about motive, I decided to press forward. "But no *physical* evidence tying him to Bev's murder or Bennett's?"

"Not yet. The letter opener didn't have any prints on it. We're waiting on forensics for the fancy sword owned by that naval officer."

"Stephen Decatur," I said.

"Yeah, well, it's a delicate matter because that sword is what they call an *artifact* and it's part of a historical collection. So, we gotta take extra care with it. That's slowing us down with our crime scene testing."

Hats off to the cause of historic preservation. That would buy us more time to figure out the real killer.

"Do you have another suspect other than Trevor?" I pressed. "Who else looks good for this?"

"We're considering all your buddies from the history conference. There's always the possibility the two murders aren't connected, although that would be an awfully big coincidence."

"I have a specific question for you," I said, noticing he'd moved onto the sour cream.

"Go ahead," he said. "I'm still eating."

Not for long, though. I'd better hurry up.

"Do you know if Bev Taylor told anyone she was going to stop by the tent the night she was murdered?" I asked.

O'Halloran finished chewing and rested the remaining half of his doughnut on a napkin. "You asked me that yesterday. Remember?"

"I do. But I think it's an important detail. Remember, we know the murderer disabled the security cameras inside the tent," I explained. "That means the guilty party knew that Bev was going to be there. If the murderer had simply followed her, when would the killer have the opportunity to turn off the cameras?"

O'Halloran wiped a piece of glaze off his upper lip. "You've got a point," he said slowly.

Having known the sergeant for a while, I knew the remark was the highest compliment I'd ever get from him.

"I know," I said. "So, do we know if Bev told anyone at the reception beforehand that she was going to the tent? I wasn't aware of it, and neither was Trevor."

"Not to my knowledge," said O'Halloran. "I don't remember anyone mentioning that in the interviews we conducted. We got witness statements from as many attendees as possible. We wanted to find out if Bev had gotten into any arguments prior to her death. In addition, of course, to the public disagreement she had with your friend."

I'm sure Trevor regretted that terse exchange of words more than he could articulate in words. What was done couldn't be undone.

"If you can check your notes, I'd appreciate it," I said. "If I'm right, then solving this murder hinges on finding out who knew that Bev was making a stop at the outdoor tent before heading home."

O'Halloran polished off his doughnut. "Of course, Bev might have told someone at the reception and the murderer overhead the conversation."

"Possibly. But the first course of action should be finding out who she told in the first place. Then maybe we can figure out who might have eavesdropped on the conversation."

The sergeant nodded. "There weren't that many people at the soirée. If required, we might be able to recreate the various groups of people and where they were situated in relation to each other."

"That sounds like a smart avenue for investigating," I said. "In the meantime, if I uncover anything else, I will let you know."

"I'll be in contact after I have an officer scan through the witness interviews. Who knows? Maybe we'll get lucky, and an important detail will turn up."

That's exactly what we needed—a little luck. For the past two days, it had certainly been in short supply.

I got up from the table and gave O'Halloran a mini-salute. "Until we meet again."

He pointed a finger at me. "I might as well say it again. Detective Glass and I want you to be careful. We don't fully understand the motivation of this criminal. The killer seems eager to show what he or she has done. Even though the murderer couldn't have had a lot of time, the crime scenes were staged. That suggests someone who isn't right in the head." O'Halloran moved his finger to tap his right temple.

"In my opinion, all murderers are deranged. But your point is valid. Also, he or she didn't hesitate in killing again when James Bennett likely uncovered a piece of evidence or overheard something."

"We may have a serial killer on our hands, Ms. Marshall. And those perps are the trickiest of the bunch. They don't kill for a particular motive. Instead, they do it because they enjoy killing people or they're compelled to do it."

A shiver ran down my spine. If that was the case, my usual deductive bumbling that previously led me to solve homicides might not prove terribly useful.

"Understood," I said. "I'll be extra careful. Please let me know if you find out anything about Bev Taylor's conversations at the reception before she left."

As I walked back to the office, I contemplated my chat with Sergeant O'Halloran. If no one had overheard Bev talking about a last-minute evening visit to the tent, how could the murderer know she'd be there? Something wasn't quite right. Perhaps the police would discover something if they identified everyone Bev spoke with and who might have been in close proximity to her. Was that even possible almost two days after the reception? Memories were short-lived.

I was about to jump on a crowded elevator inside the Cannon Office Building when I spotted Chase Wintergreen across the corridor. I might not have an opportunity to speak with him again, so I turned on my heel and made a beeline for him.

"Chase!" I called out. He was disappearing into the crowded hallway, and I was losing sight of him. But then he spun around and spotted me. He motioned for me to join him.

"I understand there was a lot of excitement last night at Decatur House after I left," he said.

"You weren't around when we found James Bennett's body?" I asked.

He shook his head back and forth vigorously. "I'd already left for home. The police tracked me down last night and I talked to them on the phone. I didn't have much to add. I have no idea why someone would have wanted to kill James Bennett. Such a tragedy."

Although Chase was saying the right words, I didn't believe a word that was coming out of his mouth. I remembered what Trevor had told me last night. Chase wanted Bev's job. In his position, James Bennett would have weighed in about her successor, and it was perfectly plausible to conclude that he might not have thought Chase was the right person for it. If that was the case, Chase had a solid motive for wanting Bennett dead. If they were alone last night, Chase might have seized upon the opportunity to take care of Bennett permanently.

"Did you leave right after Trevor spoke to you last night?" I asked.

Chase's face was impassive. "I think so. There wasn't much going on after the tour, you know. I'd chatted with everyone who was important."

Spoken like a consummate Capitol Hill operative. What was the point of sticking around if there was no one impressive to speak with?

"Both the head of the Capitol Visitor Center and the Chief Administrative Officer are dead," I said. It was more of an observation than anything else. I wanted to gauge Chase's reaction.

"The ranks are thinning by the day," said Chase nonchalantly. "It will be *fascinating* to see how this shakes out."

"Especially when the police catch the killer responsible for the murders," I said.

Chase took a step backwards. "Well, that has nothing to do with me." He pointed to himself with his index finger. "But there will be several career opportunities presenting themselves in due course."

I didn't respond. It was just as Trevor had described. Chase's ambition was almost blinding. The question was whether he had murdered two people to satisfy it.

Chase filled in the conversation gap. "Speaking of opportunities, how is your boss's Senate race going?"

I wasn't going to divulge any details about Chester Nuggets, the ongoing saga with Crypt Crasher, or anything else. He could find out those details if he looked hard enough online.

"Chairwoman Dixon is doing quite well." I mentally crossed my fingers to negate the white lie. "Of course, she'll come back in town when the memorial services are scheduled for Bev Taylor and James Bennett."

Chase waved his hand. "No need for her to do that," he said. "Representative Duncan can handle the formalities for those events. She should stay on the campaign trail, where it matters."

My temper welled up like Mount Vesuvius ready to blow. Before speaking, I took a deep breath so I could contain it. "Chairwoman Dixon wants to pay her respects to the deceased and their families. She will *not* be delegating that duty."

As much as I attempted to keep my voice even, Chase must have sensed my annoyance. He took two steps backwards and raised his hands defensively.

"Okay, no problem. I just wanted to offer Amos Duncan if Dixon needed to take a pass."

Perhaps I had been too quick to anger. After all, it was in Chase's best interests for my boss to succeed. If that happened, he'd ride the ladder up the congressional leadership chain with Duncan. Unless, of course, he had already decided he wanted a different job in Congress and had killed two people to get it. I still thought that was a strong possibility.

"You can help me with something," I said, forcing a smile.

"Sure. I'll do whatever is necessary." Chase returned my smile with a row of pearly white teeth.

"I spoke with the police sergeant in charge of Bev's murder investigation. We're trying to figure out if Bev told anyone she was making a stop at the tent before going home."

"When?" asked Chase. "At the reception at the Belmont-Paul House?"

I nodded. "Yes. Bev wasn't planning on making that stop, as far as I know. She had to change her mind about it. I wondered whether she shared that with anyone."

Chase paused for a few seconds before answering. "I'm thinking," he said. "I did chat with her at the event. But I don't remember her mentioning that she planned to make that stop."

"And no one else told you that Bev was headed there?" I asked. After all, it could be the case that someone like Chase had heard about Bev's plans secondhand.

"I don't remember that at all," he said. "What was she doing there, anyways? Do you know?"

It was best to be honest. "I think she wanted to check on everything one last time. I believe the circumstances surrounding her unplanned visit might be the key to figuring out who murdered her."

Chase rubbed his chin thoughtfully. "Interesting point. I hadn't thought of that detail." Then he smiled and pointed at me. "Is Kit Marshall on the case? I know you've helped the police solve other crimes."

I didn't want to give too much away. Also, the personal safety warnings from Maeve Dixon, Doug, and Sergeant O'Halloran ran through my head.

"Not really," I said. "A double murder has the attention of the police. They'll find out who is responsible for both crimes soon enough."

Ever so slightly, Chase winced. The untrained eye might not have noticed it, but I did.

"Of course, they will," he said. "Top-notch investigators are working on it, no doubt. Besides, you need to focus on getting Maeve Dixon to the Senate. Right-o?" Chase motioned to give me a fist bump.

I didn't relish bumping fists or anything else with Chase, who I didn't trust as far as I could throw him, but nonetheless, I touched my closed hand lightly with his.

"That's the spirit!" he exclaimed. "I need to run now. Duty calls." As he walked away, he called over his shoulder. "Let me know if I can do anything else to help, Kit."

Perhaps a murder confession? If only I would be so lucky.

Chapter Nineteen

I MADE IT BACK TO THE OFFICE WITHOUT INCIDENT. After checking emails and doing a round robin with the Dixon team, I was ready to leave for the afternoon event at the Smithsonian's National Museum of African American History and Culture, located on the National Mall.

It was about a two mile walk to the museum, which might take about forty-five minutes. Or I could take the Metro a few stops west. I looked at the time and determined that if I left immediately, I could enjoy the spring weather while strolling along the Mall and get my exercise for the day.

After walking down Capitol Hill on Independence Avenue (yes, it's an actual hill), I crossed over to the path on the National Mall alongside Jefferson Drive. Soon, I was cruising past the National Museum of the American Indian, the Air and Space Museum, the Hirshhorn Museum, and the National Museum of African Art.

I paused for a moment in front of the Smithsonian's headquarters, nicknamed the Castle. It truly lived up to its name. The building was constructed of red sandstone, and it looked like it might house King Arthur and the Knights of the Roundtable instead of the Secretary of the Smithsonian. Sure enough, the information panel outside explained that the Castle was completed in 1855 in the Norman style of the twelfth century. How about that? It was designed by James Renwick, who also designed St. Patrick's

Cathedral in New York City. For a long time, the Castle housed the entirety of Smithsonian operations. These days, it serves as an administrative office and a visitor center for tourists who want information about one of the nineteen Smithsonian museums, galleries, gardens, or zoo. It was such a magnificent building smack dab in the middle of the National Mall. I wonder how many times I walked or drove by it and never gave it another thought.

Walking to the African American History Museum was a terrific decision. Capitol Hill was my favorite part of Washington, D.C., but it's a notorious bubble. The same streets, the same people, the same buildings, the same air. *Spring Into History* was supposed to serve as a bridge for Congress to the rest of the city. Instead, we had two murders on our hands, one committed right outside the Capitol Building and the other within sight of the White House. I really hoped a break in the case would present itself, so we could salvage our initiative and establish the meaningful connections we'd aspire to create with it.

I turned right on Fourteenth Street and headed north on the Mall. The National Museum of African American History and Culture resided on a patch of land between the Washington Monument and the Smithsonian National Museum of American History. It was a perfect location. After all, George Washington was the father of the United States and solidified republican democracy by serving as both a military general and president. He was also a slave owner for most of his life. Situated between the complicated and sometimes contradictory trajectory of American history and the recognizable monument to our nation's founder, the African American History Museum completed the story. The proximity of these important sites gave visitors the opportunity to understand the complex history of our country, all easily within walking distance and, of course, free of charge to everyone.

The African American History Museum was distinctive in appearance. There had been an international competition to select the architectural design. I'd read about some key features of the building. The three tiers were inspired by the majesty of West African royal crowns. The bronze hue of the structure itself was an ornamental metal lattice that encapsulated the entire building. That feature derived from an ironwork pattern created by freed African Americans. In addition to its powerful symbolism, the exterior screen also served a practical purpose. While letting in light, it also protected the building from heat, making the entire museum environmentally sustainable.

I walked towards the main entrance, a large, covered area which resembled an extensive porch. The entrance was another design feature influenced by the culture and history of the African diaspora and African American community life. A reflecting pool framed the entrance, which undoubtedly helped to cool visitors in the summer as they approached the museum from the National Mall.

As soon as I entered the museum, I spotted Edgar, Mila, and intern Jill. The concourse was bustling with visitors. The museum was one of the most popular attractions in Washington, D.C., and the throng of people on the ground floor certainly demonstrated that rumor was correct. Edgar motioned for me to join them. I navigated between strollers, wheelchairs, and families to reach my colleagues at the entrance desk.

"Kit, you made it," said Mila, with a tone of surprise in her voice.

"Of course, I did," I said. "Why wouldn't I be here?"

"We heard that Trevor was taken in for questioning last night," said Edgar. "So, we didn't know if you would be with him. You know . . ." His voice trailed off.

"Mounting his defense? That's not necessary. Trevor didn't kill Bev Taylor or James Bennett."

Mila exhaled. "Well, that's a relief. We didn't know exactly what was going on last night, to tell you the truth."

"Maybe we will have time to chat this afternoon," I said. I looked at Jill, who was carrying a clipboard, undoubtedly with the schedule for the event.

When Jill didn't say anything, I prompted her. "Jill, what is on the program?"

"Oh, sorry. My mind was wandering." After consulting the paper on the clipboard, she answered. "A curator from the museum will take us downstairs to show us a selection of the exhibits. Then, we have a break in the cafeteria for lunch. Finally, the actual event is a public lecture in the theater."

"Is anyone else joining us for the tour?" I asked.

Jill bit her lip. "Bev and James were supposed to be here," she said. "And Trevor."

"Right," I said slowly. Our ranks were growing smaller by the day. Meg wasn't here, either. I hoped nothing had happened to Trevor since I saw him at breakfast.

A moment later, an African American woman, likely in her late twenties or early thirties, approached us with a friendly smile.

"Is this the Capitol Hill history group?" she asked.

Jill nodded. "Are you Felicia?"

"I most certainly am," she said. "I work as a curator here at the museum, and I'll be taking you on a brief tour. Then, as I understand it, we'll have time for refreshments in our cafeteria." Her eyes sparkled. "You don't want to miss our cafeteria. Trust me."

"I don't want to miss it," said Edgar, rubbing his stomach. "The food is amazing. I've been waiting all day for this!"

I couldn't decide if Edgar's enthusiasm for our snack break exonerated him as a suspect. On the one hand, would someone who just committed a double murder really be worried about what he was eating for lunch? On the other hand, it had already been established that we were dealing with a diabolical killer. Was Edgar's upbeat, breezy demeanor merely a ruse to throw us off the trail? Either interpretation was plausible. As the afternoon transpired, hopefully I'd figure out which conclusion was the right one.

"Follow me downstairs," said Felicia. "We only have enough time to view a portion of our exhibits."

We descended on an escalator to the underground level of the museum. "These are our history galleries," explained Felicia. "We have three levels that tell the story of African American history. We should have time to walk through two of the three levels. You can come back another time to explore everything else."

There was a long line waiting to enter the galleries. Luckily, we were able to bypass the line. A large, glass elevator took us down to the lowest gallery level. As we descended, the years on a vertical timeline ticked downwards on the elevator shaft until we reached 1400, the beginning of the story.

After we exited the elevator, Felicia explained, "We are starting our tour today with the origins of the slave trade. You can see that this part of the exhibit is dark and foreboding. It was designed this way to convey the appropriate context and emotion. Please feel free to examine the artifacts on display." Felicia motioned for us to explore on our own.

There is no other way to describe the exhibit than overwhelming. The various objects and interpretative displays told the story of the Middle Passage, when captured Africans were transported against their will across the Atlantic to the New World, including the land that would eventually become the United States. There was wreckage from a slave ship, a replica slave cabin, and a display featuring a statue of Thomas Jefferson with the names of the enslaved people who built Monticello written on stacks of books behind him.

Edgar approached me as I stared at the lines from the Declaration of Independence, which were etched on the wall.

"What do you think?" he asked. "Is it your first time here?"

"I'm embarrassed to say that it is," I said. "Doug has visited, but I was never available to join him."

"And your initial impressions?" asked Edgar.

"Exhilarating. I'll need to come back to spend more time," I said.

"I worked on portions of the exhibits as a lower-level historical consultant," said Edgar. "I'm always curious to learn about the reactions of first-time visitors."

"Speaking of reactions, what happened to you last night?" I asked. "We spoke at the reception, and then I didn't see you again." It wasn't the smoothest transition, but it would have to do.

"I apologize for the way we ended our conversation," said Edgar. "I know you're trying to figure out who killed Bev and now James, and it must be disturbing to know your friend Trevor is a prime suspect."

"Yes, it is," I said. "After our chat, I went inside Decatur House and that's when Trevor and I discovered James Bennett's body. I didn't see you inside the tent before I left."

Edgar smiled. "You think I had the opportunity to kill Bennett before you and Trevor found James." He put his hand gently on my arm. "Let me clarify my whereabouts for you. Mila and I were engaged in a conversation inside the carriage house area of the complex. That's the building adjacent to the courtyard, in the opposite direction of Decatur House. It's typically used for events and staging. However, since the caterers were set up inside Decatur House itself for the reception, the carriage house was empty."

"Why did you need to go there?" I asked, raising an eyebrow. "If you wanted to speak with Mila, why not simply talk to her inside the tent, like everyone else?" This was a nosy question, yet Edgar's story seemed a little too convenient, given this supposed conversation had allegedly taken place at the likely time of Bennett's murder.

"It was a private conversation," said Edgar curtly. The look on his face told me he wouldn't be offering additional details.

"Did anyone see you together?" I asked.

"I told you. It was a private conversation. By definition, no one else was there."

I'd have to speak to Mila independently to see if her story jived with Edgar's. And I needed to do it before he got to her, just in case they were in cahoots. Now that I thought about it, Mila and Edgar working together made sense. Bev didn't like either of them, and they were both ambitious historians, eager to improve their career trajectory. They might have decided to team up and get rid of a common problem. Somehow, James had figured it out, but before he had time to tell me about his suspicions, Mila or Edgar had silenced him. Or maybe they had done it together, with one of them distracting poor James while the other stabbed him with Stephen Decatur's sword. My mind began to race. Placing the sword on the piano would make sense to someone like Edgar, who had worked on historical exhibits. In a twisted way, he wanted to make sure the sword was properly displayed, even if it had served as a gruesome weapon for murder.

"Kit, can you hear me?" Edgar snapped his fingers in front of my eyes.

I'd been so deep in thought, I hadn't realized that Edgar had kept talking. "Sorry. I drifted off there for a moment."

Edgar pursed his lips together. "What I said is that you can talk to Mila, if you want. She'll tell you exactly what I did."

Drat. Obviously, they were one step ahead of me. They'd already come up with a story that provided corroborating alibis. Of course, they would have told the police the same excuse last night.

"I'll do that," I said. "I'd better find Felicia to find out if it's time to move to another part of the exhibit."

I spotted Felicia, intern Jill, and Mila. They were standing by the ramp that led to the next floor, and I hustled over to join them.

"Where's Edgar?" asked Mila.

"I saw him at the Jefferson display," I said. "He might need some more time to look around." I didn't want to tip Mila off that I'd been interrogating him.

"Edgar is quite familiar with the exhibit," said Felicia. "I'm sure he'll catch up with us. Let's go to the next floor, which focuses on segregation, Jim Crow, and civil rights."

A small cabin, built in 1853 in South Carolina, was at the end of the ramp. Constructed before the end of slavery, southern African Americans lived inside the tiny house for almost a hundred years after emancipation. The dwelling was meant to bridge the historical eras between enslavement and freedom, showing that the path to freedom was not a direct one. Many formerly enslaved people became sharecroppers and continued to live in the same dwellings they had occupied before the end of the Civil War. Behind the cabin was a segregated railroad car, which allowed visitors to walk through to better understand the inferior and separate accommodations for people of color.

I took a deep breath and proceeded along the path to the other exhibits on this floor. There was a replica 1950s Woolworth's lunch counter with large screens surrounding the stools. It was an interactive experience that enabled visitors to learn more about the civil rights movement and the social protest that took place before federal legislation was enacted.

Mila was sitting at the counter. I didn't want to disturb her, since she appeared engrossed in the touchscreen before her. However, a line of people was waiting to take their turn, and in a few minutes, Mila exited the counter and spotted me standing nearby.

"Were you able to try the interactive?" She motioned to the display.

"I spent time walking through the South Carolina cabin and the railway car," I said. "The next time I come to the museum, I will make sure to do it."

She nodded. "There's too much here to experience in one visit. Those of us who live in Washington have the luxury of coming back as many times as we want."

"That's a good point," I said. "Tourists who only have a limited time have to make the most of their one visit."

"And it's sandwiched between visits to the Capitol, the White House, the various monuments, and the other Smithsonian museums. It's a whirlwind for most people."

"Yes, but then perhaps they are excited enough to come back. Who knows? Maybe they will be motivated to live here one day. That's what happened to me."

Mila smiled. "That's an inspiring story, Kit. Did your parents bring you here on vacation?"

"No, absolutely not. However, I did travel here as part of a school group. I was so impressed by it, I vowed that I would live here one day. And I did what I said."

"Not only are you a chief of staff to a member of Congress, but you also help solve murders that happen in the nation's capital." Mila's eyes sparkled.

"My thirteen-year-old self did not imagine that amateur sleuthing would be part of the package," I said. Thank goodness Mila had given me the opening I'd been looking for. I wasn't going to squander it. "Where were you last night? I didn't see you after the Decatur House tour," I asked.

"I talked with several attendees, who had additional questions for me," she said.

"Did anyone ask about Stephen Decatur's sword?" I asked.

"You mean the murder weapon," said Mila. "Of course, the police asked me that question, and the answer is no. If someone had shown considerable interest, I would have reported it once I found out the killer used it to stab James Bennett."

Mila was a pretty sharp cookie. Not too much got past her. But I wasn't about to let her off the hook too easily.

"I didn't see you at the reception," I said. "Did you go home?"

"I was around. Obviously, I answered questions from the police, so I didn't go home."

"Were you inside Decatur House?" I asked. "Or somewhere else?"

"Look, I can tell that you want to know whether I have an alibi for Bennett's murder. And the answer to that question is that I do. I was talking with Edgar."

I nodded. "Edgar said you were together inside the carriage house, which is adjacent to the courtyard."

"That's right. That space is often used for events, but since everything was outside last night, it was empty."

"Why not talk to Edgar at the reception?" I prodded. "The food and drink were quite good, as I recall."

"There's something going on near the White House almost every night of the week. The invitations are relentless. You have to learn to say no to the reception snacks." She looked at me up and down, not bothering to hide her obvious judgment of my affinity for free finger food, cheese plates, and wine.

"Even if you weren't hungry, why not remain at the reception? Weren't you supposed to mingle as one of the hostesses?"

Mila scrunched up her face in irritation. "I'd already done my job. I took everyone on the tour and answered every last damn question about the house." She took a deep breath. "I don't need to tell you anything else."

She turned on her heel and marched away from me, leaving the lunch counter area of the exhibit. Well, that certainly went downhill quickly. I had no idea why Mila and Edgar found it convenient to sequester themselves last night, but it was apparent that neither of them wanted to tell me about it.

I perused the remainder of the civil rights movement exhibit, with pictures and films featuring the March on Washington and other key historical moments. I admired the dress Rosa Parks was thinking about sewing when she engaged in civil disobedience in Alabama in 1955. She was making the dress for herself, and eventually finished the project. But in between, she ignited a social movement that changed the trajectory of American history.

I made my way up the ramp to the next floor, spotting our host Felicia. Mila, Edgar, and Jill were already with her.

"Did you enjoy your brief tour of the museum?" asked Felicia.

"I did, but I need to come back several more times to fully appreciate the experience," I said.

"That's exactly what we like to hear," said Felicia. "I hope you've worked up an appetite. We've stuck to the schedule, so we have time for a lunch break at our cafeteria."

Edgar's eyes lit up like the National Christmas Tree. "Let's go," he said.

We marched up to the Concourse level of the museum. The Sweet Home Cafe was located immediately adjacent to the exit of the history galleries. Unfortunately, the line to enter the restaurant was a mile long. Edgar's face fell immediately.

Felicia must have seen Edgar's disappointed expression. "Don't worry. Remember, I reserved a table for us. In fact, we won't need to wait in the cafeteria line. We'll have an assortment of food delivered to our table."

We followed Felicia past the queue of hungry tourists, and she located a table in the middle of the seating area with her name on it. She motioned for us to sit down.

"I'll let the staff know we're here, and then our food will be delivered momentarily," she explained. Felicia took off, and the four of us took our seats at the table.

There was an awkward silence, probably because I'd interrogated both Mila and Edgar aggressively and they'd shared their interactions with each other.

"I'm sure the food is going to be quite delicious," I said. It was a lame attempt to break the silence, but someone needed to say something.

Edgar nodded. "I've heard great things about it. All of my consulting work with the museum was done before the doors opened, so I've never had a chance to sample the fare."

We didn't need to keep the pleasantries for long. Felicia returned with a cart of food, wheeled out by a member of the kitchen staff. After everything was placed on the table, I inhaled deeply to appreciate the enticing mixture of aromas.

"I apologize for the large quantities, but we thought we might have more people for the tour today," said Felicia.

Two people were dead, Trevor was a prime suspect, and Meg was probably too upset to do anything but worry. It wasn't Felicia's fault.

Edgar didn't seem upset by the extra servings. He leaned forward eagerly.

Before he could dig in, the kitchen staff member spoke. "Would you like me to tell you what's on the menu for your lunch?"

After we answered in the affirmative, he pointed out the array of dishes one at a time.

"We have food at the cafe representing the various regions of African American culture," he explained. "This is pan-fried Louisiana catfish, from the Creole coast. Over here, we have buttermilk fried chicken and biscuits. That's a traditional southern dish. Then, we have Son of a Gun Stew with beef, barley, and root vegetables, popular in the western part of the country when formerly enslaved people found work as ranch hands. The last entree is an oyster pan roast from New York."

"And dessert?" asked Felicia.

"We have a special today," he said. "Blackberry cobbler."

Felicia smiled. "Please everyone, enjoy yourselves. I suggest sampling everything, if you can."

She must have read my mind. When else would I have the opportunity to try such a delicious assortment of food? I took a small helping of everything and couldn't resist a fried chicken leg. I mean, you only live once, right?

I was so preoccupied with the meal that I almost forgot I was supposed to ask more pointed questions about the murder. After taking a big sip of sweet tea, I broke the silence at the table.

"I spoke to the police sergeant investigating Bev's murder earlier today. He can't figure out how the murderer knew that Bev was making a last-minute stop at the tent after the reception," I explained. "Did you hear Bev mention to anyone that she was planning to check on the tent before heading home?"

"You mean at the Belmont-Paul House reception?" asked Mila. Even she was enjoying a buttermilk biscuit. The food was too good to pass up, even for her.

"Yes. When we left the tent earlier in the day, no one was planning to stop by there again," I said. "Bev had to change her mind at the reception."

"Maybe the killer followed her there," said Edgar, in between bites of crispy catfish. "If someone had it out for her, then doesn't it make sense to tail her and find an opportunity for the crime?"

"That's what I thought initially," I said. "But the killer also had to disable the security cameras before the murder. That means he or she was at the tent *before* Bev showed up."

Edgar shrugged. "I guess that's right. Your reasoning seems logical to me."

"If that's the case," said Mila. "Then someone had to know that Bev was planning to visit the tent that evening."

"Exactly. If we can figure out who knew that piece of information, we'll be closer to finding the guilty party," I said.

Mila finished the last bite of her biscuit. "I wish I could help you, but I didn't overhear Bev mention anything related to making a final check of the tent."

Edgar scooped a big portion of cobbler for his plate. "Same for me, Kit."

Jill hadn't said anything. However, she'd been at the reception, too.

"Jill, did you overhear anything? Even if it was from someone other than Bev, we might be able to trace the conversation back to its origins," I said.

"I had no idea Bev was headed back to the tent," she said. "You were supposed to drop off the programs, but you didn't do it."

"That's right. Trevor offered instead, so I gave him the box and that's why he was at the tent right before the murder happened," I said.

"The only person who was supposed to visit the tent that night was you," said Jill. "If Bev decided to go, I didn't know about it."

"What's going to happen now with the investigation?" asked Mila. "If no one knew about Bev's whereabouts, then how will the police figure out who did it?"

I shook my head. "It's a puzzle. Right now, they're focused on those of us who served on the *Spring Into History* committee, because we all knew about the security cameras at the tent. But perhaps the police will have to widen the pool of suspects."

Felicia, who had been listening politely to our macabre lunchtime discussion about murder, glanced at her watch. "I believe the public lecture is starting soon. Should we head over to the Oprah Winfrey Theater?"

After appropriate thanks and praise for the food, we headed over to the museum's large auditorium. Felicia explained that Oprah Winfrey donated over twenty million dollars to the museum, so it made sense that the largest theater in the building was named after her.

The speaker for the program was a senior curator at the museum who described the exhibit detailing the history of music in African American culture. We hadn't seen that part of the museum today, and the details about Chuck Berry's red Cadillac and Sammy Davis Jr.'s tap shoes reaffirmed my commitment to come back when I had more time to view all of the collections on display.

By the time the lecture ended, it was almost four o'clock. The day had certainly flown by and somehow, we managed to pull off another excellent program. As we exited the auditorium, my phone buzzed. It was Meg, who wanted to know if I was still at the museum. I responded affirmatively, and she suggested we meet at the nearby Old Ebbitt Grill for its famous seafood happy hour. I was stuffed from our lunch but couldn't deny Meg one of her favorite treats. We agreed to meet at Old Ebbitt in thirty minutes. I suggested that she bring Trevor. The stress of the past couple of days had likely taken its toll and they both needed a chance to unwind. But Meg responded that he was too busy with work due to his boss's death. After all, Congress still had to function, no matter what tragedy happened yesterday. Trevor had to carry the brunt of that workload and try to figure out a way to exonerate himself from suspicion. Not an enviable position to find yourself in.

Edgar and Mila were nowhere to be found, so I couldn't say goodbye to them. I thanked our host Felicia, who offered to arrange a return visit in the near future so we could see the exhibits we'd missed today. Just as I was about to leave, I spotted Jill, near the exit.

I hurried over to her. "Jill, I'm meeting up with Meg Peters at Old Ebbitt Grill. Do you want to join us?" I flashed her a smile. "You did a great job today with the event."

Jill smoothed her medium length hair as she turned to face me. "I need to go back to the office. We're hosting that program tomorrow in the Capitol Visitor Center, remember?"

The *Spring Into History* schedule had become a bit of blur given the murders. "Can you remind me about the details again?" I asked.

A flash of annoyance passed across Jill's face, but she covered it up as quickly as it had appeared. "Bev was going to give the welcome for the event, which is a tour of the National Statuary Hall collection," she said. "I emailed you about it. Without Bev, you're going to have to give the introduction."

This morning, I had gone through my emails in such a rush, I must have flipped by Jill's message without reading it fully. It wouldn't be the first or last time that I had haphazardly missed an important email.

"Sorry, Jill. I didn't read that message. I'm glad you told me," I said. "I know something about the collection of statues in the Capitol complex, however. We had a hearing on the topic a few months ago because so many congressional delegations were interested in replacing the two statues that represented their home states."

"Then you'll be able to handle drafting the talking points for yourself?" asked Jill. Once again, the flash of annoyance appeared for a moment, and then evaporated.

"Yes, I'll be fine," I said. "I'll head back to the office after I meet with Meg to draft something up."

"Where is your husband this evening?" asked Jill.

"He's at Georgetown. I think he's got to attend an early evening reception there." I vaguely remembered Doug texting me about it to make sure I knew it was on his schedule. "Do you need to ask him about something related to our upcoming programs?"

"No, but there is a killer around, stabbing people in the back and using priceless heirlooms as a murder weapon," said Jill. "You told me to be careful this morning."

"Good point," I said. "Thanks for reminding me."

Jill smiled. "I'd better get back to the office so I can make sure everything is in order for tomorrow's event."

I placed my hand gently on Jill's upper arm. "Thank you for being so diligent about your work. I know you're only an intern, but we really would have been lost without you, especially given what's happened with the two murders."

Jill patted my hand appreciatively with the opposite hand. "I know. I'm glad everything has worked out."

I glanced at my phone. I was due to meet Meg in less than twenty minutes and I hadn't even left the Smithsonian yet.

"I've got to run, Jill. Text me if something changes about tomorrow."

"I will," she promised.

After the sizable lunch we had this afternoon, I wouldn't order seafood with Meg. But I was looking forward to catching up with my best friend, who had certainly been through the ringer the past couple of days. As it turns out, she wasn't the only one who would be tested. Not by a long shot.

Chapter Twenty

IT WAS A TWENTY-MINUTE WALK to the Old Ebbitt Grill, north of the White House Visitor Center on Fifteenth Street and directly east of the White House itself. Due to its proximity to the White House, I'd heard that prominent presidential staffers sometimes enjoyed a drink or two at the bar. However, we were too early for the West Wing (or East Wing) crowd today. Their days were longer than those of us who worked on Capitol Hill. I doubt they ever experienced an eight-hour workday.

Even though I didn't work in the neighborhood, I'd dined at Old Ebbitt many times. It was one of those iconic Washington, D.C. eating and drinking establishments that everyone patronized at one time or the other. Since Old Ebbitt professed to be the oldest saloon in the nation's capital, many presidents throughout American history had bellied up to the bar. Its location had moved around a bit, but the decor inside was reminiscent of the Victorian era, with a mahogany bar and various antique accoutrements.

It was a big place, with several separate rooms (including one named after Ulysses S. Grant) and multiple lounges. It wasn't too crowded inside, so I found Meg easily. She was seated on a corner stool and motioned for me to join her.

Since I knew Meg well, I could notice signs of strain. Her lipstick had obviously been applied hours earlier, and she hadn't bothered to freshen it. The faint laugh lines around her mouth looked more pronounced than usual. Her hair, although combed and neatly styled, seemed limp. As I approached the empty seat next to her, she got up and gave me a hug.

"It's good to see you," she said. "I feel like this week has lasted a month."

I squeezed her back tightly. "Let's call it like it is. *Terrible.*"

I noticed she was drinking something from a mixed drink glass and not her usual bubbly Prosecco. I pointed to her glass. "No wine?"

She shook her head vigorously. "I went for a gin and tonic. Tough times require tough measures."

I motioned for the bartender to pour me the same. "Did you order seafood? There's only twenty minutes left for happy hour."

"I'm way ahead of you," she said. "I ordered oysters, clams, and shrimp. Half-price, of course."

"Good thinking. I won't be able to help you much with the food, unfortunately." I recounted the feast we enjoyed at the African American History Museum this afternoon.

Meg's eyes grew as big as quarters. "I can't believe I missed it," she said. "I've spent so much time talking with Trevor and making sure he remained out of police custody, I had to stay at the Library of Congress today to make sure my real job got done."

The bartender brought my drink, and I squeezed the lime into the glass. "Shall we toast?" I asked, with it raised.

"To what?" asked Meg, her face glum. "That Trevor stays out of prison?"

"No, silly. To finding the killer and making sure the guilty person is brought to justice!"

She clinked her glass to mine. "That's worthy of a toast, for sure."

A waiter arrived and plopped down a large plate filled with fresh seafood.

"I hope you're hungry," I said. "Although everything is very healthy."

Meg sprayed her feast with fresh lemon and dug in. "I didn't have a chance to eat lunch today. I'm famished."

Meg really must have been up against it today at work. She never missed a meal. For her, it was the equivalent of a cardinal sin to forego breakfast, lunch, or dinner.

"I haven't talked to Trevor since this morning," I said. "Do you have anything to report?"

She popped a shrimp in her mouth before answering. "Nothing has changed. Obviously, he hasn't been arrested. Work is almost impossible for him, though. Now his boss is dead, and rumors are swirling that he might have been involved with his murder."

I sipped my G&T. "Yes, I can see how that might not be conducive to an optimal working environment."

Meg smiled at my anemic attempt at humor. "He's not a happy camper these days."

"I'm afraid we're at a standstill with solving the murders. I thought I made considerable progress after talking to Trevor and Sergeant O'Halloran this morning, but I still can't figure out who knew that Bev was dropping in for a visit at the tent after leaving the Belmont-Paul House reception."

Meg sucked down an oyster and gulped her drink. Upon draining it, she ordered another. After wiping her mouth delicately with the cocktail napkin, she leaned forward. "What if we're looking these murders completely wrong?"

"You may be right," I said. "I'm willing to hear new theories."

"What if Bev never told anyone she was going to the tent that night?" Meg dipped a clam into the little tub of specialty sauce and popped it into her mouth.

"That doesn't fit, though. If the killer tailed her there, then who disables the security cameras before the crime is committed?"

"But what if the killer was there for another reason," said Meg.

"Like what?" I asked. "Enjoying a beautiful springtime night in Washington? Disabling the cameras meant a crime was going to happen."

Meg thought for a moment. "The Lincoln catafalque was on display. Perhaps the murderer was planning a robbery, but Bev interrupted it."

That was an interesting theory. Yet, it wasn't plausible. "How could you steal the catafalque? It's impossible to move. It's not like filching a small artifact you can walk away with."

Meg snapped her fingers. "Maybe the person didn't want to

steal it. They wanted to damage it or desecrate it somehow. You know, like bring attention to a cause."

"That could be possible," I said slowly. Certainly, there were enough people in Washington, D.C. who were passionate about particular beliefs or policy problems. "But why Lincoln's catafalque? It seems strange. Who doesn't like Abraham Lincoln?"

"There's plenty of people in this country who still fly the Confederate flag, Kit. I bet those people aren't big fans of Lincoln."

"Fair point," I said. "It doesn't get us any closer to knowing who might have done this to Bev, however. For example, how would this person have known about the security cameras? They were hidden well inside the tent. Only the organizers knew where they were located because we oversaw the security plan."

Meg's drink arrived. She squeezed the lime into it and stirred it as she pondered my question. "You got me there. I don't have a good answer for that."

"That's okay. Thinking about these two murders in a different way is what we need to do."

"I have a feeling that Bev may have been in the wrong place at the wrong time. She stumbled upon something or someone, and because of it, she was killed."

"I assumed that because Bev rubbed so many people the wrong way, she was killed deliberately," I said.

Meg polished off her last oyster. "Trevor made for a convenient suspect since he and Bev exchanged heated words at the reception. His status as a suspect contributed to that narrative."

"Bev was stabbed in the back with the letter opener. I assumed she was running away from her attacker," I said, thinking out loud.

"But you're rethinking that assumption now?"

"Well, if she saw something she shouldn't have, perhaps her attacker snuck up on her?"

"That's plausible. However, once again, the killer needed to disable the cameras ahead of time."

"A crime was going to be committed at the tent," I said. "We just don't know if the killer planned to kill Bev, or she became collateral damage."

"It certainly does open up possibilities for other motives," said Meg. "But I have no idea how we would figure out what those motives might be without more clues or physical evidence."

Meg was right. We could come up with all kinds of inventive theories about why Bev might have been killed, but without a concrete lead, it was nothing but supposition. Our conversation meandered into other topics related to work and gossip. I glanced at my phone. It was after six o'clock.

"I'd love to catch up more," I said. "But I need to go back to the office and draft opening remarks for tomorrow's *Spring Into History* tour of Statuary Hall at the Capitol. I'm taking Bev's place."

I fished around my purse for my wallet. Meg put up her hand. "I'll get your drink, Kit. I'm sorry I haven't been so friendly these past couple of days. Trevor's situation has really rattled me."

"The reason why you're so bothered is that you care deeply about Trevor," I said. "You've come a long way, Meg, since your days of commitment-phobia."

Meg flashed a toothy grin. "I hadn't thought of it that way. It makes me feel better."

I got up to leave the bar. "I'll keep you posted if I make a breakthrough in solving the murders."

Meg stood up. "Thank you for everything, Kit. I don't always say it, but I have confidence in you. Somehow, you manage to make everything right. I'm always amazed by it."

I gave Meg a hug and left the restaurant. After I turned away, I wiped a tear from my eye. Meg's words meant a great deal. Not only about me, but about her, too. Sometimes, the worst of circumstances brought out the best in people. Meg had finally figured out what it meant to be in a serious, devoted relationship and everything that came with it— the good, the bad, the challenges. It had taken my best friend a long time to get to this point, but I was glad she had found the person who got her there.

Chapter Twenty-One

IF I HAD MORE TIME, A RELAXING WALK BACK to Capitol Hill might have been in the cards. Weather in Washington, D.C. only cooperated for a few weeks in the spring and fall seasons. The rest of the year, I was either sweating or shivering. However, I didn't have the forty-five minutes to spare. I needed to get to my office and draft those talking points so I would be prepared for tomorrow's event.

Instead, I called an Uber and within minutes, we were crawling southbound on Fourteenth Street. Mercifully, the driver wasn't chatty and instead seemed content to groove to the seventies yacht rock he had playing inside the vehicle. Unbothered by idle conversation, the brief ride gave me a moment to reflect on the day. The double murder was a conundrum. It still seemed to me that it hinged on Bev sharing with someone that she had changed her mind and was stopping by the tent before going home. Or was it something more complicated, as Meg suggested? Had Bev interrupted another crime? If so, what could have that been? Nothing had been pilfered from the tent, and the Lincoln catafalque hadn't been damaged. My mind started to click through the possibilities. We were stopped at a red light to turn east on Independence Avenue when a revelation struck me, almost like a lightning bolt from Zeus.

What if Meg was right? Had Bev been a victim of circumstance rather than a cold, calculated murder intended purposefully to end her life? Was Bev's homicide a case of mistaken identity?

We hadn't paid for a contractor to install lights inside the tent. Our only event inside the tent was the morning lecture and subsequent display of the Lincoln catafalque. We'd discussed it and determined it was a waste of money since the tent would only be used during daylight hours. When Trevor recounted his story about dropping the programs off at the tent, he mentioned that the lack of light. He said that he hadn't seen anyone, and the explanation he gave was that it was already dark.

It was likely that the murder occurred after Trevor's visit to the tent. Trevor, who was fastidiously observant on a bad day, would have not missed the presence of a body underneath the catafalque. Instead, Bev's murder had to happen after he dropped off the programs.

If that was the case, then the light in the tent might have been even dimmer due to the lateness of the hour. Bev was stabbed in the back. Had the killer seen her face? We theorized that Bev argued with the assailant and then turned to flee. But what if she literally hadn't seen the attack coming? A premeditated crime with Bev as the victim wouldn't make a difference. The killer would have still had to know she was going to drop by the tent on her way home.

However, if the murder *wasn't* planned ahead of time, it *might* be possible that Bev was an unintended victim. She was a disagreeable person, and several people could have profited from her death. But perhaps that was a convenient coincidence.

And then, the real thunderbolt struck. If Bev wasn't the intended victim, who was?

Two details from that fateful night came back to me. First, I was supposed to drop off the programs, not Trevor. I'd talked about it publicly, so anyone might have heard about my plans or passed along that piece of information. The second detail was what really got me. I flipped back to an off-the-cuff comment that Doug had made at the Belmont-Paul House reception.

She looks a lot like you, Kit.

He'd meant Bev. I hadn't put those facts together until this moment. My heart skipped a beat, and I inhaled sharply. Was it a coincidence, or had the killer been targeting me?

I'd been so busy trying to track down motives for wanting Bev dead, I never explored the possibility that the crime might have been a case of mistaken identity. But the darkness, my public announcement about making a stop at the tent, and a striking similarity in appearance stared me right in the face. As uncomfortable as it was, I couldn't ignore the glaring facts.

I forced myself to recall details about that evening. Had I told anyone that Trevor was going to take the programs instead of myself? I replayed the scene in my brain. No one else had heard Trevor offering to take the programs. It was only me, Doug, Trevor, and Meg who participated in that conversation. As far as the rest of the group was concerned, I was headed to the tent to deliver the box.

If the killer had arrived after Trevor, he or she would have seen Bev, who was probably scrutinizing the scene to make sure everything was perfect. In the dim light of the tent, without the benefit of any illumination, the murderer certainly could have mistaken her for me. We had both worn black pantsuits that day. We were about the same height and build. And our medium brown hair was similar in cut, length, and color.

My skin became clammy as we motored along Independence Avenue. My Uber driver, who was blissfully bopping along to a Hall & Oates classic, didn't notice the change in my demeanor.

What should I do? Tell Sergeant O'Halloran? I had no proof. He wouldn't offer me 24-hour police protection based upon an inventive supposition. No, it was better to calm down and act deliberatively. After I had written my talking points for tomorrow, I would draft all the details about my theory and text it to O'Halloran. That way, I could think about the scenario I was outlining and present the best possible case to him. After all, my revelation didn't get me much closer in figuring out who the guilty party was. However, it did eliminate several potential suspects, like Mila and Edgar. There was no way that either of them wanted me dead. We had worked together well on *Spring Into History*. They might have had a beef with Bev, but there was no plausible motive for killing me.

If Edgar or Mila wasn't the murderer, the suspect pool was

rapidly dwindling. The only remaining, or living, members of our group was myself, Meg, Trevor, and Chase Wintergreen. By process of elimination, that only left one person.

Chase Wintergreen was the killer.

My brain flipped back to the conversation we had earlier today. He hadn't seemed particularly out of sorts. But the facts fit. Chase had a motive to want me out of the way. If I was eliminated, his path to become the committee staff director would be smooth sailing. There would be no serious competition for the position if I was dead. There was also James Bennett's murder to consider. The killer might have done away with Bennett to silence him. Or, it could have been premeditated. Once he realized he'd killed Bev instead of me, he might have thought the top position at the Capitol Visitor Center was attractive. Who knows? Perhaps Chase went to Bennett and asked him if he would support his bid for the job. When Bennett refused, Chase might have become enraged. Then, he used the event at Decatur House to get rid of Bennett. As far as the odd displays at both murders, I didn't really know exactly what that meant, but Chase did have a flair for the dramatic. Perhaps it was merely a diversion, an attempt to throw the police off the scent of the real killer. Or maybe he was deranged. Deep in thought, I hadn't realized we'd arrived at our destination until the Uber driver spoke.

"Ms. Marshall, we're here." He looked back at me through the rearview mirror with his one eyebrow raised. Every Uber driver must dread a passenger who acts oddly, much like I was now.

His words jolted me back to reality. "Oh, I'm sorry. I was in another world." I didn't want to tell him that it was the world of a double homicide.

I gathered my purse and exited the vehicle directly outside the Cannon House Office Building. Despite the late hour, there was a lot of traffic going in and out of the building. People were working late, many ducking out for a happy hour or dinner and then reluctantly returning to the office for a few more hours of work.

As I went through the security check and metal detector, I wondered again about contacting Sergeant O'Halloran. My ideas were purely hypothetical. With no hard evidence tying Chase

Wintergreen to either murder, would O'Halloran wonder why I was bothering him? The police sergeant was tolerant of my sleuthing, but he didn't appreciate fanciful conjecture. I needed to ponder my next move. Once I was inside our office, no one could harm me. There were too many people inside the congressional office buildings. I would be perfectly safe.

I let myself into our suite, locked the door behind me, and took a speedy walk around the perimeter, including Maeve Dixon's office. I even checked her private bathroom. No one was here. With the door closed and alarmed, there was no lurking murderer to worry about. But I did have to draft those talking points for tomorrow, or else I risked looking like an idiot in front of a crowd of people eager to learn about the history of Statuary Hall inside the United States Capitol.

With the help of a Congressional Research Service report that spelled out the history of the featured sculpture collection within the United States Capitol, it only took twenty minutes to craft opening remarks. After all, the real historical lecture would come from an expert curator of the collection. I just needed to provide the welcome and set the context. As I wrote, I exchanged texts with Doug. Surprisingly, he was next door at the Library of Congress, capitalizing on evening researcher hours. We agreed to meet up after I was done with work so we could drive home together. He asked about my progress on the investigation, and I explained that I'd experienced a recent revelation and wanted to tell him about it this evening. Best to keep it brief so he could get back to his researching and I could finish the draft of my remarks for tomorrow.

As I was putting the polishing touches on my talking points, my desk phone rang. The identification of the number said the call was coming from within the Capitol Visitor Center. That was odd. Curiosity got the best of me, so I picked up.

"Kit, it's Jill. I'm glad I caught you."

My conscientious intern was undoubtedly calling to make sure I had actually followed through and written the opening remarks as I promised. I couldn't blame her. After all, I had forgotten the email she'd written me about it.

"Don't worry," I said. "I'm finishing up my script. I can email it if you want to read my remarks."

"That's fine," she said hurriedly. "There's been a change of plans for tomorrow. I found out that there's a possibility of providing Capitol dome tours to a select number of attendees."

Something didn't exactly sound right. "Doesn't the Architect of the Capitol require a sitting member of Congress to host a dome tour? We don't have an elected member of Congress planning to attend tomorrow."

In our congressional office, we received requests for specialty United States Capitol tours all the time. When I became chief of staff for Maeve Dixon, I learned that even as a high-ranking staffer, I couldn't substitute for her. Consequently, we rarely offered them to constituents because my boss found it next to impossible to fit the tours into her busy schedule. The dome tour was particularly exciting, because it walked participants through the bowels of the Capitol dome, culminating in a beautiful view of the city from a small observatory deck immediately below the Statue of Freedom.

"We received special dispensation due to Bev's death," said Jill. "We'll have an official Capitol tour guide join us. They said we can do several rounds of tours so that everyone who is interested can have a chance to do the tour."

"That's surprising," I said. The Capitol Visitor Center and Congress were creatures of habit. They didn't easily reverse practices or bend rules. It was part of what gave the institution its character, for better or worse.

"I know," she said cheerily. "The reason why I called you is that the Capitol Visitor Center tour guide agreed to give us a preview. Have you ever had the opportunity to climb the dome?"

I checked the time. It was only six-thirty. Doug would probably want at least another hour at the Library of Congress. Since he'd taken on a primarily administrative role at Georgetown, his time to conduct his own research had diminished. He truly cherished the moments he could spend absorbed in the historical materials that helped him write his books.

"It's been years. I went a long time ago with my former boss, Senator Langsford," I explained.

"If it's been that long, then you should take the opportunity tonight," said Jill. "I don't think it will be possible tomorrow. Too many attendees from the general public will want to do it."

"Okay," I agreed. "Where should I meet you?"

"In the Crypt," said Jill.

"I'll be there shortly," I said. "I'll bring a draft of my speech and maybe you can take a quick look to make sure I'm covering the critical points."

"Sure," said Jill. A dial tone rang in my ear.

That was abrupt. When things were back to normal, I'd have to counsel Jill on proper phone etiquette. Younger people were so used to texting, they often forgot that when they were speaking to someone, politeness was important.

After printing out my remarks, I grabbed my purse and my phone. When the dome tour was done, I'd head right over to the Library of Congress so Doug and I could drive home together. Then I'd be able to tell him about my theory of mistaken identity and get feedback from him about what I should do next.

The Crypt sounds like an ominous place to meet, but it's really a misnomer. No one is actually buried there. Located directly underneath the rotunda, it's a large circular room in the center of the United States Capitol, filled with elaborate neoclassic columns.

Although there's no dead bodies (that we know of) in the Capitol, the Crypt got its name due to burial plans that never came to fruition. When the Capitol was being constructed, Congress passed a resolution to bury George Washington in a tomb directly underneath the Crypt, two floors below the rotunda. According to Congress's plan, visitors to the Capitol would look through a glass floor from the Crypt level and would be able to see Washington's tomb. The problem was that George Washington specified in his last will and testament that he wanted to be buried at his estate, Mount Vernon. Washington's descendants honored his wishes, and George never made it to the Capitol. Apparently, the designers of the Capitol tried to change the name of the Crypt to the "Vestibule," but it never caught on. The area designated for Washington's unused tomb housed Lincoln's catafalque for years. Now, most days, the catafalque was on exhibit display inside the public area of the Capitol Visitor Center.

Most tourists had already left the Capitol for the day, yet there were still a fair number of congressional staff throughout the building. It took ten minutes to walk from my office to the Crypt on the first floor of the building. The tall Doric columns inside the circular vestibule initially obscured my line of sight, but then I spotted Jill standing in the center of the Crypt. I hustled over to her.

"I made it," I said, a little breathless. I'd have to get back to my regular jogs when life got back to normal. Perhaps if we got Clarence back on track, he would join me.

"We'd better get going," said Jill. "Before we lose the natural daylight."

"But where's our tour guide?" I asked, scanning the area.

"She'll meet us inside the rotunda," said Jill. "She wanted a head start up the stairs."

"It's not like I'm going to be going that fast up them," I said. "How many are there?"

"Almost three hundred to the observation area underneath the Statue of Freedom," said Jill. "But I don't know if we're going up that far." She motioned toward my purse. "Are you sure you want to take that with you? It's a big climb."

I'd never warmed up to the tiny purse fashion craze. I carried a big Kate Spade bag with me wherever I went. The difficulty was that it often weighed me down.

"I'll keep it," I said. "Besides, I don't know where we could leave it safely. All of the visitor desks are closed by now."

Jill shrugged and started walking in the direction of the small Senate rotunda. "The staircase we need is over here," she said.

The small Senate rotunda had been added to the building after the British burned the Capitol in 1814. Benjamin Latrobe, the architect, decided that while rebuilding, the space would be better utilized to circulate air and provide light. He built a small rotunda in the old Senate wing, complete with slender columns decorated by the leaves of tobacco plants and a glass oculus in the ceiling.

I hustled to keep up with Jill. She opened the door to a small circular stairwell.

"We need to go up four flights until we move inside the dome itself," she said.

"Is that where we'll meet the guide?" I asked.

Jill didn't answer and kept climbing the stairs at a breakneck pace. Her internship had not gotten in the way of her cardio fitness.

After climbing four flights, we arrived at the attic level of the Capitol. We entered another staircase, where there was a diagram showing the path of the climb. There were also several photos, providing a short history of the Capitol Dome. It was going to be quite a hike. I pulled out my iPhone and snapped photos of the display. After ascending that staircase, we arrived at the top of the dome roof. Now, we were inside the dome itself.

Iron staircases zig-zagged between the inner and outer domes, and as we started to climb the steps, I remembered the tour I took years ago with Senator Langsford. The first dome of the Capitol was finished in the 1820s. It was a low dome, and when the Capitol Building grew to add more space, it was perceived as being too small for such a regal and iconic structure. It was removed in the 1850s and the Architect of the Capitol at the time provided a new design that included two domes, an interior and exterior. He built the Capitol Dome that everyone recognizes today as one of the most famous, iconic American symbols of democracy.

We ascended several flights on the iron staircases and then ducked into the first visitor's gallery, which was really a narrow aisle with the Capitol rotunda to our right and glass windows facing the Supreme Court and Library of Congress to our left. Jill was several paces ahead of me and wasn't looking back. I called out to her.

"Jill, wait up!" I exclaimed. "Where's the guide?"

She didn't respond and kept going. I took a brief pause. I was definitely feeling the climb. My gaze drifted downward. Even though the Capitol was closed to tourists at this hour, there were still numerous staff crisscrossing the rotunda below. I could still make them out, but they seemed far away. I snapped another photo of the view and resumed the climb. There was only one way in and one way out, so thankfully, there was no danger of getting lost. Maybe Jill was concerned that we were late for the tour guide and wanted to catch up.

The next portion of the climb moved us into the interstitial space. In other words, we were now between the two domes of the Capitol. White trusses were all around us, supporting the gap between the inner and outer structures. The steep and winding staircase, illuminated by interior lights, snaked through these huge supports, almost like we were making our way through the hull of the Titanic. I could barely see Jill ahead of me. She was effortlessly taking two steps at a time, almost like she was out for a springtime sojourn at the park. I paused to take a few more photos and fiddle with my iPhone before resuming the climb.

Finally, I reached the final staircase. I could see the door leading to the second visitor's gallery, which was located immediately underneath the ceiling of the dome. This vantage point was directly below the painting of the apotheosis of George Washington, a fresco painted by Constantino Brumidi situated around the dome's center oculus. Brumidi's masterpiece was spellbinding when viewed from the floor of the rotunda, almost two hundred feet below. But as I recalled, it was simply spectacular to see it up close. I trudged up the last flight of stairs, eager to see the masterpiece up close once again.

I emerged through the door frame and moved right on the narrow walkway that encircled the interior dome. I looked downward. The staffers walking hurriedly through the rotunda were much smaller in size. It was eerily silent up here. I looked for Jill but didn't see her. Where did she go? She had been ahead of me on the ascending stairs, so why wasn't she on this level? And where was the guide? A sinking feeling in my stomach told me that a vague hunch I'd had earlier in the day, when we were at the Smithsonian, had proved prescient.

Jill wasn't in front of me on the walkway. Did that mean she was behind me?

I turned my body to the left, back towards the doorway. Sure enough, she was standing between me and the exit, with a boxcutter in her hand.

"Kit Marshall," she said. "Welcome to the United States Capitol dome. Take a good look at the scenery. It's the last view you'll ever see."

Chapter Twenty-Two

I PUT MY HANDS UP IN THE AIR, a natural reflex to the threat Jill posed. At the same time, I took several steps backwards, but she advanced forward.

"Jill, what on earth are you doing?" She had a strange look in her eyes, which freaked me out almost as much as the weapon she was wielding.

"You still have no idea, do you?" She whipped her auburn hair around as she waved the boxcutter in front of me. I backed up again.

"I suspected you might have been involved with the murders," I said. "To tell you the truth, I have no idea why."

"And why did you suspect me?" she sneered. "I can't wait to hear the revelation from the great Capitol Hill detective."

"It was more of an observation that didn't quite fit," I said, trying to keep my voice calm. "You mentioned at the Smithsonian about someone getting stabbed in the back. That was Bev, of course. But that detail was never released to the press or public. The police have been quiet on the specifics of the deaths, just in case they were dealing with a serial killer. I had to wonder how you knew about it. I never told you how Bev was killed."

"But you still don't know why I did it," Jill said. Her face was flush. She was enjoying watching me squirm, so I took a deep breath to steady myself. Jill was the same person I'd worked alongside the past couple of months, but the expression on her face made her almost unrecognizable. It was filled with anger and hate.

"No, although I did work out that Bev's death might have been a case of mistaken identity. I was supposed to drop off the programs at the tent that night. A comment from Doug that night reminded me that I resembled Bev in height and build. In the dark, the killer might have mistaken her for me."

Jill stepped closer to me, and I retreated. We were now a quarter of the way around the circular dome walkway. Maybe I could keep going and eventually make a break for the door.

"You're right about that detail," she said. "I didn't mean to kill Bev. Even so, I didn't lose any sleep over it. She was just another example of Capitol Hill arrogance. No one liked her. Everyone might pretend to mourn her death now, but she wasn't dead for twenty-four hours before people were plotting to replace her."

While Jill was speaking, I caught a glimpse of the rotunda below. At least two Capitol Hill police officers were standing guard, and staffers continued to crisscross it. If I was going to try to draw attention to my situation, it was now or never.

I made a fast break so that I could put some distance between me and Jill. As I was running, I screamed as loud as I could. "HELP! HELP ME! LOOK UP! SOMEONE IS TRYING TO KILL ME!"

Jill caught up to me and lunged with the boxcutter, but I sidestepped her.

"For a chief of staff who supposedly knows Capitol Hill inside and out, you're not very smart," said Jill. "Why do you think I lured you up here?"

I continued to move backwards as she advanced. "The loudest scream can't be heard from this level," she said. "I made sure when the tour guide brought me up here a few days ago. When I learned that convenient fact, I decided this was where I wanted to finish you off. I could kill you in plain sight, and there's not a thing anyone can do about it."

Now I was halfway around the circular pathway. If I could get a little closer, then maybe I could reach the door. Even if I made it to the walkway exit, I'd still have to outrun Jill down the winding staircase, which seemed like a crapshoot, at best. Buying time was in my favor, because if I was lucky, help was on the way.

"I still don't know why you want to kill me," I said. "I realize I didn't spend as much time as I should have with you during the internship."

Jill threw her head back and laughed. It was a deranged cackle, which confirmed my deduction that she was mentally unstable.

"The internship was part of the plan. You still don't know who I am, do you?" She shook her head. "I'll give you a hint: Senator Lyndon Langsford."

That was a name I hadn't heard in a while. I took a careful look at Jill. Her facial features were twisted, yet was something oddly familiar about the angular cut of her jaw and her deeply set eyes? Who did she remind me of? My brain flipped through a mental rolodex back to my working days in the Senate. After a few moments, it finally hit on a possibility.

"Jeff Prentice," I muttered. "You look like him."

Years ago, the first murder I helped solve ended in a cataclysmic underground Senate subway chase involving the killer who had murdered my former boss, Senator Lyndon Langsford. Jeff Prentice was a lobbyist who was a likely accomplice to the murder, but as far as I knew, the police never could prove his involvement in the crime.

Jill clapped her hands together in a taunting manner. "Congratulations. The super sleuth does not disappoint!"

I put two and two together. "You're Jeff's relative?" I said.

"I am his younger sister," she said. "Do you know what happened to Jeff after the murder investigation?"

"I don't," I said. "I never saw Jeff again."

"Exactly!" exclaimed Jill. "He wasn't charged for any crime, yet he suffered the consequences. He lost his job at the defense lobbying firm and no one would hire him, in government, the military, or elsewhere. He ended up moving back in with the family."

It sounded bad, but there must be something more. "Is he still living there today?"

Jill waved the boxcutter erratically. I could feel my pulse accelerate. "Some days he's there. Other days he never makes it home from his benders."

My heart sank. Jeff had turned to drugs or alcohol, maybe both. "I'm sorry to hear that, Jill." I extended my hands in a conciliatory gesture. "Maybe we should talk about it."

Jill laughed. "We're beyond talking about it. There's one thing my brother is clear about, even when he's under the influence." She pointed the boxcutter directly at me. "You are the reason for his demise. Your so-called sleuthing cast a cloud of suspicion over him, and he never recovered from it. Do you know what addiction does to families? It wrecks them."

"And you blame me for Jeff's problems?" I asked.

"My brother blames you for it, and I blame you for it," said Jill. "I worked with him to plot our family's revenge. You destroyed us." As she said the last sentence, she pointed at me with the boxcutter.

Despite my dire circumstances, I couldn't help but note the irony that my amateur sleuthing had metaphorically come full circle. And now I was physically close to coming full circle, too. I was three-quarters of the way around the dome's walkway. I had to buy more time.

"Why did you kill James Bennett?" I asked. "Did he know too much?"

Jill shook her head. "I hadn't planned to hurt Bennett. I arrived early for the event that evening and called Jeff. I thought I was by myself inside the house, but when I turned around, I spotted Bennett. He tried to sneak away, but I knew he'd overheard my conversation."

"James worked on Capitol Hill for years. He would have remembered Jeff and the fact that the police suspected his involvement in Senator Langsford's murder. James must have heard enough to realize who you were."

"He had to be eliminated. I told him I had a good explanation for what he'd heard. He was too trusting. I'd already placed the sword upstairs. I staged the murder just the like the other one. Don't ask me why." Her beady eyes blinked rapidly as she sighed. "It just felt *right*."

I was slowly inching my way around the perimeter of the dome. Jill must have noticed that I was aware of our location on the circular path. "Enough talking," she said. "Now I'm going to finish what my brother should have done years ago." Jill reached for my arm and tried to pull me closer to her. Instead, I blocked her advance and then kicked her backwards. This was my chance.

While she was off balance, I sprinted around the walkway for the door. I had no idea if I would be able to fend her off when we reached the staircase, but it was my only hope. Unless, of course, my last-minute notification had reached its intended audience and he'd known what to do with it.

Jill was right on my heels when I was only steps away from the exit. All of a sudden, the door swung open, and Sergeant O'Halloran appeared.

He was in a perfect position to intercept Jill, who was already lunging forward with the boxcutter. O'Halloran swung his right hand around in a clockwise motion and hit Jill's wrist just at the right angle. The boxcutter flew out of her hand and dropped eighteen stories to the rotunda floor. I looked over the railing. Two police officers had rushed over to the object and pointed up at the walkway. O'Halloran put handcuffs on Jill and went through the drill of reading her rights.

He turned to me. "You're one lucky lady," he said. "You have a smart husband who realized you must be texting him pictures of the Capitol dome for a good reason."

"I wanted him to know where I was," I said. "He knew I was close to solving the murders, so I hoped he would interpret it as though I was in pursuit of the killer. It also helped that my last text said 'help' in capital letters."

"You should have turned around when you realized something was wrong," said O'Halloran.

"This was my only chance to prove what she'd done," I said. "Otherwise, it was all circumstantial. There was no hard evidence. I had no choice. I had to take the bait."

"Do me a favor, Ms. Marshall," said Sergeant O'Halloran.

"Anything," I said. And I meant it. He'd saved my life.

"If you want to take the bait, go fishing in the Chesapeake. Stay away from murderers from now on, okay?"

Without hesitation, I said, "You've got a deal."

Chapter Twenty-Three

A WEEK LATER, THE SPRING SUN was shining brightly as I gazed westward, taking in a spectacular view of the National Mall and Washington Monument from the Speaker of the House's outdoor balcony in the United States Capitol. *Spring Into History* had concluded without missing a beat. Despite a double homicide and the fact that our intern had been fingered as the killer, the program had been a resounding success. So much so, Representative Dixon had asked the Speaker if we could use her valuable real estate for a small celebration and she had readily agreed.

No one passed up an opportunity, particularly on such a pleasant weather day, to enjoy a glass of wine on the Speaker's balcony. That meant the gang was all here. I'd even managed to secure an invite for Sebastian. Unfortunately, Lisa had to return to her FBI training, but there was good news to share.

Doug raised his glass. "We have much to celebrate. Our first toast is for my brother-in-law Sebastian, who is now engaged to Lisa, a soon-to-be FBI agent in its prestigious K-9 unit. Congratulations!"

Everyone joined in the toast and Sebastian's face turned pink. My brother might be a fearless protestor and activist, but he didn't like the spotlight directed on him.

Meg chimed in. "What are your plans for the future, Sebastian?"

My brother inhaled deeply before speaking. "We need to wait to find out where the FBI assigns Lisa and Murphy. Fortunately, the nonprofit I work for will allow me to work remotely, so I can move wherever she's assigned. Everything has fallen into place."

Of course, I understood the reality of Sebastian marrying Lisa. I was wildly happy for my brother. It did mean that he would probably leave the Washington, D.C. area once Lisa received her first official post from the FBI. My heart hurt that Sebastian was likely leaving our orbit, but I was so thankful we had reconnected and spent time together. He was in a good place these days, even if it meant his physical location was going to change.

"And Sebastian helped us solve one final mystery," I said.

"What's that?" asked Meg.

I pointed towards the floor, where Clarence was sitting obediently. "We figured out what was making Clarence depressed. It turns out he missed having another dog around. Once Murphy came for a visit with Lisa, he was his old self."

"I'm also afraid to ask what that revelation means," said Trevor, looking skeptically at Clarence.

"That's right," said Doug. "We're going to look for a canine brother or sister for Clarence. We'll start with our favorite local rescue organizations next week."

Clarence seemed to understand Doug's pronouncement. He appropriately wiggled his butt in excitement and licked my fingers. Clarence would be up to his old tricks again soon, and now he'd have a permanent accomplice.

Mila and Edgar strolled over to join us. "Thank you for asking us to join you today," said Edgar. I noticed he and Mila seemed to be standing awfully close to each other.

"My boss orchestrated it." I gestured to Maeve Dixon. "Despite everything that happened, *Spring Into History* was a major success. She hopes it will become an annual weeklong celebration of American history."

Mila grinned. "We'd certainly support that," she said. "Edgar and I are going to be seeing a lot more of each other."

Edgar slipped his arm casually around Mila's waist.

"Congratulations," said Doug. "The four of us will have to plan a double date soon."

Three historians against one. That would be one deadly night out on the town. Somehow, I'd figure out a way to survive. Before I could chime in and offer my congratulations to the couple, Chase Wintergreen sidled up to Maeve Dixon, who was now standing next to me.

Chase cleared his throat before speaking. "Chairwoman Dixon, can I ask how the campaign trail is looking for you these days?"

My boss plastered a smile on her face. Only someone who knew her facial expressions could tell it was less than genuine. I'd seen it many times before when she was forced to placate sycophants.

"It looks promising," she said. "I don't like to get ahead of myself, however."

Chase's voice oozed with an ingratiating tone. "We will certainly miss you when you're in the Senate. Particularly on the committee."

Dixon's eyes sparkled. "I intend to leave my chairmanship of the committee in good hands," she said. "In fact, I've personally spoken to the Speaker of the House about succession."

Chase blinked rapidly. "How impressive," he choked.

"Not just the chair of the committee," she said. "I mean on the staff level, too," Dixon pronounced.

I winced. She'd gone right for the jugular. Chase's face drained of color. He faltered for a few moments, and then he recovered. "I would like an opportunity to speak to you about your recommendations," he stammered.

Dixon looked pointedly at Chase. "This is not the time or the place, Mr. Wintergreen. All in due time. Now, I must greet our other guests. It was particularly generous of the Speaker to offer use of her balcony, and I want to make sure everyone is enjoying it." Dixon walked off and joined another conversation.

Chase lowered his head, his chin trembling. I took pity on him. "Don't worry too much about it. We'll just have to see what happens with the Senate race and what decisions Maeve Dixon makes after that."

He nodded and placed his wine glass on an empty tray. "I think I'll take off now. See you later, Kit."

Despite Chase's disappointment, I had a feeling that things

would work out for him, as long as he played his cards right in the coming months. He was a smart guy and once he thought about the conversation, he'd figure out what to do. After all, Washington, D.C. was a like a giant chess game. It was worth thinking about your opponent's next move before making your own.

The glass door to the balcony opened and Sergeant O'Halloran and Detective Maggie Glass emerged onto the balcony. Maggie Glass was unflappable, but even she couldn't hide her amazement of the spectacular view before us.

"Thanks for joining us," I said. "After all, you saved me from a very tricky situation. If Jill had executed her plan, the fresco of George Washington in heaven might have been the last thing I ever saw."

O'Halloran shrugged. "I've seen this view before. We do security checks up here all the time." He chuckled. "You know, when the actual Speaker of the House is using the balcony. But Maggie hadn't ever been up here, so I told her we should come."

"It was definitely worth it," said Glass, who had pulled a smartphone out of her jacket pocket and snapped several photos. She turned to face me. "Before I forget, I do have a question or two for you, Ms. Marshall."

I was expecting this. Despite the celebratory nature, we always managed to talk about murder at these soirées.

"Fire away," I said. "No time like the present."

"Did you know that Jill was the murderer when you entered the Capitol dome with her?" asked Glass. "If so, why didn't you call me or Sergeant O'Halloran?" She crossed her arms. "I know darn well that you have both of our numbers programmed on speed dial."

"That's correct. I do have your numbers at the ready," I said. "I knew that Jill had slipped up and provided a detail about Bev's murder that hadn't been publicly shared. However, I didn't know whether she might had overheard the detail somehow in conversation. More importantly, for the life of me, even though she had the means and opportunity, I didn't know her motive until she revealed it to me at the top of the dome."

Glass shook her head. "You should have erred on the side of

caution. Even so, why did you decide to text your husband when you were climbing the stairs?"

"What tipped me off was the tour guide," I said, taking a deep breath. "There wasn't one. After we had reached the first visitor's gallery and the tour guide didn't appear, I knew something was up. Normally, a member of Congress must serve as the escort for guests during a dome tour. There was no way Jill, a lowly intern, would have been allowed to show me that protected, secret area of the United States Capitol without authorization. That's when I knew something was wrong, and I'd better let Doug know where I was."

"You snapped a few photos, which seemed perfectly innocent for someone on a super cool tour," said Meg.

"Jill might have seen me, but that didn't seem out of place. What she didn't notice was that I was sending them to Doug with a quick SOS text attached to them."

"Smart thinking on your husband's part to know where you were," said Detective Glass.

"I'd been on the dome tour before, when I was the director of the scholarly center at the Library of Congress," explained Doug. "Kit knew that I would recognize her surroundings, particularly when she entered the area between the inner and outer domes. Nothing else like it exists in the entire city."

I put my arm around Doug's waist and squeezed. "Sometimes having a historian for a husband pays off."

He gave me a peck on the top of my head. "Glad to be of service," he said sweetly.

"What's going to happen to Jeff Prentice?" asked Meg.

"We'll finally be able to charge him for acting as an accomplice to murder and attempted murder," said O'Halloran. "He'll be headed to prison for a long time."

The police sergeant's words comforted me. Prentice had always been a loose end. Unfortunately, two people lost their lives in the process of apprehending him. He'd also managed to ruin his sister's life, too.

"It's hard to believe that the first murder you investigated actually came back to haunt you." said Trevor. "You weren't even an amateur sleuth yet when you solved that one."

"I was definitely not a sleuth of any sort," I said. "But I had to clear my name, as you might recall. I was a suspect in that murder investigation."

"It was touch and go for a while," said Meg. "The police had you in handcuffs for a few minutes. Isn't that right, Sergeant O'Halloran?"

O'Halloran perked up. He'd been feasting off the canapé tray sitting along the edge of the balcony. He never indulged in an alcoholic drink at these events, but he did feel as though it was fine to gulp down several appetizers when offered.

"I can't quite remember." O'Halloran's face was impassive, so it was difficult to know whether he was telling the truth or not. "However, I do know that Ms. Marshall promised me that she was going to stop making herself the target of murderers." He took a bite of the fried mushroom he was holding. "Or she *promised* when I stopped that maniac intern from killing her."

Meg's eyes grew wide. "Kit Marshall said that she was going to stop sleuthing?"

I took a deep breath. "Well, I did say that in the heat of the moment. After all, Jill had come quite close to finishing what her brother started a few years ago."

Meg's smile widened. "See? I knew Kit wasn't giving up solving mysteries. She has a knack for shining a fresh light on thorny problems."

Meg's words rang true. I was a fixer, and a darn good one, too. I straightened up and placed my finger in the air for emphasis. "However, there is a kernel of truth to what I said."

O'Halloran raised his eyebrows. I doubted he thought my dome confession had been truthful. After all, we had gone back and forth over the past several years about my amateur detective excursions.

Trevor narrowed his eyes. "We're waiting, Kit. Don't keep us in suspense."

"I plan on taking a break, but that doesn't *necessarily* mean I'm giving up on sleuthing entirely," I said. "A fiction writer has approached me. She wants to write about the amateur detective adventures of Kit Marshall."

Meg's eyes fluttered. "Someone wants to write a book about you?"

"Yes, and she wants to write the stories as novels," I explained. "She read in the newspaper about the murders we've solved. She thinks there's definitely enough for a series of books."

Meg squealed. "Certainly, I'll be a main character." She smoothed her blonde bob and licked her lips. "I hope this writer will portray me accurately."

I put my arm around Meg and gave her a squeeze. "Don't worry. That's why I might not have the bandwidth for solving new murders. I'll be spending a lot of time with the novelist, making sure she gets everything right."

Trevor wrinkled his brow. "Who is this person? For your sake, it should be no one less than Louise Penny or Tana French." Trevor shrugged his shoulders. "Perhaps Laura Lippman."

Good old Trevor. His elite sensibilities would never abate.

"She worked for years in the legislative branch and teaches at Georgetown," I said. "She approached Doug about the idea. Although she hasn't written fiction before, she's eager to try."

Trevor sighed. "I would not trust a novice to write a fictional account of my life." He glanced at me and must have noticed the look of disappointment on my face. He took a deep breath. "However, if you spend considerable time with this budding novelist, I trust you'll make sure she gets it right."

"It's so exciting," said Meg. "I *will* require several consultations with her. There's a lot to discuss. If my character isn't spot on, then the whole enterprise might fall apart."

Doug smiled. Meg had certainly matured over time, yet it was good to know that some things never change.

"I look forward to the books hitting the bestseller list," said Sergeant O'Halloran. "Although it will be odd if Kit Marshall doesn't show up at my next Capitol Hill homicide scene."

My eyes locked with Doug, Meg, Sebastian, Trevor, and Clarence before I responded.

"Truth is stranger than fiction," I said. "And I'm looking forward to the next chapter in our story together."

Epilogue

I PULLED INTO THE SURFACE PARKING LOT on Capitol Hill and turned off my car. After collecting my purse and a stack of folders, I got out of the vehicle and turned to face my destination. Beyond the office buildings stood the alabaster Capitol dome, one of the most enduring symbols of democracy in the world. What transpired inside those walls was often messy and almost never perfect. Yet, the United States Capitol stood for what mattered to most Americans: the promise of striving towards a "more perfect Union." My goal was to be part of the solution, the drumbeat that took us closer to realizing the best America had to offer.

Most days, it wasn't that glamorous. In the process of walking to my office that spring morning, I almost dropped the pile of documents I was carrying and nearly tripped over the curb leading to the congressional office building where I worked. It wasn't even eight o'clock in the morning. Luckily, Congress was not known for its "early to bed, early to rise" routine. No one saw my clumsiness except a few Capitol Hill police officers patrolling the grounds. And believe me, they'd seen much worse than an agility-challenged staffer trying to make her way inside the office in one piece.

I entered the building and stared for a few moments at the massive Alexander Calder statue inside the lobby. The fifty-feet high steel structure, which was a modern interpretation of mountains, greeted me every morning. It was both austere and comforting, imposing and familiar. Strange combinations of emotions, yet they seemed to epitomize my time on Capitol Hill.

I exited the elevator on the sixth floor and mechanically turned left. I had to rummage through my cluttered purse to find the office suite key. I was the first person to arrive this morning, so there was no staff assistant to greet me at the front desk.

The silence in the office was eerie and misplaced. Normally the hub of activity, the lack of noise made me feel uneasy. I headed straight to my modest office and sat down in my chair. There was an important memo I had to get to the boss this morning, and I wanted to make sure it was placed on her desk before she arrived.

I unlocked my desk drawer, placed my purse inside, and rifled through the stack of papers, which I'd reviewed last night at home. I finally found it, affixed my initials to the "CC" line, and rose from my desk to deliver it. My boss's office was adjacent to mine, separated only by the desk of our scheduler, who held the keys to the kingdom. No one walked into the head honcho's office without the express written consent of the sacrosanct scheduler. However, I was here so early this morning, I'd beat everyone else to the office.

The senator's office door was ajar, and I pushed it fully open so I could enter. I glanced toward the sitting area of the spacious office. A hand rested on the blue wheeled armchair in the corner of the room, facing the sizable window and a beautiful view of the Capitol grounds. I'd mistakenly thought I was the first to arrive at the office this morning. But I was wrong. My boss had beat me here.

As I stood in the doorway and surveyed the scene in front of me, my mind flashed back to years ago. I was a junior staffer, reporting to work early inside this congressional office building. I had arrived before everyone else, diligently hoping to provide Senator Lyndon Langsford with a memo before he started his busy day. It had been an exercise in futility. Much the same as this morning, I spotted his hand resting on a stately armchair. He was already dead, a victim of murder. His death had altered my life forever. I was still a congressional staffer, but I found another vocation: seeking justice for those who had been the victim of injustice.

What was the old axiom from philosopher George Santayana? Those who cannot learn from the past are condemned to repeat it. Here I was, standing motionless before my fate once again. I hadn't encountered a dead body or a murder victim in over a year. Had my good fortune ended? Had someone ripped away another person I cared about under the most tragic of circumstances?

I stepped forward, tentatively at first. Then, my fear melted away. Why was I hesitating? I wasn't the Kit Marshall who cowered from danger and conflict. I'd left that woman behind years ago. With renewed confidence, I charged ahead.

When I was halfway across the room, the chair spun around.

Maeve Dixon stared at me.

"You're here early, Kit. What's on the agenda today?" she asked.

Without missing a beat, I handed her the memo and sat down in the seat opposite her.

"Senator, I'm ready to discuss this policy proposal when you are."

The day began, and neither of us ever looked back.

THE END

COLLEEN J. SHOGAN has been reading mysteries since the age of six. A political scientist by training, Colleen has taught American politics at numerous universities. She previously worked on Capitol Hill as a legislative staffer in the United States Senate and as a senior executive at the Library of Congress. Currently, she's a Senior Vice President at the White House Historical Association. A member of Sisters in Crime, Colleen splits her time between Arlington, VA and Duck, NC.